Alison DeLuca

- April, 2013

unique electronic & print books

Published by Myrddin Publishing
ISBN-13: 978-1939296184

Credits
Cover design and layout: Lisa Daly
Editor: Connie J. Jasperson
Illustrations: Ross Kitson

CROWN PHOENIX:
The Devil's Kitchen
by Alison DeLuca

For Lesley and Lisa
Best sister, best friend

Table of Contents

BONUS CHAPTERS FROM
CROWN PHOENIX: LAMPLIGHTER'S SPECIAL -

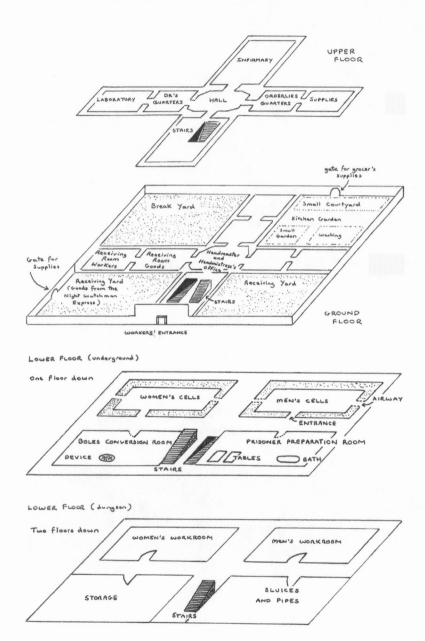

PROLOGUE
The Crown Phoenix

From Theodosia Marchpane, to Miss Barbara Cantwell

31st of July, Anno Domini 1906

My very dear Barbara -

I received your telegram and I suppose you are right. If you feel that it is necessary for Simon to stay with you and dear Valiant near the city for the time being, I must agree. I do hope the poor boy doesn't miss his loving Mother too much, however. Do see that he has an extra blanket at night and some nice warm woolens for when he goes out so he doesn't take cold in the chest.

I have some very good news. We have at last located the Crown Phoenix typing machine. That Awful Girl, Miriam, had the thing in her bedroom all along. I am certain that she had no notion what the machine can actually do. She was always far too stupid to understand such matters.

Virgil has attempted some tests with the Crown Phoenix, and it seems to work perfectly. The boat with Mana Postulate, That Dreadful Hussy, was able to leave through the Passage when we activated the Machine. I am very glad to be rid of her. Not only did she insult you, but also it was always so unsettling to have a native in the house. I must say she was a good governess at the time, and by that I mean the woman could keep Miriam quiet and somewhat civil. Now that the girl has gone as well, however, we have no more worries on that score.

Virgil also believes that we can begin expedited imports of the bolemor trees this very day. And, dear Barbara, we shall import the boles themselves for processing by the workers in Devil's Kitchen. To that end, Virgil feels that Valiant should go to Lampala and set up a regular import schedule with that Person on the throne there. I can never remember his name. Atol, I believe it is.

It is all very exciting, and I only wish I had my darling boy by my side in our hour of triumph. However, I am certain that you and Valiant will take the very best care of him. To that end I am enclosing a cheque for anything Simon may want. Please indulge his every need with it, and write to me if you need more funds.

I remain, dear Barbara,

Your friend and partner,

Theodosia Marchpane

CHAPTER 1

On the Night Watchman Express

The Night Watchman train swayed and chugged along through the countryside. Miriam stole a look at Simon's grim profile, sighed slightly and tried to shift into a more comfortable position. Since they sat on a floor made of dimpled iron, this was next to impossible. The windows in their carriage were boarded up with planks of roughly hewn wood, so there was no way to tell what time it was, or whether it was even still dark outside.

Her head drooped with weariness and hit the hard, wooden side of the train, and it woke her with a start. Sleep stole over her once more, and her head banged against the wall again. After a few more bumps, Miriam sat up and rubbed her eyes with one hand. She felt as though the inside of her lids had been filled with fine sand. In order to stay awake, she considered trying to talk to Simon, but his gaze was fixed at the wall opposite them, and he had a stern frown on his face. She wasn't in the best of moods herself; certainly they would only end up in another argument.

She folded her arms against her stomach and thought about a story she wanted to write when she got off the train. It was set in a country where there was a crystal globe called the Birthright, which protected the people and the lands in some mysterious way. However, the king of the country, who wished for quick riches to satisfy his own evil greed, sold the precious bauble. The land began to die slowly; the trees lost their leaves, even though it was still summer, and the rivers turned black and were filled with slimy, wriggling creatures.

Miriam felt a chill on her back as she imagined the pale, armless, boneless things that would fill the springs and wells and fountains in her imaginary country. *Ugh. That would be the last straw for Tom, the farmer's son who loved to fish and swim in the ponds on the farm. No! Make that the last straw for Thomasina, the farmer's daughter.* Miriam glanced at Simon triumphantly, as if she had just scored a point against him.

"Why must you smirk at me like that?" he demanded.

"I have never smirked at anyone in my life!" Miriam retorted. There you go, she thought. She knew they would only quarrel if they talked. "Be quiet if you can't be polite."

"Why are you trying to stay awake?" he asked, curling his lip. "You yawned so much just now that my ears nearly popped. You might as well just go to sleep, since we have no idea when we'll arrive, or even where we're going."

"Well thank you very much for that incredibly intelligent suggestion, but I can't sleep. My head bangs against the side of the carriage when I do."

"Oh for heaven's sake. What an idiot." Simon inched nearer and nudged her with one elbow. "Here, you might as well lean against me. Well, go on, I won't bite."

After an instant's hesitation, Miriam moved closer to Simon and gingerly put her head on his arm. That wasn't so bad. In fact, it was rather warm, and quite comfortable.

Simon looked down and watched Miriam's eyes flutter and close. She snored gently and put one hand on his arm.

He felt a tickle in his throat and stifled a cough. The floor of the carriage was filthy. In fact, there were some large stains in one corner that looked like dried blood. He looked away and strained his ears for any sounds from another carriage. All he could make out, however, above the constant rattle of the rails, was an anonymous intermittent rumble that could either be conversation or the pipes backing up. It could even be the conductor who had refused to listen to him earlier.

Well, no matter. When they arrived at wherever they were headed, he would explain to whoever was in charge the mistake that had obviously occurred, and he and Miriam would be sent home quickly. That fool of a ticket collector would have a great deal of explaining to do... he might be put in jail, or even deported... – Ouch! In between musings, he had fallen asleep and banged his own head on the side. Simon rubbed his head and remembered that he had called Miriam an idiot for doing that exact same thing. He shifted and experimentally tilted his head against hers so that they leaned against each other. Hmm... that was a bit better. Soon, he was snoring too.

The door opened with a sudden bang. Miriam looked up and blinked sleep out of her eyes. Beside her, Simon stirred as well. She realized with a jolt of something like shock in her stomach that they had fallen asleep curled up together.

"Disturb your kip, did we?" The odious conductor tapped a pencil against one leg and grinned. "About to have some company, you are." He looked out of the doorway and shouted to some unseen companion, "Bring the lot of them in! Sleeping Beauty and Prince Charming was just waking up."

It seemed they had stopped at a station. A large man, whose arms were bound behind his back, stumbled into the carriage as if he had been given a hard shove from behind. A thick chain at his feet connected him to another prisoner, who followed the first man closely. Another man entered, and another, all connected by the same chains.

Four prisoners altogether. Miriam swallowed. They didn't look like the types to inspire a friendly chat. The first hadn't shaved in weeks and wore a huge tattoo inscribed on one arm. He slid down, crouched on the floor opposite her and stared at her with bright blue eyes.

The other prisoners squatted beside him. Their chains clanked as they settled themselves. One, a smaller fellow with dark hair that beetled back from a low forehead, said to the conductor, "Oy! I wants my breakfast!"

"Yeh," the man next to him agreed. There were grunts of agreement from the others. Miriam reflected that she could do with some food herself.

The conductor emitted a short bark of laughter. "What would you lot prefer today, the poached eggs or smoked kippers? Or perhaps just buttered toast? Get out of it." He aimed a kick at the dark one and left, still chuckling. After a minute, the train screeched and began to move again.

The dark haired man nodded and said, "I didn't expect no more than a pig's squeal. Still, no harm in asking."

"That's right, Frank," the one with blue eyes agreed. He looked at Miriam again and asked, "And who might you two be?"

"We are –" Miriam began, but Simon interrupted her with his own explanation.

"We were put on this train by mistake. As soon as we arrive at our destination, we'll let a person of authority know of the error. Naturally, we'll be sent back to my parents right away."

Frank hooted. "Hark at Young Muck!" he said, baring his gums. Miriam saw, with a shudder, that most of his back teeth were missing. Simon opened his mouth again, but he obviously decided not to reply.

Blue Eyes stared at them with an unblinking stare. "You ain't going anywhere, either of yiz," he said after a moment's thought. "You're on your way to Devil's Kitchen, sure as eggs."

Devil's Kitchen! The name made a horrible chill slide down Miriam's spine. "What is Devil's Kitchen?"

"Where you're going," Frank said. "Shouldn't doubt you'll be there the rest of your days, running the mills and sweeping the floors."

"Packing the cases and driving the nails," the man next to him agreed. He had a scar that ran right down his face, from eye to chin, that snaked across nose and mouth.

"Carrying the water and sifting the sludge," the last man said. His voice was nothing but a hoarse whisper.

"Saying goodbye to fancy balls and servants," Blue Eyes said with a last chuckle. "Now, stow it, lads. I want to catch a few winks." He leaned back and closed his eyes, and the rest of them fell silent, although Frank leered at Miriam whenever she looked at him.

Obviously, she reflected, Blue Eyes was the leader, if you could call it that. She noticed that although his head also struck the back of the carriage when the train began to pick up speed, it didn't wake him at all. He must have been exhausted; indeed, all of the men had dark shadows smeared under their eyes.

Simon sat upright rigidly. Miriam stole a peep at his face and saw that he was doing the same thing as her: trying not to look at the men. He must have been embarrassed by the reference to his posh accent, and he tried to hide it by with a scowl at her when she looked at him.

"What?" she asked. "I didn't do anything."

"Shut up," he replied. A moment later, he whispered, "What do you think Devil's Kitchen is?"

"No idea, but it doesn't sound too promising."

He sighed. "A masterful understatement."

"Well of all the-" she started, when Frank interrupted.

"What are you two on about? Blowing kisses in her ear, are yeh? Eh, young buck? Couldn't I just show you how to fancy a girl in my time? Couldn't I just!" He winked outrageously at Simon and let a pink slice of tongue show through his teeth.

A slew of responses tripped to Miriam's tongue ("Be quiet, you horrible, dirty old man; I wouldn't let him blow kisses in my ear if he begged for it; mind your own business, you old leatherhead,") but she foresaw a losing fight as the only possible result of any argument with Frank. With great self-control, she kept her mouth closed.

Simon was probably going through the same inner battle. His face turned purple from the effort. Frank must have seen this, as he chuckled, leaned over the man with the scar, and nudged Hoarse Voice.

"Lay off it, Frank," Hoarse Voice wheezed.

Frank opened his mouth to retort, but the train rounded a turn and began to slow down.

"Maybe we're almost there," Miriam said.

"At last," Simon responded. "I can talk to someone with some education and let them know what severe trouble they are in."

"I just want to know what happened to Mana." Miriam tried not to shiver.

The door to the carriage opened again, and the guard thrust his head in. "On your feet, you lot," he said to the prisoners. "You too." He nudged Miriam with one toe.

"Leave her alone!" Simon spluttered, but the guard had already left. "Idiot," he said to the closed door.

"It's all right," Miriam said. "Soon you'll be able to talk to someone in charge, as you keep saying."

The prisoners stood up slowly. Miriam could hear their joints crack as they straightened their spines. Blue Eyes opened his eyes with a slight snore and came to instant awareness; he stretched and rose to his feet.

"Perhaps we had better get up," Simon said in a low voice to Miriam. "I want to be prepared for whatever comes next."

The train slowed further and stopped with a jerk. This caused Simon, Miriam and the prisoners to tilt forward and snap back upright. The door opened again and the guard shouted, "All out! Come on, you horrible lot!"

Blue Eyes took this in stride. He pushed Frank and the others slightly and they began to move out, their steps shortened by the chains around their ankles. Miriam waited until they had left, and she got up and followed them.

"Have a nice stay," the guard said as Miriam passed him. He winked and elbowed her as she passed by him.

Oh, for heaven's sake, Miriam thought. She ignored him as she followed the line of men, and the guard walked close behind her and Simon.

"Going to buy me a present?" The odious guard stepped right behind Simon's shoulder. "After all, you've got connections in high places, don't you, young muck? Hope you brought your paint-box for some fancy watercolors! Won't want to forget a minute of your stay." He continued in this vein, and Miriam could feel Simon get warmer with aggravation. *Be quiet, Simon,* she willed. *Don't say a word.*

Only one train door opened to the outside. Another conductor pointed the way off the train. "Exit this way, you lot," he said to Blue Eyes and the prisoners. The men kept their heads down in stoic silence and descended, and after a moment, Miriam and Simon followed. The sky overhead was dark with clouds, and it had started to rain. The drops sluiced down her neck with a weary intensity.

The train had stopped, not at a station, but at the back of the back of a large, dark brick factory. The rails ran behind the place, separating it from a scrubby field filled with gorse and what looked like bits of old washing that had been torn off someone's line with the wind. Miriam stepped over the train rails and stood behind the other prisoners.

The building in front of them was surrounded by stone that was dark as slate. The factory was the largest structure in the mean little street, and it had several large, doors set into its dripping, dank walls. It had to be the place known as Devil's Kitchen.

One of the gates opened, and someone stepped out. Miriam stretched on tiptoe to see, but a trick of the light or the lack of it caused the person to look like a tall, dark silhouette against the brick wall. The face was entirely in shadow, until it turned to her, and the eyes flashed, the only visible feature.

Miriam gasped and stepped back. Simon put a hand on her sleeve and whispered, "That must be the one who is in control here. We'll be home in time for tea, just like I've said all along."

"Just a second," Miriam hissed and grabbed his sleeve. "I've seen this place before. I know I have."

"Bring them here to the gates," the figure declaimed in a somber voice, and Miriam realized that it actually was a very tall woman. The conductors prodded the chained prisoners and pushed Simon and Miriam, and they all shuffled towards the figure.

The figure looked down at them. Her hair, what there was of it, was scraped back from a face so bony as to appear skinless and bloodless. Her eyes were a light color, but the brows were heavy and black, descending towards the brow in accusing question marks. Hoarse Voice, who was first in line, stopped abruptly, and the other prisoners bumped into each other. Frank immediately said to the man behind him, "Oy, watch it!"

The woman's dark, bloodless head snapped towards him. The dark, little man was watched in silence for a long moment, and she spoke to someone behind the door. "That one," she said.

Two huge guards appeared behind her. "Yes, Headmistress," one said. They lumbered towards Frank and gripped him with huge hands, and pulled him into the dark, brick building. The other prisoners followed by necessity, as they were all still connected by thick chains.

There were no more complaints.

The Headmistress' light eyes regarded Miriam and Simon. "What is this?" she asked. "We didn't expect the girl just yet, and the boy shouldn't be here at all."

One of the conductors answered with a shrug. "They was dumped on the train back where we rounds the coast, weren't they. We was told to bring 'em, so we brung 'em." The other conductor nodded in agreement.

Simon stepped forward and held out his right hand. "Good day, madam," he said. "My name is Simon Marchpane, and there has been a terrible mistake." She ignored his proffered hand, and after a moment he stuffed it in his pocket. "My father is a businessman," he continued, clearing his throat, "an extremely wealthy business man, and he'll be wondering where we are. I'm certain that the authorities are on a hunt for us now."

The Headmistress stared for a moment longer, and she spoke again to the door. "This one as well," she said.

Another huge guard appeared and bore down on Simon. "Wait!" Miriam cried. "Just listen to him for a moment – it's the truth!" She stopped.

The guard's enormous fist exploded outward, caught Simon on the edge of his jaw, and dropped him to the alley. The guard watched him fall without expression, and Miriam bit down, hard, on her tongue so she wouldn't scream. The man picked up the boy, tossed him over one shoulder, and followed the other guards and the prisoners into

Devil's Kitchen.

The Headmistress and Miriam confronted each other. The woman stretched out one long arm and gripped the girl's shoulder. "Come inside. Be quiet. Not one word. You have now seen what will happen if you try to speak."

Miriam stumbled through the door. Just before it slammed shut behind her, she saw the marks on the dark wood. They were long scratches, and they looked as if they had been made by human nails.

CHAPTER 2
In the Devil's Kitchen

O n the other side of the door was a small, sanded yard, surrounded by four heavy, tall brick walls. The dirt underfoot was the damp, gritty sort that instantly gets into one's socks and causes dull, grinding discomfort. The bricks in the walls were stained an ugly dark brown, either from the smoke in the factory itself or from the dirty air in the alleyway.

"Where is Simon?" Miriam looked around her. The prisoners and the guard who carried Simon's limp body had disappeared, probably through one of the heavy, iron doors that lined the walls.

The Headmistress ignored her and put a whistle that hung around her neck on a silver string to her lips. She blew it once, a long, loud, piercing blast that echoed around the yard. Miriam shut her eyes and tried to cover her ears. The sound was horribly familiar.

One of the doors opened, and a man, as tall and thin as the Headmistress appeared. The Headmistress turned to Miriam and addressed her directly for the first time. "This is the Headmaster," she said. "You will do everything we tell you to do. Without argument."

"How many arrived today?" The Headmaster spoke to the woman and ignored Miriam.

"Four men from the prisons and two children. The boy has been taken to the Infirmary. This one needs a uniform and a cell."

The Headmaster nodded. "We'll put her in the one on the West Side. It's been vacant since the girl from the main island had to be evacuated."

The Headmistress nodded. "That will be fine. Do it now."

The Headmaster gripped Miriam and dragged her towards another set of the doors. He inserted a large key into a lock on one and opened it. Miriam stumbled as he thrust her into a narrow hallway that was lit by two insignificant lanterns that left plenty of shadows and dark corners. By their light, however, Miriam could just discern a steep staircase that descended into the dark.

His fingers felt like damp chicken bones as he pushed her down the flight of stairs. "You don't have to squeeze me," she said, exasperated, and she tried to shake his hand off. "I saw what your goons do to us if we don't obey you." The only response was a tighter grip.

At the bottom of the stairs, the Headmaster steered her to the left, down another narrow, dark passage. Drips ran down the walls, and she could hear a metallic clanking sound, rather muffled by the thick walls. The air was cooler down here but smelled stale.

The Headmaster suddenly stopped her and made her turn to face another door. Taking out another key, he opened it and said, "In here."

Miriam squinted her eyes, as the tiny room was well lit compared to the dark hall. The Headmaster took out a whistle like the Headmistress' and blew two long blasts and one short one. Instantly, a woman appeared from a door in the opposite wall. Miriam, her hopes rising, saw that she had the same brown skin as Mana, the same dark hair, and the same black eyes. The eyes of the woman, however, were dull and listless. When she saw the Headmaster, she dropped her head and began to nod in a strange, rhythmic way.

"Clean her," he said. "Take her to Tache's old cell." He turned and walked out of the room.

Miriam started forward and asked, "Are you from the Island? Oh, you must be! Do you know Mana?"

The woman looked up for a moment, but she shielded her eyes. "Oh no," she said. "Oh no." She continued to nod and repeat those words to herself as she turned to an old desk in one corner and removed a large pair of shears.

"What is your name? My name is Miriam," she told her, speaking slower. "Look, I'm not supposed to be here. You were probably kidnapped too, weren't you? Maybe we could help each other."

The woman merely beckoned. Miriam followed her through the door in the opposite wall, still hoping to break through. "Do you know of a way out of here? Are there any other stairways to the outside?"

"Oh, no." The woman waved the shears. Miriam went with her into a larger room where more women, all with white skins, bustled about in silent, meaningless tasks. One was counting a mass of folded, gray shirts on some shelves. Another poured a stream of water into a tin bath.

The woman said nothing but pushed Miriam forward and pointed to the bath. "What?!" Miriam said, her voice rising. "I'm not going to undress here – oy, stop that!" Two of the women had come forward and seized her. Her pinafore was pulled over her head, her dress unbuttoned, and her shoes and stockings were pulled off. Before she could protest, Miriam was popped into the bath. The woman from the island disappeared, leaving Miriam with the other workers.

One seized a cake of soap and Miriam's arm. "Hey!" she protested, as she was scrubbed with a stiff brush.

The other worker spoke for the first time. "Keep your mouth shut, or yizz'll be eating soap." She snickered.

"Look what she's got here." A woman in the corner shook out Miriam's pinafore and pulled out Mana's wooden comb.

Miriam stretched out her hand, covered with greasy suds from the heavy soap. "Let me have that – please!"

"Oooh, must be precious," the woman said. "What should I do with it, Mrs. Siddons?"

The woman who scrubbed Miriam's back spoke up, her voice jerking as she plied the brush. "Throw it out. Headmistress'll have our hides if she sees such a thing."

Another one sniffed in a disapproving manner. "Looks dead heathenish to me."

"No, wait, please! I'll hide it, and I won't let the Headmistress find it, I promise." Miriam said, twisting to look at Mrs. Siddons. "It was a present from – from a friend. It's all I have. Please?"

Mrs. Siddons shook her head. "Oh, give her the silly thing, Dora, do.

You kept your Samuel's picture for the longest time in your own cell, until they moved you. Now, you, girl. Shut your mouth as you were told, and mind you share your rations with me when I tell you, since I've let you keep your precious comb."

She jerked Miriam's face around, considered her for a moment, and added, "Pity to lose them curls. Hand me those shears, would you?" Taking the scissors in one hand and Miriam's hair in the other, she cut it off with two short, rapid strokes.

Miriam was hauled out of the tub and dried with a stiff towel that looked more like a piece of an old oats bag. One of the shapeless gray garments was slipped over her head; it was rough, but at least it was clean. Miriam thrust the comb down the front of the dress.

The dark-skinned woman reappeared. "Oh no. Oh, no." She pointed at the hallway.

"It's Oh No again." Mrs. Siddons gave Miriam's garment one last, sharp tug. "Take her along with you, Oh No."

Miriam was guided out of the room. She and Oh No made another left turn to more steps that went straight down. Miriam, who had been trying to construct a map of the factory in her head, realized that she was now hopelessly lost.

The passage opened into a wide chamber, constructed with the same greasy, stained bricks that appeared throughout the place. More doors lined the walls, each one with a grille and a small opening on the bottom. They looked like a row of prison cells.

Oh No brought her to the only open door and pointed inside. Miriam turned to her. "Look, we can help each other, really! I could make sure that you get make to Lampala, with your family."

The woman looked up at that, but there was a screech from one of the neighboring cells. "Save your breath, dearie! That one's flying with the dragon!" This was followed by a burst of maniacal laughter.

"Oh no, oh no." The woman shook her head.

Giving it up as a bad job, Miriam walked into the cell and the door was closed on her. An instant later, the key grated in the lock.

There was a cot in one corner of the room, and Miriam plopped onto it. Mana's comb skittered to the floor, and she picked it up. She felt the shorn hair at the back of her neck; it seemed to be terribly jagged and prickly. Suddenly it all seemed too much – the train ride, Mana's disappearance, the cut hair, the disgusting cell she was in. With the comb in her hand, Miriam lay down, stuffed her face into the thin, hard pillow and felt scalding tears burn her eyes.

"Mana!" she sobbed. "Mana – where are you?"

CHAPTER 3
A Strange Place

D espite the red, thumping ache in his head, Simon could smell a delicious odor of soup, violets, and fresh bread. He opened one eye.

He had an idea that he was lying in a huge bed, his head propped up with luxurious pillows, and there seemed to be several people in one corner. He couldn't really tell, though, because the curtains were drawn and the room was dark. His general impression was that wherever he was, the room was very expensive and very clean.

"-waking up-"

"-better leave -"

There was the sound of a door opening quietly, and one of the figures left the room. The other came to his side, and he struggled to open both eyes fully. It was a woman in a white, starched dress, with a white cap on her head.

She put one hand on his forehead and said, "No use rushing things, now, you poor dear. Just close your eyes, and when you're ready, I'll give you some beef broth."

Simon opened his mouth to protest, but his eyes were closing against the material of her white uniform. Her dress almost seared his eyelids with its brightness. She smoothed his forehead again with one cool hand, and he fell back to sleep in a single instant.

It was either one minute or a very long time later that he woke up again. He had been dreaming, but he could remember nothing of that dream. He only knew that there had been something that he wanted very badly to get done, and he had been unable to do it.

When he turned his head on the pillow, the lady in the white uniform appeared again. No, it was someone different, but in the same clothes. How odd! This nurse was smaller and thinner, but she smoothed his forehead in the same way. "Don't struggle," she said in a low tone. She turned to the table and brightened the lamp on the table beside the bed.

Simon could now see that the room was even larger than he had thought, and it was very richly furnished. The velvet curtains at the windows hung down and puddled on the floor in soft folds, and the bed was canopied in white silk, embroidered with scarlet. Large paintings hung on the walls, portraits of foreign royalty next to large landscapes. There were bookshelves on either side of the bed, filled with volumes bound in green, scarlet, and gold leather, and inlaid with gold letters.

The woman in the white uniform brought a tray to his bed and put it on the round table. "Maybe we'll try some soup now," she said.

Simon was about to protest, but he stopped when she uncovered the silver tureen and spooned some of its contents into a bowl. A curl of steam emerged along with the rich smell of beef, and herbs, and sherry. His mouth watered suddenly, and he tried to sit up and reach for the spoon.

"Now, now, let me," she said. She pressed him back on the pillow and carefully held a spoonful to his mouth. "Not too quickly, there, that's it –" The soup was hot and delicious. Still, something nagged at Simon's memory. Wasn't there something terribly important that he had forgotten?

"Where am I?" He tried to prop himself up again.

She pressed him back and blew on the spoonful to cool it. "Don't worry about that now."

"I must find out-" his words were cut off as she popped the soup into his mouth. "It's good," he couldn't help saying. "But please, just tell me where I am."

She interrupted him again. "Just get your strength back now, and we can talk more later. More? Yes?" She fed him the rest of the bowl and held a crystal tumbler of something cold and delicious to his lips. After he had swallowed, she said, "No use getting into a fuss, is it? Just rest now."

His head swam. That seemed like a good idea. He closed his eyes and slept.

The room was suddenly lighter with a few bright streams of sunlight piercing the heavy curtains. Simon sat up fully and winced as he moved his jaw. Raising one hand, he found that it was still swollen from – what the hell *had* happened to him, anyway?

Shaking his head as if that would help to clear his memory, he looked around. He was in the large bedchamber, but the linens on the bed had been changed. They were now a light blue, and they retained the smell of a hot iron. His pajamas had been changed as well. In fact, he himself seemed to have been washed. He must have slept for well over twenty-four hours, and yet he felt quite clean. As an experiment he sniffed. Yes, he had been bathed at some point.

The door opened and the first lady came in, bearing a vase full of flowers. She smiled delightedly when she saw Simon sitting up and exclaimed, "Feeling much better, aren't we? How nice! Let me just put down these flowers, and we can take a look at you." She removed one vase full of blossoms on the bedside table, although they still looked as fresh though they had just been picked, and replaced them with the new container of yellow roses, peonies, and snapdragons.

"Where am I?" Simon asked. His voice was a bit garbled, so he cleared his throat and asked again.

"In the hospital, of course, dear. You had a nasty knock on your head."

"This is a hospital?" Simon looked around in amazement.

"A private hospital. Now, just stick out your tongue for me – ahhh – that's right."

Simon pushed her hand away. "Ouch. Hey! I remember now! That guard knocked me on my jaw. Back in that horrible place, just off the train. That was it. And what happened to Miriam? They took her into that dreadful factory, the Devil's Kitchen. I simply must find her." He thrust one leg out of bed and immediately felt woozy.

"Oh dear, standing isn't a very good idea, now, is it?" She chuckled and pushed him onto the pillow, but he resisted her touch and sat up again.

"Look, I've got to find my friends," he said. "I tell you that Miriam is being held prisoner in that terrible place, that factory, and heaven knows where Neil is."

"Is that right? Tsk, tsk." She widened her eyes and shook her head as she clucked her tongue with elaborate concern. Simon knew she didn't believe one word of what he had just told her.

"Look, it really is the truth, miss – what is your name, anyway?"

"Why don't you just call me Nurse," she said. She smiled, and two deep dimples popped into her cheeks.

"Nurse, I have *got* to get up and get dressed, and get the police, and find them! Now!" Panic began to surge in his chest.

"I know, dear." She walked to the door, carrying the discarded vase of flowers. "But wouldn't it be best for you to get nice and strong and healthy, and you can find your friends when you feel better? How about that idea? Isn't Nurse clever? Now, I am going to get you a nice breakfast of buttered toast and coffee, and maybe I'll fetch you some ham if you're good." She opened the door and slipped out before Simon could say anything.

As soon as she shut the door behind her, he threw back the sheets and blankets. There was a pair of red leather slippers on the floor. They sat beside a little set of steps necessary to get into such a high bed.

He swayed with the effort, but he managed to climb down and thrust his feet into the slippers, which were his exact size. His legs felt horribly weak and shaky when he stood up, though, and he leaned on the marble and mahogany bedside table before he dared to take a few steps.

Simon tottered to one of the windows and brushed away the curtain. He was able to look out, or rather, down. The room was at the top of an extremely tall house. In fact, the walls were so high up that he felt he was in the ice tower in Miriam's story, the one she had been writing in the window seat. It seemed like a very long time ago now. Far below, he could see a deserted park that led to a deep, dark forest.

He tried to open the window, but the catch would not move. Nothing happened when he tried to lift the sash. Of course, he told himself, he was still terribly weak.

He dragged himself to the other window, but the view was the same. Oh well, Simon thought. He'd simply walk out, even though he was dressed in pajamas, and find a village somewhere. Every village had to have a policeman, or at least a post office where he could send a telegram.

On a chair by the door there was a silk, padded dressing gown. Silently blessing the person who had furnished the room, Simon put it on and tiptoed to the door. He seized the handle, but even though he tried shaking, twisting, and rattling, it wouldn't budge. The door was locked.

"*Hey!*" he yelled, beating one hand on the door. "Hey!" His voice seemed ineffectual against the solid oak, and the heavy door solidly absorbed his kicks and blows. He felt as though he was in one of those diving machines he had read about at school, trying to shout for help through walls of thick glass and miles of water.

Giving it up, Simon weakly fell into the chair from which he had snatched the dressing gown and looked around. The room was beautiful, it was clean, and he was dressed like a prince. But despite the luxury, he was in a prison cell. There was no question about that.

CHAPTER 4
Hidden Treasures

Miriam lay on the bed and rubbed the comb's smooth wooden surface against her cheek. She sat up suddenly, however, when she heard slow, steady footsteps coming in her direction. Miriam hid the comb under the thin mattress, and she sat up and tried to push her hair back from her face as the door was unlocked and opened.

The Headmistress entered the cell and looked down at her. It seemed as though the woman never stood in full light. From that angle, her light eyes gleamed like ice in the center of two black puddles.

"Stand up when I am before you," she said after a long moment.

Miriam stood and looked up at the woman. "Why am I here?" she asked. "When can I go home?"

There was a pause, and the Headmistress responded, "You will not talk to me unless I ask you a direct question."

Miriam felt a rush of anger. Once, at a dinner party that her father had given, she had been allowed to squirt some soda water from a large siphon into a glass and taste it. Some had gone up her nose in her haste to drink the unexpected treat. The prickling, stinging sensation in her nostrils was just like the fury that she felt now.

"You will work for the factory here," the Headmistress said. "Mrs. Siddons will show you your duties tomorrow. You will start at the very bottom of the task list and, if you do as you are bid, you might possibly work your way up to a better position. *Do you understand?*"

Miriam gritted her teeth. She'd be damned before she gave this woman the satisfaction of an answer.

27

There was a hiss of in-drawn breath, and the Headmistress darted forward and put one long, icy finger under Miriam's chin and jerked it up. "Perhaps you do not understand your position," she said. "You no longer have any family, nor friends, nor any contact with the outside world whatsoever. The Headmaster and I are now all you have to rely on in this world. You will do everything that we tell you, you will work hard and be obedient, and you will give me no trouble. I shall ask you once more. Do you understand?"

The question was designed to intimidate her, but on Miriam it had the opposite effect. She jerked her chin away and said, "You don't frighten me. Try it on someone your own size, you great, tall - hulking - broomstick!"

The Headmistress' thin lips spread upwards. "Ah," she said. "I've seen your sort before. You'll do as I wish in the end. Your type always does." She stepped closer to Miriam and continued, "Although your behavior is disgraceful, I will allow you to be fed tonight. Otherwise you will be no use on the Floor tomorrow. Put that bowl and cup out when they come round and knock at your door in an hour. Don't be late, or you will go hungry."

"Where am I?" Miriam shouted. "Tell me where I am! This is England! You can't just kidnap people, and hold them against their wills, and cut their hair off, you dreadful old hag!"

The Headmistress looked at Miriam for another long moment, until the girl, to her chagrin, found that her lips were beginning to tremble. The woman seemed to know the precise moment when the girl began to weaken. She smiled, stepped closer and swung her large hand and smacked Miriam's face, on both sides, with two loud, hard, deliberate slaps.

There was silence for a moment. The woman opened her thin lips and spoke again. "Once you have worked off your uniform and your food for the week, you will be paid a decent wage. You are working for Pearson's. We abide by the law here." With a quick movement she exited the room.

Miriam moved from where she had been standing, stunned, when the Headmistress slapped her. She reached the door just as it was shut in her face and began to scream, "Pearson's! That's my father! I am Miriam Pearson! Open the door at once. I shouldn't be here!"

There was no response but the Headmistress' steps as she walked away. Miriam shouted again, and someone in the cell next to hear said, "Oh, give it up and keep quiet, do. They'll never listen to you, no matter what pack of lies you tell them."

"But it is nothing but the truth!" Miriam screamed.

"Shut your hole," another voice in another cell bellowed, "or I'll give you more of what you just got from the Headmistress tomorrow when we are all on the Floor."

Miriam opened her mouth to shout back. With a supreme effort she closed it again. She recalled Mana saying, "You can run at a wall with your head and bash into it, but it's certain that all you'll get is a sore head. Or you can study the wall and check for its weak points, and when you find them, you can knock it down."

The women in the other cells continued to yell, threatening her with slaps, kicks, and other punishment. Miriam went to the bed and felt for the comb under the mattress. It had been a lucky thing that no one had found it, or that the Headmistress hadn't taken it into her head to search the place.

Where on earth could she put it? There was no pocket in her uniform, and she didn't want to carry it in case she dropped it and broke it when she was working tomorrow on "the Floor," whatever that meant. She was certain that if the story got out that she had it, the comb would be taken away from her.

The room was a mean little cell, lined with the stained brick that she had noticed in the passages of the Factory. Miriam gazed hopelessly around, and looked under the bed, which was empty except for a few curls of dust and a stained chamber pot. She couldn't hide it in there; that much was certain. The first person to search her cell would find the comb and confiscate it.

She sat back on her heels, defeated, and looked under the bed again. Moving the loathsome pot, she crawled underneath and looked closely at the bricks. By some miracle, there was a large crack in the wall where the buildup of smoke and dirt had worn the cement away.

Miriam probed the bricks with her finger and found that one brick was broken in half and wobbling in its place in the wall. Holding her breath, she maneuvered it and managed to slide it out of the wall, leaving a dark hole behind. *What was inside it? Rats, mice, or centipedes?* She nearly jammed the brick back into the hole, but she mentally shook herself. *Oh, stop it*, she chided. *Anyone would think you were the fainting victim in a novel.*

She put her hand into the space and felt around cautiously, in case it opened to a sluice that led directly to the sewers or something worse. The hole was not much bigger than the brick, however. She quickly jerked her hand back when she felt something furry, and her knuckles scraped painfully against the rough edges of the wall.

Brrrrrr! She pictured mice, or rats, or a rotting corpse of some other kind of rodent. Chills of disgust ran down her back, but she curled her hand in again and touched the thing. It didn't *feel* alive, or even seem as if it had ever been alive. Exploring a bit more, she touched paper and a great build-up of dust.

She drew the thing out and saw that it was a small, ancient book, stiff with age and yellowed around the edges. Still lying on the floor, propped up on her elbows, she blew the dust off and opened it. Inside were some entries in a round, untrained hand.

There was a clanging from outside and a voice yelled, "Come on, ladies! Get those bowls and cups out through the doors if you want any supper!"

Miriam quickly put the brick back in the wall and, getting up so quickly that she saw spots dance in front of her eyes, thrust the book and the comb under the mattress. She could hide them both later. At that moment she was starving. She grabbed a tin mug and dented bowl from a small, rickety table near hear bed, and put them down near the slot at the bottom of the door. She could hear the other bowls being filled, and the women next to her start to chew and suck at the food.

The small slot slid open, and Miriam put out her bowl and cup. A moment later they were handed back and the door closed.

Miriam took them and went to the bed. The cup had been filled with tea, and the bowl was heaped with a thick green soup. A slice of bread and cheese was balanced on the top.

Miriam tore into the bread, tearing it off with her teeth and not noticing how stale it was. There was no spoon for the soup, and she considered shouting for one, until she reflected that it was better to keep quiet. Probably they weren't allowed to have any kind of utensils, anyway.

Tilting the bowl, she was able to slide some of the thick soup into her mouth. The bread could be used as a type of shovel, too.

She swallowed some of the soup and drank the tea until the edge had been taken off her appetite. The soup was tasteless and made from dried peas – some of the beans hadn't been soaked well and they cracked under her teeth like pebbles. The cheese curled on both sides from age. Still, the food was thick and plentiful, and she couldn't remember the last time she had eaten. She managed to swallow half of the soup and most of the cheese, as well as all of the cold tea.

Once she had finished her strange meal, Miriam lifted the mattress and took another look at the small notebook. It was filled with misspelled entries. One said, "Ellie ows me tenne pense. Will notte paye." Another read, "No bred thys nitte. Ellie stol it." The author held a great grudge against the unknown Ellie.

Miriam got back to the business of hiding the comb. She slid back under the bed and found the loose brick. She removed it and dusted out the space as well as she could with one corner of her uniform. She held the wooden comb, all she had left of Mana, against her cheek for one moment and felt the smooth wood and the ornate carvings against her skin. No, no one at the factory must find the precious thing. Miriam, with great care, put the comb between the pages of the book and placed both objects back into the hole.

Once she had returned the brick to its place, she stood up and looked with dismay at the stains on her hands and on gray garment she was wearing. There was a cracked bowl of tepid water on the rickety table, and she used it to wash herself as best she could.

There was nothing more she could do, so she lay down on the bed and closed her eyes. She remembered Thomasina, the farmer girl that she had invented. What had her heroine been up to? Oh yes, she had ridden away from her farm disguised as a boy, to see if she could find the Birthright.

"Lights, ladies," a loud voice proclaimed outside Miriam's cell. The lanterns hanging in the hall were darkened and extinguished, but Miriam didn't notice. She was no longer in her cell. In her mind, she rode a black charger through a dappled wood, wearing a man's cloak, with the wind blowing the dust from her cropped hair.

CHAPTER 5
Travelers from Lampala

T hose who worked at the docks had seen so many ships come in from the Lampala islands lately that they didn't even notice them any longer. When a modest schooner was tied up along the quay in the mist of early morning, no one stopped unpacking crates or loading boxes long enough to give it a second look.

After everything was made ready on the ship, the passengers began to disembark. The boy with wire spectacles coming down the stepped plank caused no comment. Anyone could see he had been studying somewhere abroad since he looked bookish and was wearing native dress.

The tall, heavily veiled woman descending the plank made some workers stop what they were doing to watch her slim figure and rich attire. One man put down his fish barrow and leaned against a hitching post to strike a match, hoping that he could catch a glimpse of her ankles. She disappointed him, however, by climbing down gracefully and holding her skirts close about her.

When her companion, or guard, or footman, disembarked after her, every worker at the dock stopped and gaped at him. No one had ever seen such a dark, foreign person before. He was dressed in embroidered robes that left one heavily muscled arm bare, and his face bore an expression of almost insolent pride. Was he a servant? The lady seemed to be on excellent terms with him and walked towards the main road at his side, to continue a warm argument they were having. And not only was he dark, and foreign, the man was incredibly huge. The boy with glasses followed them, and he stopped only to give a final direction to one of the porters.

"Disgusting," said the boatswain who had stopped for a smoke, spitting out some shreds of tobacco into his beard and jabbing a finger in the direction of the pair. "Oughtn't to be allowed, that kind of carry-on in front of decent folk what minds their own business." He saw one of the sailors from the group's vessel descending with a large trunk balanced on his head, and he caught the man's arm. "Who were they?" he asked, gesturing at the group.

The sailor dropped the trunk into a waiting barrow and shrugged. "No idea. Got a light, mate?" The boatswain leaning against the post proffered a match, and the sailor sucked at his pipe with an unsteady hand. "Cheers. Needed that." He blew out a huge cloud of smoke. "Ain't half glad that journey's over!"

"Why do you say that?" the man on the post asked.

"Don't want to be on a ship where Things as shouldn't be moving go walking at night," the sailor said, breathing out a wreath of smoke. "Oof, I need a drink."

"Things?" one of the dockworkers asked.

"Aye. And where you hears Sounds where none should be heard, if you catch my meaning."

"Tom Nugget!" An enraged cry came from the prow of the ship, and the sailor dropped his pipe.

"Got to finish unloading," he said, looking around him. "Suppose I have to earn my keep." He pushed his way back up the ladder onto the ship, still muttering about Things. The swain leaning against the post shrugged, spat, and looked curiously after the group that had disembarked.

The threesome reached the end of the pier and disappeared into the busy streets. The man spat again and prepared to return to his work.

"Pearson's has two places of business. One is in the heart of the city where the accounts and orders are kept. Most business is done there.

There is also one storage place, but it is only used for holding supplies." Mana pointed to a small alley on the map of London that was spread over her and Kyoge's knees on the carriage seat.

Kyoge nodded. "The obvious place to start would be the one in the heart of the city." He tapped the map and looked into Mana's eyes.

She smiled at him, swaying a bit with the movement of the carriage. "And, since the factory in the heart of the city is the obvious place to look..."

"...we should start with the other," Neil finished for her in triumph.

Mana shook her head. "It is in a very mean part of London. There were some nasty rumors about the place before Henry ever bought it."

"Henry?" Kyoge raised his eyebrows.

"Miriam's father."

"We cannot allow a little danger to put us off!" Neil bent over the map and peered at the spot Mana had indicated.

"We can begin with the larger place and not get our heads cracked open."

"The most intelligent thing to do, however," Kyoge objected, "is to watch both places. We should have brought some of my guards, as I had wished."

"We caused quite enough of a stir as it was on the docks, in case you didn't notice. Kyoge, we will have to get you some clothes for the mainland as quickly as possible, so you don't get noticed quite so much. A suit in gray, or in black perhaps. Yes, I think it should be black."

"And give up my robes?" Kyoge was horrified.

Neil smiled at the thought of the huge man dressed in a broadcloth suit with a top hat; he would still stand out but in a magnificent manner. He sighed and looked out of the window at the shop windows rolling by, thinking of Riki. She would have loved this adventure. The sights of the City, the maps, and above all, the plans would have enchanted her. He could just picture her delighted smile. For a moment he felt Riki sat on the seat beside him in the swaying carriage. She would stare out the window and jabber constantly about what she saw. She would annoy him no end. And he would give anything to have her there, he realized.

"We'll also have to hire someone to act for us," Mana said. "I refuse to go to Pearson's lawyers. I never trusted them when Henry was still alive. I'll have to find someone who is young, and therefore hungry enough to act for us, but who is also completely respectable and hard-working."

"Sounds like an easy person to find," Kyoge commented, sitting back and looking at her out of the sides of his eyes. "Good luck with that, my queen."

She smiled again and looked back at the map. "It's in a disgraceful part of the city," she said, pointing again to where the storage warehouse was located. "Still, perhaps we can find a house to rent nearby that is clean and safe."

"Where are we going to go in the meantime?" Neil asked, coming out of his reverie.

"We'll stay at Lloyds until we can find something. It's a good hotel, but not too fashionable. In other words, no one will ask any questions. And Neil, one more point." Mana looked at him severely. "We must also discover what has happened to your family, and we must rescue them, if need be."

Mana, Kyoge, and Neil were shown into a small suite of rooms at Lloyd's. If the clerk had not wanted to let rooms to a lady hidden behind a veil and her large companion, it vanished when she produced a large sheaf of bills and put them down on the desk. "And could you give us the name of several attorneys in the area?" Mana asked as the clerk handed her a key.

"There's Viceroy's, and Pipstone, and Watley's," the clerk answered. "They're all on Sweetwater Street, just down there."

After thanking him and adding a large, gold coin to the heap of money she had left, Mana swept up the stairs to the suite which, if not luxurious, had the merits of being clean and quiet.

"Well," she said, sitting down and removing her veil with a relieved sigh, "we didn't cause *too* much commotion, I suppose. Kyoge, you will have to go and get yourself measured at a tailor's today. Neil, you will go with him, and I'll go and look for a lawyer."

"My queen!" Kyoge protested. "You have just finished a most trying time, not to mention a long sea passage! You should rest, and have some tea, and bathe."

Mana laughed. "Yes, and sniff some smelling salts while Neil pats my temples with eau-de-cologne? Certainly not. I waited long enough in that infernal cage on that cliff as it is. I must find Miriam as soon as possible."

"Em," Neil said, "sorry to interrupt, but, that is, I really don't need new clothes. If you find my parents, they'll have some things for me at their house. Honestly, I'll be fine."

"My dear Neil," Mana said, "I owe you so much already that a few new suits of clothes will hardly serve to lessen the gap. Besides, if it makes you feel better, look upon it as a loan."

"But-" Neil thought about how much he owed.

"Enough," Mana said, waving one hand at him. "You'll simply hold up our rescue of Miriam and Simon with your foolish arguments. I may have plenty of energy, but I don't have enough time to listen to such nonsense."

Completely vanquished, Neil shut his mouth. Beside him, Kyoge said, "My queen, forgive me, but I insist that you must be very tired after the voyage."

"And didn't I tell you before to stop calling me 'My queen'? We are equals on the Mainland, Kyoge, and you must treat me as such. Furthermore, didn't I just say I have plenty of energy?"

The man bowed deeply, although he sniffed in an offended way. "As you wish."

Mana opened her mouth, but shut it again as someone rapped on the door. "That will be our luggage," she said. "Neil, show them in, would you? We all need a quick wash and a change, since we're snapping each other's heads off."

Once the porter had been tipped and sent away, Mana disappeared into one of the rooms in the suite and closed the door. After a second's pause, Kyoge did the same in the other room.

Neil found another small bedroom and washed quickly. He dressed in one of the white silk Lampalan suits that looked more like a pair of pajamas than actual clothes. As silly as the clothes appeared on the Mainland, the Lampalan style was definitely more comfortable than any English clothes, Neil thought, remembering his school uniform with the high, buttoned jacket and woolen trousers to match. He slipped his feet into the curving sandals that were embroidered to match the suit, trying not to think of heavy leather boots that laced up above the ankles.

When he came back to the small sitting room, Mana and Kyoge were already dressed. They were sitting at a table, discussing something in a low voice. When he saw Neil, Kyoge stepped back and bent his head. "Are you prepared, sir?" he asked.

"I, ah, that is, yes," Neil said.

Mana shook her head. "Kyoge, if there was a fire, and people were running out of the building, you would wait behind until both of us were saved, and you would still call us Sir and My Queen."

Kyoge bowed slightly. "But of course."

Mana's cheek dimpled slightly for a moment, before she resumed her former, severe expression. "We'll meet back here in several hours. Kyoge, take this," she added, handing him a thick envelope.

He bowed again and put the envelope in some inner pocket. He nodded to Neil, and they followed Mana out of the room.

Carrying several large boxes and followed by two porters with more parcels, Neil and Kyoge returned to the rooms a very long time later. The fittings had not gone well, although in the end they had succeeded in getting everything they needed. Kyoge had caused the problem. The large man had lost his polite mien in front of what he considered his inferiors and had looked on the tailors who had measured his large frame with deep suspicion. He and Neil had been booted out of one shop and had settled on another, less fashionable establishment that put up with Kyoge's manner, thanks to the contents of Mana's envelope.

She had already returned. The Queen of Lampala sat at a settee in front of a large tray, sipping a cup of tea. "Ah!" she exclaimed as they walked into the room. "I see you were successful. Put those down over there," she added to the porter, who was gazing at her in shock.

The poor man dropped the bundles at his feet and gazed back and forth at Mana and Kyoge. "Does the manager know about these here goings-on?" he stammered.

She rose to her feet, standing nearly as tall as Kyoge. "Put them over there, I said." She pointed with one long finger at a green and gold-striped settee. In an off-handed manner, she picked up a few gold coins from the table and began to pour them from one hand to the other.

The porter brightened, and deposited the bags where she had requested them. Seizing his sizable tip, he fled.

"Well, now we have made rather a spectacle of ourselves," Mana said, sitting down again. "All of London will now know we have arrived. Nothing to be done about it, however. At this moment, I'm sure you both must be hungry. Sandwich? Scone?"

"Gosh, yes please," Neil said, coming forward with alacrity and taking an egg and cress sandwich.

"I am not hungry," Kyoge growled.

"Yes, I thought you'd say that," Mana responded. "There is a meal in your room, since you won't eat with me. But we'd get along much faster without these fastidious manners. Go on and eat, and we can arrange things when you return."

Kyoge bowed again and left, and Mana took another sip of tea, looking at his departing back with her intelligent stare.

"He's not in a good mood," Neil whispered to her. "We got thrown out of Bates."

Mana's dimple reappeared. "I can just imagine," she said. "Well, I, on the other hand, had a most successful afternoon. I think I found someone to work for us. His office was not on Sweetwater Street, needless to say. None of those attorneys would allow me to stay in their office once they saw my skin. But Philips is a new lawyer, looking for business, and he'll be honest. He's going to find us a house."

"So, things are going to start moving now," Neil said, his heart lifting for the first time since he had left Riki.

"Yes, I really think they will," Mana said, taking another sip of tea. She took a small bite of a cress sandwich, but she also continued to watch Kyoge's closed door.

CHAPTER 6

In the Sickroom

There was a schedule in the sickroom, Simon found. Nurse came during the day and brandished her dimples and blond curls at him whenever Simon mentioned leaving the room or going out on his own. Nanny replaced her at night, the older, thinner woman who was, thank goodness, not nearly as overbearingly kind as Nurse but just as ruthless in her attentions. Simon quickly grew to loathe the sight of both of them.

In a few days, he found that he could get out of bed easily on his own. Nanny came in one morning with the usual change of flowers and nearly dropped them when she saw him standing by the window.

"What are you doing?" she gasped, as she steadied with one finger the bottom of the vase she held in the other hand.

Simon turned and frowned. "I am looking out of the window, what does it look like?" He was pleased to notice that he had caused her dimples to disappear.

Nurse put the flowers on the ground and bustled over to him. "Now, don't make Nursie angry at you!" she said. She took hold of one of his sleeves. "You must get back to bed this instant – do you hear me! If you have a relapse, that would be-" This thought appeared too horrible to contemplate, and she tugged again on his pajama sleeve.

Simon shook off her hand and strode to the door. "I'm really doing fine," he insisted. "I appreciate your kindness, or the concern of whoever it was that hired you in the first place, but now I am ready to leave," he insisted. "Get me my things now, please."

41

Nurse flew to his side. "Yes, yes," She took hold of his arm again. "And stop mauling me!" Simon growled.

"See now?" she said. "You've got yourself all worked up into a fret, poor dear, and your fever must be soaring dreadfully. Just let Nurse take your temperature, and if it's low enough, we'll see."

Simon sighed. He didn't have much choice, since she had wedged herself between him and the door. Short of knocking her down, the only way to get out was to comply. "Very well," he said grudgingly.

Nurse smiled at him, and out popped the dimples. Simon sighed. "There, I knew you were a good lad," she said. "Now, come over to the bed and sit down, yes, that's right. Allow me to make certain the fever thermometer is clean. One moment - now!" She put the thermometer under his tongue and Simon closed his mouth over it, grimacing at the bitter taste. "Who is it?" he asked, his words garbled.

"Who is what?" Nurse had returned to her original task, that of changing the fresh flowers for more fresh flowers.

"You know, the one who hired you and had me brought here. Is it that foul old woman at the factory? Or one of her goons?" He swayed suddenly and put one hand up to his forehead. The room got hotter all of a sudden. Simon felt the sweat break out on his brow.

Nurse picked up the old jug of flowers and turned to him. "What did you say, dear?"

"I wanted to – I wanted to know-" The room suddenly swam in front of his eyes.

"Did you want to know when you would be better?" Nurse asked, coming over to his side and removing the fever thermometer from his mouth. "As soon as you start being a good boy and cooperating, I should dare say. Now, if you listen to Nursie, and do as you're told, and stay in bed, and take your medicine..."

Simon opened his eyes. He was back in bed, and the room was dark. The thick curtains were drawn on the large windows. Nurse had disappeared, and Nanny bent over his bedside table. She picked up one of the medicine bottles on a silver tray and held it up to check the level of the liquid inside. He turned his head, and Nanny put the bottle down.

"How do we feel now?" she asked. Nanny always called him 'we.'

Swallowing and blinking his eyes, Simon looked around. "What happened?" he asked. "I was just talking to Nurse, and she disappeared."

"Ah." Nanny picked up a chart hanging off the end of the bed. "It's written here that we had a bit of a relapse – apparently we got out of bed without permission?" She looked at him, her dark eyebrows raised.

Simon turned red. She reminded him of his own governess, who had bossed him and taken care of him until he had left home for Firbury College. "I just – that is, I thought I felt better." His eyes adjusted to the darkness, and he saw a large, bulky mountain of a man standing by the door. "Who is that?" he asked, sitting bolt upright.

Nanny turned. "Who is what? Oh, you mean Jenkins over there? He's just here to assist me and make sure that you don't hurt yourself."

Make sure that I don't escape, you mean. Simon plopped back against the pillows and looked up at the ceiling. *I got out of bed, and they realized that I had recovered a bit, and that I wouldn't cooperate. Now they've added guards to the ranks of Nurse and Nanny, in case I try and push one of those blasted women down and rush off on my own.*

Something else made his heart beat faster. *That thermometer must have had some kind of beastly drug on it,* he thought. *I was feeling fine until that woman put it in my mouth. It tasted bitter, too.*

"Do try and have some nice broth, dear," Nanny said, sitting in a chair by his bed and taking the cover off the usual silver tureen.

Simon turned his head away. "Don't want any," he said, pushing the spoon away from his mouth. It spilled some soup on the smooth linen sheets. "I feel tired, and I have a headache."

"Oh, dear me!" Nanny said. "We aren't doing well at all, are we? My goodness, and we have made a mess of the bed. Lie down now, and we'll see about your medicine." She opened one of the bottles and poured out a dark, thick liquid into another spoon.

Infuriated, he was about to hit the spoon of medicine and splash it all over her impeccably white shirtfront. A thought struck him.

Obediently he opened his mouth and she popped it in.

She tidied his bedclothes, tut-tutting over the soup stains on the sheet. Finally she picked up the tray and walked out of the room. The massive guard followed her.

There was no pretense this time. Simon heard the key turn in the lock.

He waited for a moment, hopped out of bed, and pulled the chamber pot out. He gagged and spit out the disgusting stuff in his mouth.

It tasted foul on his tongue. There was a carafe of water by his bed. Simon took a big sip and rinsed his mouth out again and again. Thank heavens she hadn't decided to stick around. He couldn't have held that in much longer.

He hopped back into bed just in time. Nanny returned with an armload of linens. The dark bulk of Jenkins followed her, Simon saw from under his eyelashes.

She pulled the quilt off the bed and began to strip the sheets off, turning his body cleverly so that she could remake the bed while he was still in it. He remained as limp as he could throughout the whole operation.

"What if the tyke tries something?" Jenkins growled.

"Nonsense," Nanny replied briskly. "He'll be out for hours. I gave him a double dose. We won't have worry about him tonight, at any rate! Now, I'll just finish changing these sheets, and I'll close this window. He mustn't breath in any of that nasty night air." She closed a window, and the deliciously cool breeze that had been sliding around the room abruptly ceased.

"How long?" the man in the corner of the room asked after a long pause.

"Will they keep him here? Goodness, I don't know." Nanny sounded annoyed. "As long as they need to, I should imagine. That's not for me or you to speculate; we just need to do our jobs as best we can and keep him in here." There was a sound of linen being flapped in an aggrieved manner.

"Just asking." The mountain by the door sounded out of sorts as well.

Simon smiled to himself. He hadn't learned much, but they had started to snap at each other, and he knew for a fact now that he was being held as a prisoner. Very well. They wanted him to be an invalid. An invalid is what they would have on their hands. He could play that part.

When Nurse came in the next morning, Simon was in bed, tossing back and forth. He had pulled off most of the sheets and they were wound around his legs.

"What is the matter?" she asked. She dropped her bag on a chair and ran to the bed. Jenkins was with her, of course. By day he proved to be a large man with hair that had melted off his head into fat, dripping sideburns and a coarse, hairy neck. He stood by the door and watched, and his small eyes darted between Nurse and Simon.

"I feel hot," Simon complained, "and I feel cold at the same time." He rolled his eyes up at her in a piteous manner.

"You poor dear!" she said with a cluck of her tongue. She felt his forehead with one hand. "Yes, you are a bit hot. Dear me, that will never do. Won't you have a bite of breakfast just to make Nurse feel better?" She stuck her lower lip out, making a moue.

"Oh, Nurse, you are so funny," Simon said. "I'm not hungry. Can't I just sleep some more, and maybe I'll eat later?" He stuck his lip out at her as well, making her giggle.

"Well!" she said. "I'm sorry to hear that." Her dimples flared in her cheeks. Obviously, she loved having this new, pitiful patient instead of the previously uncooperative Simon.

"Thanks, Nurse," he whispered, with what appeared to be the end of his strength. He closed his eyes.

She kissed his cheek with a loud smack and left, followed by Jenkins, who turned and gave Simon a quick glare. He even went so far as to stick his tongue out at the boy before he closed and locked the door, Simon saw from beneath his eyelashes.

Waiting until he heard their steps die away, Simon got up again, opened the window, and breathed deeply. Ahhhhh. Finally, he thought, fresh air.

He was very hungry. Nanny had taken away the soup the evening before, and he had spent much of the night walking around his room. He found that he had to stop continuously to sit down and rest, since his knees had a tendency to feel like jellied eels.

It was a great stroke of luck that Nurse had left the breakfast tray behind her. Simon inspected the contents eagerly, finding lemon sponge, porridge, and thin wafers of toast instead of the bacon and sausages he wanted. He wolfed down as much as he dared, and after a small meal he stirred the contents of the bowls so they appeared to be full.

His hunger somewhat blunted, Simon walked around the huge room a few times. He swung his arms and breathed deeply. His legs felt stronger than before, and his jaw no longer hurt from where that goon at Devil's Kitchen had smashed him a few days ago. Even though he had to stop and rest after a while, he was able to stay on his feet longer than the previous night.

He'd wait another day and get his strength up, and maybe he'd be able to do the exercises that Sergeant Major Whatsit had the students do at Firbury every morning before lessons. Soon, he'd be strong enough to work on an escape.

CHAPTER 7

What Happened Underground

Miriam followed the line of fellow prisoners out of the area where they slept in their cells. The inmates, some older women who probably had families somewhere, some older girls, all were dressed alike. Each one wore the same shapeless gray uniform Miriam had on. They even walked in the same way, with their shoulders hunched, eyes cast down, arms hanging by their sides.

"Wonder if Frank'll come up t'yards tomorrow afternoon," one coughed. "I owes him half-a-crown."

"He'll be there, in that case," another responded with a loud belch.

The line shuffled down one of the long hallways lit with the dim lanterns. Miriam looked around with interest, trying again to discover where they were in relation to where she had been forced off the Night Watchman. Had the people who ran the Devil's Kitchen burrowed underground, under the scrubby camp that she and Simon had seen beyond the train track, or were the prisoners still under the sandy factory yards?

A large hand caught her a stinging blow on the side of her head. "Quit your staring about and get a move on," Mrs. Siddons said. A few of the women sniggered, and one began to sniff loudly.

"Hoo hoo hoo!" she said, pretending to be Miriam. "I'm the new girl, I am!"

Miriam felt the angry prickles in her nose again. Those bloody women! She wanted to scream at them, but she had a strong notion that it would be of no use.

The hallway widened into a large, square chamber. Miriam had a confused notion of huge cogs, great flywheels, and large belts that turned around and around, twisting something brown and pliable in the process.

The line divided into two. Some of the women went over to the large machines and tapped other workers on the shoulders to relieve them. "Ta," one of them said as she stepped back from an iron spiral with sharp edges that spun next to her unprotected fingers. "I could just do with a cup of tea; been working all night."

"All right, get on with you," Mrs. Siddons said, and she pushed the line of women who hadn't gone forward to take a station in the room. "Over there," she added to Miriam, who looked around, wondering what Mrs. Siddons meant. She realized the woman had pointed to a small passage between two of the machines. "Take care of her, Elsie; she don't know where she's going."

Elsie, a thick, lumpish girl not much older than Miriam, pushed her towards the passage and Mrs. Siddons took her own place in front of one of the machines. "Don't we work here?" Miriam asked Elsie.

The girl hooted. "Not much! You and me are picking boles, and don't you forget it. They'll expect at least a basketful by this morning from every one of us." They were in the passage, which opened into another narrow stairs, leading down. The steps were so narrow here that some of the workers, Elsie among them, had to descend sideways in order to accommodate their girth.

At the bottom, there was another room shaped just like the one above, only darker and filled with baskets in one end and crates in the other. "Come on." Elsie pushed Miriam towards one of the crates and picking up two empty baskets on her way. "There you go, one for you and one for me. Friendly, isn't it? Aren't I a pip? Tomorrow you'll do this on your own, right? And we can go our separate ways, and I won't have to talk to you again. So's I hope you're minding what I say. No one's coddling you here."

She plumped Miriam's basket beside one of the crates and sat on the one next to it. "You gets one of the sticks inside the box, see, the crates are loaded with them, and you've got to pick them, see."

"Pick them?"

Elsie sighed and rolled her eyes. "Just watch me." Her thick fingers peeled the thin bark from the twig, revealing some white pods that clung to the core. Elsie pointed at them. "See those? That's what you put in your basket. And you don't want to squeeze too hard, or they'll burst, and the sap'll get all over your hands, and a right bugger it is to get off, too. And Mrs. Siddons'll have your head."

Miriam nodded. "I see. I'm very obliged to you."

Elsie stared at her for a moment, and hooted. "Very obliged! I bet you are! A fountain of charity, I am! Here, I'm leaving this one to come and sit with youse. Shift over, Sally." She picked up her own basket and moved towards a group of workers who had gathered around another crate. There were a few glances in Miriam's direction and more stifled laughter.

Cut off from the group of girls, Miriam scrubbed the back of her hand across her eyes when she thought no one could see. She picked up one of the branches. At least I'm not upstairs in that nasty machine room, she thought, as she peeled the bark back from one of the branches in the crate. A sharp, spicy smell made her sniff and close her eyes. She knew that scent. Yes – the wood they "picked" were pieces of bolemor trees.

So the Devil's Kitchen *was* part of her father's business. It didn't seem right, however. She had visited his factory when he had been alive. One of his undersecretaries had led her through the large rooms, pointing out the different steps of the manufacturing process.

In that workspace, Miriam remembered, the bolemor trees were refined and polished by machines that workers in spotless aprons fed with planks, and everything had taken place above ground, in an airy, light-filled room lined with windows. In fact, she had overheard something about Pearson's winning an award for their innovative factory design that aided production and catered to the workers' safety.

It had been completely different from this dark, musty cellar that she was now in. Miriam looked around at the dark walls and back at the twig she was holding. There were the white pods, just as Elsie had said. Carefully she picked them off, and put them into the basket. They were sticky, and she had to wipe sap off her fingers before she stripped another branch.

She quickly discovered the drawback of picking boles from the bolemor sticks. The bark, although soft and easy to peel back, was lined with fibers that sliced her fingers if she wasn't careful. Miriam suffered several cuts, the most painful of which were right under her nails. She didn't want to stick her thumb in her mouth to suck on it, though, since she had an idea of what was in the sap boles that they were gathering.

This was her father's business, but not the one he had established. No. It was the new pharmaceutical branch, led by vile, fish-faced Uncle Virgil and those disgusting Cantwells, Valiant and Barbara. Miriam had the idea that there, in that dark, cellar room, she and Elsie and the rest of them were involved in creating something horrible. Some drug, she thought. Perhaps the Cantwells hoped to sell it to society ladies, or young rich bucks, the society types who were always bored and looking for a new thrill.

Miriam shivered and remembered the sad look in the eyes of the woman who kept saying, "Oh, no." What could make someone so hopeless, and so lost? Whatever it was, it frightened her.

As she thought about this, her hands soon cramped from the work. She had no choice but to keep at it. She was comfortable enough sitting on one of the crates, and she had eaten part of a large breakfast of bread doorstops slathered with lard and jam that had been thrust into her cell much earlier. She had even slept well on the thin cot mattress, unhampered by nightmares, since the night before that she had only snatched a few hours rest on the train.

Soon, her mind drifted back to Thomasina, who had reached the edge of the kingdom and had to cross a bridge into the neighboring country. In order to do so, the farmer's daughter had to solve a puzzle involving a fox, three ducks, and seven barrels of grain that had to be carried across the river in a small boat before she could ride on to the palace to demand the Birthright for her own country.

Miriam worked out the answer in her head, smiling a bit to herself. She had to write that down later, but what could she use? She had paper in the ancient copybook that she had found. Now if she could only filch a pen and a bit of ink.

"Dinnertime," a voice called down the stairs.

"And about time, too," Elsie said, getting up from the crate. There was a pounding of footsteps down the stairs, and two girls burst into the room carrying large bowls covered with stained napkins.

"'Lo, Elsie," one of the girls carrying the lunch said.

"Back at you, Minnie," Elsie said. She looked under the napkin. "Bread and cheese – what a surprise! Here, Sally, catch." She tossed a chunk of bread and a wedge of cheese to Sally, who caught them with a grin.

"Any ale?" Sally asked, nudging the girl next to her, which happened to be Miriam. Looking down and seeing the new inmate, Sally frowned and moved away.

"No, it's champers today, girls," Minnie responded quickly, making the others shout with laughter. She lifted a jug with one huge arm and grinned, showing a large pink gap where her teeth were missing in front.

"Thanks, Minnie! That'll go a treat with the pigeon pasties!" someone called. Minnie grinned again and made a show of licking her lips, flashing that hideous toothless gap again.

The girls crowded forward with their mugs in hand, and Minnie expertly filled them. Miriam, who hadn't thought to bring her mug, hung back and accepted a piece of bread and cheese from the bottom of the bowl, even though they looked terribly dry.

"What's the matter? Didn't bring your cup?" Minnie asked. "Here, I've got a spare. Give it back to me tomorrow in the yard, mind, or it'll be the worst for you." She thrust out a mug. Miriam tried not to flinch as she took it. What did she think would happen, anyway? She wouldn't catch some terrible toothless disease from the girl's mug.

"Thanks," she said, as the mug was filled with bluish milk.

"She's much obliged, Minnie!" Elsie called, her mouth full. Sally found this remark an example of the highest wit, throwing her head back in order to laugh and choking in the process.

"Woo-hoo-hooooo!" Sally said, wiping her eyes. "You made a bite go down the wrong pipe, Elsie."

"Lay off," Minnie said, shoving Elsie. "She's just a kid." She put her fists, which were roughly the size of cottage loaves, on her hips and glared at Sally.

"Didn't mean nothing by it." Elsie picked up her mug and crammed the rest of the cheese into her mouth.

"See that you didn't," Minnie threatened. Picking up the bowls and the empty jug, she made for the dark stairs, followed by the other girl, who had stayed quiet during the entire episode.

Casting dark looks at Minnie's retreating bulk, Elsie and her cohorts gathered back at the crate and began to peel twigs. Miriam quickly swallowed the rest of her milk and cheese and did the same, peeling the bark back and placing the pods into the basket. Once the basket was full, a dark, thin woman called Wilson whisked it away and replaced it with an empty one. This appeared to be Wilson's only duty.

As she started her afternoon shift, Miriam was transported back to her own kingdom. After making her way to the Palace, Thomasina managed to talk her way into the king's chamber of ministers with her ready wit and quick charm. The king refused to part with the birthright, but he offered to gamble for it. If she lost, Thomasina would become a slave in the mines, just like Miriam.

Of course she won easily. The king was enraged and demanded a duel, not realizing that the "boy" was a farm girl in disguise.

The afternoon quickly passed. By the time Thomasina had won the duel, and the king had discovered that she was really a woman, and Thomasina had won the king's heart, Elsie and Sally stood up from the crates. Elsie put her fists on her spine and rubbed her back.

Mrs. Siddons appeared at the top of the stairs. "Right, girls, inspection," she called. "Line up."

Miriam popped the last of the pods into the basket. She grabbed Minnie's mug and stood at the back of the line.

The girls marched up one at a time to Mrs. Siddons, who ran a practiced hand over their clothes and through their hair. She even had them open their mouths and stick their tongues out, checking their names off a list as she did so. Only were they allowed to go up the steps.

"What is she searching us for?" Miriam whispered to the woman in front of her, the dark thin one who had collected the filled baskets.

Wilson started and turned with a hunted look in her eyes. "What? What do you want? Why did you ask me that?"

"Sorry!" Miriam said. *Keep your hair on,* she added mentally.

The line moved forward slowly. Finally Mrs. Siddons checked Wilson, squinting closely into her mouth.

"Check her armpits," she ordered brusquely. "Go on, Wilson, slip off your shirt."

"Why do you want to do that for?" Wilson cried, opening her mouth. A white pod popped out from between her teeth.

Mrs. Siddons stared at her for a moment, and she picked up the pod with a look of disgust. "This was your last chance, Wilson," she said. "You'll have to pack up your things."

"What? No, you can't! I've got a man and a kid to feed!" Wilson cried. She twisted like a salamander in Mrs. Siddons tight grip.

"You knew what would happen, so it's your own fault. Now, come along there, Wilson, that's a good girl. Don't make things harder – ouch! You little cat!"

Wilson had leaned forward suddenly and bitten Mrs. Siddons' hand. With a wild gasp the woman pounded up the stairs, the two inspectors close after her.

Miriam looked around the deserted room. The silence was sudden, punctuated by Wilson's muffled screams as she was chased on the floor above.

Something lay on Miriam's toe. It was a grubby sheet of paper, nailed to a rough plank - the list of names that Mrs. Siddons had been checking off. And under it lay not one but *two* pencils.

Miriam picked them up. She hardly dared to breathe. They were stubby and had been licked and bitten, but she could write with them. Or, she told herself, one of them.

Retrieving the list, she put one pencil in Minnie's mug and climbed the stairs to look for Mrs. Siddons.

Among the machines in the workroom upstairs, Wilson had been caught and was now getting towed off to her cell. Mrs. Siddons, breathing hard, tucked one wisp of hair back and rolled up a sleeve. "She'll never learn," she said to the silent group of workers, who were watching Wilson's exit. "You don't fool with that stuff, see. It's poison, that is."

"Em, Mrs. Siddons." Miriam came forward tentatively and held out the list. "You left this on the floor downstairs, just now."

Mrs. Siddons became aware of Miriam's existence, and her thin lips widened in a smile. "Oh, ta very much," she said, grabbing the list. "Headmistress would have my hide if I lost that." Miriam held her breath, afraid that someone would notice that there was a missing pencil, but the inspectors started up the stairs, followed by the workers who grouped themselves in a neat line.

Miriam fell in behind Elsie, who turned around with a glare and hissed, "You're doing all right for yourself, aren't you? No flies on you today, now, are there?"

Miriam shrugged and stuck her tongue out at Elsie's back. She might be alone and have no friends, but at least now she could write down Thomasina's story.

CHAPTER 8

A Quick Escape

In a few days, Simon was able to run around his room. His knees no longer grew weak and his heart didn't flutter in his chest, even when he leaped about as fast as he could. His jaw regained its normal size, and he was able to chew easily

In fact, food became his primary concern. He wanted to pretend that he was still an extremely ill patient. If he ran around the room before the scheduled appearance of Nurse or Nanny, it caused a heartbeat that was fast enough to convince them that he really was suffering. "Hectic color," Nurse said after a particularly athletic morning, "and a warm, perspiring brow."

The warm brow was actually due to hopping from corner to corner and not a fever. All of this, however, also increased his appetite. He was still being served an invalid's meals of jellies, blancmanges, sponges, weak tea, and dry toast. As well, he had to leave enough food on his plate to convince the nurses and their attendant guard that he really was very weak and they could relax their supervision.

Jenkins continued to accompany the nurses as a guard, and he glowered at Simon during the nurses' visits. Whenever Nanny bent over Simon to change a dressing or wash his face, or coax him to eat a little more "for her sake," Jenkins frowned and waved a fist at Simon. The big man didn't seem to care so much about Nurse, but he watched every move Nanny made.

One evening, at the end of her shift, Nanny wiped Simon's forehead with a cool cloth and stood up from his bedside. "You look better," she sighed, "but your energy is still sadly lacking. You have an imbalance of the vital liquids, perhaps. We really should have a physician come in and look at you."

Simon sat up in alarm. "I feel much better," he stammered. "With your excellent care, Nanny, and a few more days in bed, I'm sure I'll be able to think about getting up soon." Over her shoulder, he saw Jenkins pull down the corners of his lips and silently mouth Simon's words, "With your excellent care, Nanny!" in a hideous, mocking fashion.

Nanny laughed and touched her curls with one hand. "Well, perhaps. But it really is time to start to think about a doctor. I suppose we shall see." She kissed Simon briskly on the forehead (Jenkins' eyes nearly bulged out of their sockets) stepped back, and picked up his discarded tray. Simon followed it with wistful eyes. His plate still contained a square of cheese and half an apple that he could have devoured. At the thought of the food, his stomach contracted in a long, loud rumble.

Nanny was too busy with his linens to notice. As she gathered his napkins and draped them over his plate, Jenkins emitted a low growl. "What you want to plant kisses on him for?" His brows descended over his eye sockets.

Nanny looked up in surprise and frowned. She bustled to the guard's side and hissed, "Stop that at once! It is going directly against orders!" She glanced back at Simon, but he faked unconcern, glancing at the flowers by his bed in an idle way.

"Blast their orders." Jenkins uncurled a long, hairy arm and wound it around Nanny's waist. "When are you going to come out walking with me again?"

She laughed, a silvery little tinkle. "But don't be silly – open the door for me, do, like a dear – of course we can't be seen together while I'm on a case! Now hush, the child will hear –"

Simon could see their two forms, silhouetted now against the hall light. Jenkins looked down at Nanny. The guard had the appearance of a huge, misbehaving child as she raised one finger and shook it at him. The door closed behind them and her diatribe continued as they walked away, muffled by the thick walls.

However, with that argument going on, *they had forgotten to turn the key in the lock*. Simon hopped up as soon as Nanny's voice died away and felt for his slippers. He climbed down from the bed, grabbed the thick dressing gown that hung from a hook on the wall, and crept towards the door.

The handle turned easily. Simon poked his head out and looked down the passage in both directions. The hall was lined with doors and was deserted. Nanny and Jenkins had either gone below or into one of the other rooms in the hall.

Without stopping to think, he stepped into the passage. It felt good to be able to move on his own and not to be in that scabby room anymore.

He'd find a way out of the house, he thought as he strode down the hall, and he'd set off for a police station. He would get hold of his parents and demand that they release Miriam from that hellhole where she had been mistakenly delivered by the Night Watchman Express. Finally, he'd find Neil and make certain that all was well with him.

Still, he reflected, if he saw some food on the way out, he'd grab a bite. He could just do with a large ham sandwich, or a huge beef pasty, or a Scotch egg.

As he pondered these matters, he reached a little stairway that led downstairs. It twisted so sharply that he couldn't see where it led, but Simon plunged down the steps without any hesitation. With any luck he would find a large pantry or a scullery at the bottom.

The stairs turned several more corners and passed landings that looked identical to the one he had left behind. The house had to be huge, with ten or twelve floors of rooms. It seemed more like an old palace or estate than someone's actual residence.

The staircase ended at a floor tiled with rough, orange squares worn down in the centers with years of use, lit from above by a dim lamp. Simon crept forward. He sniffed. He thought he detected the delicious smell of roast chicken and new potatoes.

The room was a large kitchen, just as he had hoped. He could find something to eat and bolt out the back door. On a sideboard there a large plate covered with a cloth. He lifted one corner of the napkin and saw the remains of someone's tea: tomato, egg, and cucumber sandwiches.

Seizing two in each hand, Simon took a huge bite of egg and cress and began to search for a door, munching as he looked. The only exit, however, was through what appeared to be a stately dining room, which opened onto a large hall.

He swallowed a huge lump of sandwich and crossed the hall, feeling as though someone was watching him as he did so. Nonsense, he said to himself; it's just your imagination. Still, he felt a bit silly carrying the sandwiches, and he stuffed them into the pockets of his dressing gown.

There was a large front door with a brass handle set directly in its center. Simon made for it. His heart thumped in his chest, and he tried not to let his slippers scuffle on the marble floor. He reached the door without incident and was pleased to find that this handle, as well, turned easily in his hand.

"Oh, I don't think you should do that, Simon," someone breathed in his ear. He jumped, turned, and gasped with fright.

Barbara Cantwell, her orange eyes narrowed against the overhead light, stood behind him. As usual, she was dressed to perfection; her hair was piled up on her head and cascaded over one shoulder in long curls, and she wore a loose chifferobe of creamy brocade that exactly matched her skin.

"Barbara," Simon panted, seizing her shoulder. "Barbara! It's really you! Thank goodness... I hoped I'd find someone I could trust! Listen, I'm in the most awful fix. My friends are missing, and I have to get a message to my parents somehow. Heaven only knows what they're thinking!"

"Hush, now," Barbara said, one corner of her exquisite lips turning up in a smile. "And, if by 'my friends' you mean that scutty little girl and the bespectacled swot I had the misfortune to meet in your house, don't worry about them."

Simon's mouth opened and a red wave of fury passed over his vision. Trembling, he spoke to her in a low tone. "I advise you not to speak of Miriam and Neil in that way ever again."

Barbara's lips lost none of their curve, but her eyes sparked dangerously. "Now, really, Simon. Don't tell me that you actually have some sort of affection for that girl! Didn't we discuss this already? As it happens, you have pushed back our plans a trifle when you ran off in this fashion, but I forgive you. In fact, now you and I needn't worry about that tiresome arranged marriage of yours any more, since what's-her-name has disappeared. It's quite a godsend, actually."

"Miriam," Simon said, and he curled his hands into fists.

"Miriam," Barbara agreed. She moved a trifle closer to him. "Do you know, Simon, you've grown more mature during the past few days. I've thought about you so often. And now to see you so suddenly, and you look like a real man! I must admit I'm rather devastated. Do you remember when you used to turn my music pages for me, when we were staying together?"

Simon jerked his hand away from hers. The disgust that he felt for her must have been clearly written on his face.

Her own face never lost its alluring smile, but her eyes narrowed. "I see that you have been overcome by an unfortunate attack of conscience," she said. "How utterly boring. We'll just have to see what we can do to rescue you from such a terrible thing. Valiant!" she called. She kept her eyes on Simon.

Her brother appeared in the hall, holding his customary cigar. "What's toward, Babs? Couldn't convince him to behave with your wiles, my love?" He smiled and lounged against one wall.

Barbara turned to respond to her brother sharply, and Simon leaped for the door. He opened it and made to run out, when cigar smoke choked him, and he felt an appalling spot of heat against one cheek.

"Absolutely not, old chap," Valiant said in Simon's ear, with the same confident candor that his sister used. "I'm holding my cigar against your handsome face, and it would give you an extremely nasty burn if you moved. I'm going to hold it against your eyelid now. Like that. Now, you'll find that you'll lose an eye if you so much as flinch. Don't do it, there's a good fellow."

The smoke and the heat of the burning made Simon lose track

of logical reasoning. Before he could twist away, or yell for help, his arms were clamped behind him and someone expertly tied his hands together.

"You can look now." Valiant stepped away and puffed out a long cloud of smoke. "Barbara's an old hand at tying people up; don't know how she acquired that little skill; eh, old boy?" He dug one elbow into Simon's ribs and winked.

"Oh, really, Valiant, you are disgusting at times," Barbara said. She let go of Simon's hands and threaded one arm through her brother's. "I wish you would put that thing out." She pouted her lips at him.

He looked down at her and winked again. "But it's just so delicious and decadent, to smoke a cigarillo that I've used as a torture device," he said.

"Let me go," Simon said with a shudder. "You're foul, the both of you. When I get away from here, I hope to never see either of you again, except in the hands of the law."

Valiant laughed and raised one eyebrow. "Oh ho!" he laughed. "You seem to have lost your young swain, Barbara!"

She wound one arm around her brother's neck and brought her lips to his ear. She whispered something, and one small dimple appeared at the curve of her red lips. Valiant nodded at her and laughed again. His attention snapped back to Simon and he became serious.

"Time for business," he said. "I'll call that fellow, Jenkins, and tell him that he and the Nanny woman will lose a week's wages for leaving the door unlocked. And," he added, "they had better get Simon here back in bed. He's looking a little overheated! Get the joke, my love? Overheated?" He waved his cigar in her direction.

Barbara nodded, not laughing. "You and I will also need to accelerate our own methods." She reaching forward and felt in Simon's pocket, although he tried to back away from her. With a delicious moue of distaste, she held up the remains of one sandwich. "Hungry, were you? What a shame. *I think you'll be a great deal hungrier before the end of this week*," she suddenly whispered, and she darted her head at Simon like a snake about to attack a hummingbird.

Unnerved, he couldn't help flinching and pulling his head back. Her face was contorted in a terrible grimace. He had never seen anything as evil in his life. He blinked, and her expression returned to her usual delightful smile. She laughed, a husky note in the darkness of the hall, and kissed her fingertips at him.

CHAPTER 9
The Headquarters

P hilips, the lawyer whose services Mana had retained, gestured to a house with one arm. The sleeve of his jacket rode up, revealing his shirt cuff. "It's a small house, but the neighborhood is the best to be found in this vicinity. The street is quiet, and working-class families make up the bulk of those who live here. The house is also furnished, although quite plainly."

Mana looked up at the front of the house, which was dark with a newly painted yellow door. "It appears to be exactly what we need, Mr. Philips," she said, pushing her veil away from her face. Two small boys paused in the act of rolling a hoop past the house and stared at her.

"Cor!" one said loudly. He had the plentiful remains of a jam sandwich smeared over his face. At the implied insult to Mana, Neil felt his face grow hot and his glasses began to steam up; he prepared to double his hands into fists should either of the little horrors say anything else to her.

Kyoge, however, settled the matter. He stepped forward and took off his new bowler hat. He merely stared at the boys for a moment without saying anything. After a short time they appeared to recall some other pressing engagement and hurried away, casting curious looks back over their shoulders.

"Well," Philips said, clearing his throat, "shall we go inside?" He produced a key, and opening the little gate to the house, he marched up to the steps and opened the door.

Mana, Kyoge and Neil followed closely. Once indoors, the house smelled clean enough, although the wallpaper hung in long strips in one corner of the entrance. The hallway was lined with bookcases filled with old volumes. Two doors on either side of the hall opened to a sitting room to the left and a small dining room on the right.

Mana started up the stairs, which were covered with a runner that had worn down to mere threads in the center of each step. Philips came behind her with Kyoge at his shoulder.

Neil left them to it. Instead, he went to the back of the house, where he found the kitchen. The floor was clean, although the tiles were cracked in spots. There was a wooden table on one side, and a few sad-looking plants languished on the windowsill behind the sink. Looking outside, Neil saw that the house included a small kitchen garden with a tiny square courtyard. The house must have been the residence of a retired university professor, or perhaps a bluestocking lady fallen on hard times.

The others came back down the stairs. Neil went to meet them in the hall. "It will suit us admirably, Mr. Philips," Mana said. "I must commend you for your excellent work in finding it so quickly. And can you also find someone to cook and dust for us?"

Philips straightened his tie, which was made of rather battered black linen. "Actually, my sister's eldest is looking for a place for a short time before she is married. She is a good girl, and hard-working, but I must tell you..." He whispered something in Mana's ear.

Mana nodded. "That shouldn't matter in the slightest, as long as she feels well enough to work for the next few weeks. Well," she added, drawing on her gloves, "all that remains is to move our things from the hotel."

Philips bowed. "I have already engaged a porter, madam. And some fresh linens have been ordered for delivery this evening."

"Very impressive!" Mana smiled, showing her white, even teeth. "My goodness, Mr. Philips, you certainly were a good find. Well, shall we all go and have a bit of lunch somewhere?"

Neil suddenly realized that he was very hungry. "Yes, please," he said emphatically.

They exited the house, Philips first locking it carefully and handing the key to Mana. "I would be very careful in this area, if I were you, madam," he said.

Kyoge nodded. "I'll protect her. Any ruffians who wish to enter her house will have to deal with me."

Well, reflected Neil, as he watched the big man descend the steps, *I would give a lot to see that.*

They walked back into the street. The boys had returned, their faces smeared with more jam, and they had found a stick, which they banged against the railings. "Going to live here?" one boy asked, pushing his hat back on his head.

"What if we do?" Neil responded.

The other boy burst out laughing. "Keep your knickers straight, yeh gloomy toff!"

Mana put a hand on Neil's shoulder and said, "Yes, we will live in this house as of today. Perhaps you could keep an eye on the house for us for an hour or so and watch for a delivery. I expect it should arrive any moment." A few coins appeared in her hand.

Both boys dropped their sticks. One grasped the gate with a filthy paw. "We might be free," he answered, his full attention on the clinking coins.

"You appear to be knowledgeable, intelligent men," Mana continued, looking at the two boys. "Maybe you could also give us the name of some small restaurant nearby, clean and with good, plain food?"

They looked at each other. The one wearing a hat pulled on some dried skin on his lower lip with a forefinger and thumb. "There's Rosie's," he offered. "She does a fair meat and gravy pie."

"Meat and gravy pie." Mana smiled. "As it happens, that was the very thing we are hungry for."

She handed them a coin each and started in the direction indicated, when the boys called her back. "Hey! Missus!"

"Well, what is it?" Kyoge asked, looking down at them from his huge height.

"Just wanted to warn you," one boy said, looking up at Kyoge as if he were talking to an equal. "Ever since that one –" he pointed to Philips – "started nosing around the house a few days ago and asking questions and such, there's been a haunt on it."

"What do you mean – a haunt?" Neil burst out.

"Just what I say. There's lights that go on, and off, and we've heard things move about; for the past few days, it's been going on."

"Stairs that creak," the other boy said. "And windows and doors what should be shut found open, see."

"Well," Mana said with firm determination, "thank you both very much for that important information. We do appreciate your time. Now, Rosie's was the name of the café, you said? Excellent. Come along, Neil." Without looking behind her, she strode off, pulling her veil back in place over her face.

"Cor," one of the boys said again. "For a darkie, you'd think she were the queen. Er, no offense meant," he added hastily, tipping his scurrilous hat at Kyoge, who stared back at him for a moment before following Mana.

As they sat over the remains of their meal, Mana balanced her teacup in both hands and took a thoughtful sip. Looking at her, Neil thought he knew what was in her thoughts. "Do you really think there's a haunt on the house?" he asked.

Kyoge shook his head and put his hand flat on the table. "No such thing," he declared. "Ghost stories are always derived from fact, and often for someone's profit. Look at the legend that Atol spread about the tunnel through the mountains on Lampala, to explain the cries of his victims in the cage."

Mana put down her cup and shivered. "Very true," she agreed. "It certainly prevented anyone from finding me for some time, until Neil was clever enough to discover where to look."

Kyoge scowled at her. "Such a thing will never happen to you again," he said, and he clasped a fork in his huge fist as if he still held his Lampalan spear.

Philips wiped some crumbs from his lips with his napkin. "Still," he said, "even though I am a lawyer and therefore continually on the search for a logical argument for everything I hear, I have been told some strange stories. There was a blue light that appeared in the graveyard where my great-aunt is buried, some few miles from here, and our maid told us that the dog used to watch something invisible climb her stairs every night at the same time, when I was a child."

"Is that really true?" Neil stuffed one last bite of piecrust (it was flaky and delicious) into his mouth and sat forward. "We heard some stories as well, on the docks where I grew up. There was a ship that was said to appear once a year, with no lanterns and a silent crew. Someone said they saw one of their faces, and their eyes were nothing but dark, empty sockets."

"Stop that at once," Mana said with great determination. "No need to work ourselves up over what is undoubtedly a foolish tale, invented for the purpose of keeping thieves away."

Kyoge nodded in agreement. "You are in the right, My Queen – that is, Miss Postulate. I have often heard these tales, but I have never seen anything strange occur myself."

Mana laughed. "Exactly! They always begin, 'I have heard,' or 'It is said' or 'I know a friend who told me.'"

Philips smiled. "Perhaps we should head back? If you're not afraid of the ghosts, that is." He reached for his wallet, but Mana forestalled him.

"It is my privilege." She put a gold coin on the table.

The lawyer turned slightly pink. "Really, I insist. As my client, you should-" He spoke to empty air. Mana was already striding to the door.

The boys were still in front of the house. One swung on the gate, and the one with the hat had resumed his game of banging his stick. "Gennelman's here," they shouted as soon as they saw Mana. The boy on the gate jumped off and they both ran towards her.

"We told him to wait on the steps," one said importantly.

"Well, that was exactly right." Mana climbed the steps where a porter was standing beside a tower of boxes with an expectant air. The two boys, who had obviously adopted Mana as their own property, followed up the steps and watched the proceedings closely.

Coins were handed out all round, and the porter and the boys were sent off, well satisfied. "Now we can begin," Mana said in a low tone. "Come inside, all of you, and we'll decide what should be done first."

They trooped into the house and, by common consent, sat in the small sitting room. It was furnished with deep, squashy sofas and several rather creaky chairs. Philips' niece was already there, laying a fire, and she turned and gave them a cheerful smile as they filed in and sat down.

"I'll have the hearth ready for you in a moment," she said briskly, "and I'll start on the bedrooms." Neil noticed with a start that she was very pregnant.

Mana nodded. "Thanks very much. I'm sorry, I didn't catch your name."

The girl laughed. "Janet. That's my name. Right, that should do you; now I'm going to get those linens and make the beds."

Once she was gone, Mana turned to Kyoge and said, "I have explained our situation to Philips, so we can speak freely in front of him. I have an idea that he will be of great assistance."

"That could be true," Kyoge objected, "but we shouldn't tell our story to everyone we meet. No offence meant, Mr. Philips, but we know nothing about you."

The lawyer grinned. "None taken, Mr. Kyoge, and a very admirable position it is that you take. The facts are that I've watched the occurrences at Pearsons' for some time. An acquaintance of mine, Pierpont Fortescue, is the attorney for the Pearson family, and I have seen some papers prepared by him that were not, well, shall we say, exactly within the confines of the law."

Mana sat forward. "You mean to say that Fortescue is a thorough villain," she said. "I have long suspected it myself."

"Well," Philips began. "I wouldn't put it quite - that is to say, I have worked with him in the past, and he has used some methods that I would not employ myself."

"Just as I thought. A thorough villain. Could you investigate his offices on our behalf, and find out anything pertaining to the Pearson family, in particular, to Miriam Pearson's situation? In the meantime, Kyoge, you should try and get as close to the main factory as possible. In fact, perhaps you could apply for a job there."

"And me too?" Neil asked, leaning forward and clasping his hands on his knees. "I bet they'd hire me."

"Perhaps," Mana said. She looked at him and smiled. "Yes, that might do very well. You could start as a junior clerk or some such thing. While you're doing that, I will start to look for the Cantwells and see if I can encounter them in society."

"You? In society?!" Philips ejaculated. "Er, that is, begging your pardon, but-"

"I am a queen, as Kyoge enjoys reminding me at length," Mana said, smiling. "That will be my entrée. Some aspiring hostess is always looking for an exotic royal pet to produce at a soiree or dinner party. I intend to play the part of some wealthy woman's society pet."

Kyoge frowned again at her, but she shook her head at him. "No use giving me that suspicious look of yours, Kyoge. You will dirty your hands and work ten or twelve hours a day," she continued. "I intend to do as much as I can for our cause as well. I will have to put up with some curiosity, but you will have the more physical job."

Kyoge lowered his brow further, but at length he sat back. "Very well. But if anyone at those parties tries anything with you, they will have me to answer to."

That night, Neil lay in the small bedroom that had been allotted to him. The bed was small but comfortable, and Janet had put fresh sheets on the beds. The pillow was soft, and he should have been asleep, but the horrors they had discussed over lunch tumbled through his brain, causing him to start at the wind blowing the leaves on the courtyard outside, and the faint tick-tick of the clock by his bed. Finally he fell into an uneasy doze, punctuated by strange dreams of trying to find Mana, and Miriam, and Riki.

He sat up suddenly, his heart pounding. He thought that he had heard a noise. Yes, there it was again! A soft tread pounded down the stairs and stopped at the bottom.

It's only Mana. Perhaps she decided to have a cup of warm milk, Neil reasoned to himself. However, he decided to get up and open his door. The moonlight lay on the threadbare rug, as well as the bookshelves that lined the hallway. It appeared that the previous owners had been great readers.

Neil crept to the top of the stairs and stopped. There were muffled sounds as of metal moving against china, and cupboard doors opening and closing. He breathed out a sigh of relief. It *was* Mana, or more likely, Kyoge, overcome with hunger in the middle of the night and off to the kitchen to look for some food.

He crept back to his room and glanced at the bookcases. Tomorrow, after he had applied for a job, he'd look for something to read before bed so he wouldn't be woken in the dead hours of the night. Something historical and long-winded, designed to make the reader fall asleep. Yes, that would do the trick.

CHAPTER 10
Break Time

M iriam looked up in surprise as Mrs. Siddons came down the stairs. The appearance of the older woman signaled the end of the shift. Miriam had managed to get into a rhythm, and the boles popped off the twigs as she devised an end to Thomasina's story.

"Line up, you lot!" Mrs. Siddons shouted. "It's Break Time in twenty minutes, and I want to get my own rest and repose!" She turned and elbowed Minnie, who stood beside her to help with inspections, and wheezed out a laugh.

"Break Time," Elsie echoed, as she pushed into the line of women. "Where's Sally? I almost forgot it was today!"

Break Time! What did that mean? Miriam wondered. Did they actually have a free moment when they didn't have to work or be watched? She could use the time to write her story, and perhaps even to think about making an escape plan.

The line filed up the stairs slowly as their names were ticked off the list, and as she passed by, Miriam handed the borrowed mug back to Minnie. "Thanks again," she muttered.

"'S nothing, love," Minnie replied. "That's the lot, Mrs. Siddons!"

"About time too," Mrs. Siddons replied. "I need to tot up the wages before I steps outside."

Miriam stumped up the stairs to her cell. She wondered if some of the women were allowed outside into the city. Maybe, if she could gain the Headmistress' confidence, and get promoted or some such thing, she could go outside and escape... She heaved a big sigh, realizing that her plan probably involved years of filthy labor in that dungeon. No, she had to somehow, some way, find a way to Simon and Mana much sooner than that.

Still deep in thought, she hurriedly washed the dirty sap from the bolemors off her hands and filched the copybook and pencil out from their hiding place in the wall. She sat on the bed and licked the pencil, but suddenly a key turned in the lock to her cell.

Thrusting the book and pencil into one leg of her knickers for lack of a better place, she jumped up and put her hands behind her back. The woman from the islands, the same one who had locked her up the first day in Devil's Kitchen, beckoned to her and said, "You. Come."

Unwillingly, Miriam looked out of the door. The other women were lined up again, talking loudly. "I'm off to give Henry what for when I sees him in the yard!" one said.

"Why's that?"

"He spent the money I gave him last week; I heard from Minnie!"

"Well, why'd you give it to him?"

"He's my man, ain't he? What else am I going to do with it?"

"Hurry up, girl! Don't dawdle!"

This last was directed to Miriam. With a gasp, she looked up and saw the Headmistress' pale eyes boring into her, as if they could read her thoughts or even see the contraband hidden in her pants. The woman from the islands gestured again and disappeared. Quickly Miriam skipped into line and the workers moved up the stairs, still chattering.

Upstairs, they were herded down a long, dark corridor, lined with more lamps that flickered in the gloom. At the end there was a large door, and it was actually open to the outside. The women moved out into the open, and Miriam squinted her eyes at the unaccustomed sunlight. She scrubbed her lids with one fist and looked around for a means to escape.

They were still enclosed, however, in a large, square courtyard that looked like the one she had been brought into when she had first arrived. There was the same damp, heavy, clinging sand underfoot, and the walls were stained with soot and lined with more doors.

One of these, a large, wooden affair, swung open and revealed a group of men. The Headmaster was behind them.

"No fights today, gentleman," the Headmaster said. He stood to one side and swung a huge key in his skeletal hands.

"You all know the rules," the Headmistress continued in a cold voice behind Miriam, making the girl jump. "No nonsense. Mrs. Siddons, the wages."

The workers began to mutter something, as Mrs. Siddons walked to the men and women in the yards. She handed out small, thin packets, which were quickly stowed away. Some of the men slowly drifted into the women's courtyard where Miriam stood, and a group of girls, Elsie among them, rushed into the men's yard.

"Nothing for you this week," Mrs. Siddons said to Miriam, having handed out the last packet. "You've got to pay off your clothes and training, see."

Miriam hadn't expected any money, but it was still infuriating to be told that she had to actually pay for Elsie's insults and half-hearted instruction. Mrs. Siddons walked to the door that led to the men's yard, and Miriam, looking around, found that most of the other female workers had melted away into the men's side of the yard. The Headmistress and Headmaster stood by the gate, but they conversed in low tones, their heads close together.

Taking advantage of the unexpected freedom, Miriam wandered to an empty corner and sat on the damp sand. Shielding herself by the wall, she took out the book and pencil from the leg of her knickers (thank goodness they hadn't fallen out on the way up) and thought for a moment before she began to write quickly.

As usual, she lost all sense of where she was. The sandy floor, the stained walls, and the closed doors all disappeared, and she was transported to Thomasina's kingdom and the search for the Birthright. The story, shaped already in her mind, flowed easily, and she had to chew the point of the pencil frequently to keep up with her fingers, racing across the page.

"What have you got there?" a voice accused suddenly. A shadow fell across the book. Miriam looked up and was recalled to reality. Elsie was standing over her, peering at the copybook.

"Nothing," Miriam said, closing the book. "It's mine."

"Where'd you get that pencil from? I could use one of those, and the book too. Sally, let's grab her arm and take the lot."

Furiously, Miriam flung the book down and faced them. "I'd just like to see you try," she said. Her voice shook with anger.

"She's going to cry!" Sally howled, delighted.

"No, I'm not," Miriam said more firmly. "But no one has the right to touch my things."

"Yes, we can," Elsie said. She pounced and grabbed the pencil. "Sally, you get the book! Let's see what the little swot's been writing!"

"Give that back!" Miriam said. She doubled her fists and stepped right up close to Elsie.

"What's going on here?"

Elsie shrieked and turned around. Perhaps she was afraid that it was the Headmistress. Miriam's vision cleared, and from behind a red haze of fury she saw Blue Eyes, the prisoner she had talked to on the train. It seemed like ages ago at that point.

"Ow, Mack, you gave me a real fright!" Elsie said. She simpered at him. "I thought you were the Old Stick herself! How are yeh? Having yourself a time?"

Blue Eyes, or Mack, ignored her. Speaking to Miriam, he said, "You're a right little bantam, aren't you. These two giving you any trouble?"

"No trouble," Miriam replied with spirit, "as long as they give me my things back."

"You stole something from this here?" Mack wheeled to face Elsie.

"Just borrowed," Elsie said in a subdued tone.

"Right, return what you borrowed, and be hasty about it." Mack's blue eyes glinted in the watery sunlight.

"Oh, have the filthy thing," Elsie said, and she pushed the pencil at Miriam with a flounce.

"And you," Mack said, turning to Sally, who looked to Elsie for support. Finding none, she handed the copybook over to Miriam. "Right. Now go on, the both of yiz – scarper!"

The girls took off and glanced back at Miriam with evil stares. "Er, thanks," she said to Blue Eyes, or Mack.

Mack squatted down and fished in his shirt with two fingers. Drawing out an extinguished half-smoked cigarette, he put it between his lips and scraped a match on the heel of his boot. He jutted his head at the copybook. "What's in it?"

"Oh, just – nothing."

He looked up at her quizzically, and blew out a long stream of foul-smelling smoke. "You weren't about to fight over just nothing," he said. "Go on, let's have it."

Miriam squatted down beside him and picked at one fingernail, which was splitting from picking the boles. "It's just a story I was writing."

"Is that right! I allus liked a good story. Go on, read us a bit." Mack picked a fleck of tobacco off his tongue and leaned back.

"No, it's silly. I mean, it's a fairy story. You know, for children."

Looking amused, he widened his eyes and whispered, "You saying I'm too old, missus?"

She couldn't help smiling back. "Of course not!" she said. "Very well. Stop me if you're bored." She opened the book and, settling herself more comfortably, began to read, "'The king found that his kingdom wasn't enough to keep him happy. He was handsome, and he was rich, but he was also bored. Therefore, one day, when the fortuneteller in the square saw five ravens in her glass, he decided to sell the Birthright...'"

Mack leaned back and closed his eyes, and she stopped, but he gestured with one hand. "Go on, don't stop. What's the Birthright?"

"I'm about to tell you. 'The Birthright, a large golden globe, had always belonged to the kingdom. Some said that the original ruler had received it from the Elf Queen, and others said that one of his knights had stolen it from a dragon, deep in the mountains. One thing was clear, however, and that was its age. The Birthright was very, very old indeed.'"

The courtyard disappeared again, and Miriam found herself in the

Kingdom, looking at the beautiful globe, supported by four angels made of gold. She read on, her voice growing more confident, and Mack listened closely, punctuating the tale with an occasional "Ah," or "Hm."

"'...Thomasina found that the water in the pond where she loved to fish had grown black and stinking, and the fish themselves had been replaced by slimy, wriggling things with no eyes.' And that's as far as I've gone," Miriam concluded.

"Not so bad, is it?" someone said. Looking up in surprise, she saw the other prisoners from the train. There was Scar Face, and beside him stood Hoarse Voice. Frank, with an expression of studied unconcern, leaned against the wall as well.

"Oh, I didn't know you all were there," Miriam said, with an embarrassed laugh.

"When are you going to finish it?" Hoarse Voice asked. "By next week?"

"I don't know," Miriam hedged. "We don't have much free time. Maybe I'll have another chapter ready, anyway."

"Ah." Mack got to his feet and felt in his shirt again. "Got a fag, Bill? Ta. Look forward to that, I will." Hoarse Voice, or Bill, handed Mack a cigarette.

"Do – do you know what we're doing here? I mean, in the factory?" Miriam asked, emboldened by the men's interest in her story.

Mack blew out another long stream of smoke and said, "Work, innit?"

"But why?"

"Because those two –" he jabbed his cigarette at the Headmistress and Headmaster – "paid off the prisons to send their undesirables, meaning us, to work for next to nothing in their stinking pit." He spat with a flourish.

"But why us?"

Mack shrugged. "Don't know." He began to whistle through his teeth.

"I heard something." Surprisingly, it was Frank who spoke up, revealing his missing teeth. "One of the inspectors said that we make medicines, or some such, and the Big Mucks don't want workers with papers."

"Medicines!" Hoarse Voice, or Bill, said.

"You know, for rich people. Those snobby, snooty types who get bored and look for some mischief to get into. The arty people, and the wives of dooks, and that sort of thing."

"You mean, medicines like opium?" Miriam ventured.

Frank nodded violently. "Exactly what I do mean. It's some kind of – what did they call it, Mack? – some sort of sap, that comes from trees. Like resin, see."

"Don't know anything about all that." Mack shrugged. "Look, time's up. We've got to go. See you next week, miss."

"My name's Miriam," she said with a smile.

"Miriam," he repeated, and he gave her a wink. "Cheers." He stubbed out his smoke on the wall and headed to the men's side of the wall.

The women were already lined up. Elsie, instead of hurrying to the front of the line as she usually did, hung back and hissed at Miriam. "What were you talking about with that lot for so long?"

"Wouldn't you like to know?" Miriam responded smugly. In frustration, Elsie opened her mouth to argue, but the Headmistress blew two blasts on her whistle, and the line began to disappear back into Devil's Kitchen.

CHAPTER 11

His Only Friend

S imon was dragged back up the stairs by Jenkins and Nanny. This time her dimples did not appear. She frowned and remained tight-lipped as Jenkins hauled him up the steps by his collar, a leer on his face.

Instead of taking him to his original room, they continued up another flight of stairs to a floor of dark attic rooms. There Nanny fished in her pocket, withdrew a key, and opened a narrow door. "In here," she said.

Jenkins' grin widened and he wrapped a large arm around Simon's neck. "You're *my* bits and pieces now," he whispered into Simon's ear before he pushed the boy into the room.

Simon flew into a tiny, stuffy garret with no windows and fell heavily on the floor. He picked himself up from where he crashed and ran back to the doorway. Jenkins blew a loud raspberry at him and slammed the door. An instant later, the key turned in the lock, and loud, angry footsteps marched away.

Simon looked at the door. He knew if he pounded on it and yelled it would be no use. Instead, he turned around and looked at his new prison.

It was a small room. Perhaps it had once been used as a scullery maid's bedroom; there was a narrow bed with a striped ticking and a bundle of coarse sheets thrown on top, as well as a tin chamber pot in one corner. Simon hastily turned away from it and sat on the bed.

This is about the lowest I've come to yet, he reflected. More than anything, he wanted to put his head down and howl, but something stopped him.

If it's the lowest, he thought, *there's only one way to go from here, and that's up. They have locked me in here, but they haven't tied me up. Yet.*

Wearily he stood up and stretched. He ran in place for a bit, and he touched his toes a few times. The regimen made his heart beat faster, and his hopes were raised a bit. Maybe I can still get out of here, he thought.

He could do exercises and get stronger, he mused. And, of course, now, he could eat all the food he wanted. The truth was out; Nanny and that great lug knew he wasn't sick. That thought made his stomach growl again, since he had only had a few bites of the sandwich that from downstairs in the kitchen.

He dropped to the floor and did some press-ups, and he got to his feet. The exercise made him feel brisk, at any rate. Right. Simon stripped the sheets off the stained mattress and turned the bedding over. The other side wasn't very clean, either, but it was better. Rather clumsily, he made the bed. It was a poor attempt, but he tucked in the sheets as best as he could. He stood back to look at the effect. Not too bad, for his first try at making a bed.

Simon went back to the door and pressed his ear to it to try and listen for anything, like footsteps of someone bringing him a meal. Hearing nothing but muffled silence, he shrugged and decided he might as well rest up.

He stripped off his dressing gown and as there was no place to store clothes, he folded it and put it in the least dusty corner. Yawning from hunger, he blew out the candle on the floor and lay down. His mind raced, but eventually his eyes closed and his breathing slowed.

Suddenly, a terrific banging started outside his door. Simon started up, his mouth open, pushing back a lock of hair that had fallen into one eye.

The sound was a drum, which pounded its way into a crescendo that introduced a loud military march, complete with tubas and bassoons. The music was so loud that the gramophone might have been directly outside his door. Giving up the attempt to sleep, Simon threw the sheet back. He winced and covered his ears.

The march grew louder, accompanied by joyous trumpets and bugles.

The invisible drummer was having a great time as he thumped his baton with gusto against the drums; he was really putting his heart into it, Simon thought bitterly, dropping his head into his hands. What type of torture was this?

The march eventually wound down, and Simon collapsed back onto the bed, but it was soon replaced by a particularly soppy waltz, complete with harps and violins. When that finally ceased, Simon ran to the door and shouted with fury, "Hey! Stop that! I'm trying to sleep!" The only response was a loud, operatic aria.

With a loud, desperate groan, Simon went back to bed and tried to cover his ears. The opera singer, an unknown soprano gifted with magnificent lungs, wailed loudly in a foreign language. He clasped the pillow over his head and ground his teeth.

After several hours of loud music, Simon somehow managed to drop off to sleep. It seemed like a few moments later when he was awakened by the goon Jenkins. The large man grinned and shook Simon hard by both arms. "Wakey-wakey," he trilled in a high voice. At least the music had stopped.

Nanny popped into the room, but she didn't smile at Simon. Her eyes were red, and she sniffed as she put a tray down on the floor by his bed. "Look, I'm sorry if they stopped your wages," Simon said to her. She simply shook her head without looking at him and left the room, still sniffing.

Jenkins' smile dropped, and he grabbed a fistful of Simon's pajamas. "You don't talk to her, see?" he threatened, and he thrust a fist the size of a small ham under Simon's nose.

"Leave me alone!" Simon shot back, as he glared at Jenkins. The goon smiled his unpleasant grin, looked down at Simon's tray, and deliberately stepped right into the middle of the plate. His large foot, shod in a thick boot, shattered toast, knocked over a cup of milk, and squished a pile of scrambled egg. He walked to the door, leaving a line of eggy footsteps behind, and opened it. As usual, he had one last comment. "Nyah, nyah," he said, and slammed the door.

Simon stared at the plate for a moment, absurd tears pricking at his eyelids. He had been so hungry. One drop slid down his cheek and he dashed it away angrily. *You're a girl!* he said to himself, disgusted. *No, not a girl. Miriam wouldn't cry about this, nor would Mana. They'd simply find a way to survive.*

He wiped his face with one sleeve, picked up some of the less shattered pieces of toast, and looked at them with loathing. However, there was nothing else for it. Simon put the disgusting food in his mouth and forced it down, trying not to vomit at the thought of Jenkins's huge boot in his eggs.

After that unsatisfying breakfast, Simon got up and tried again to run in place, although his eyelids drooped and he felt more and more disheartened. *Come on,* he said to himself fiercely, *exercise is the one thing you've got left. Come on, softie!*

He forced himself to do some jumping jacks, although it was difficult to feel energetic wearing dirty pajamas. After that he tried to clean up some of the mess Jenkins' boot had left on the floor, using his napkin as a washrag.

There was nothing else to do, so he lay on the bed and fell asleep. Instantly, a loud concerto started again outside his door.

Boiling with fury, Simon bounded from the bed and ran to the door. "Shut it off!" he yelled. "*Stop that noise! Stop it!*" He looked at the ceiling, the tears pricking the inside of his eyes again. "Please," he added in a whisper.

The musicians, who were still in fine form, worked their way through the allegro with many flourishes and began the largo. "Stop it," Simon moaned, and went back to the bed. He curled up and hid his head under the pillow. His entire body ached, as though he had been physically beaten.

Nurse, looking grim, served lunch. She was joined by the inevitable Jenkins. Simon was careful not to say anything to either of them, and

Jenkins contented himself with a chant of, "Simple Simon," before the goon locked him in.

Did you think of that all by yourself, you slimy lug?" Simon thought, picking up the luncheon tray. A piece of ancient cheese curled on a wilted lettuce leaf, next to a heel of hardened bread. A glass of water was the only accompaniment. Simon forced it all down, however, cramming the food into his mouth as if someone was going to snatch it back from him before he could eat it.

It wasn't nearly enough, but at least it filled his stomach a bit. He fell back on his pillow, not even noticing the extended symphony that had replaced the concerto, and instantly started to doze.

"Oh, no, we can't have that," someone said loudly in his ear. Simon started and sat up. Nanny was pouring a dose of something purple into a small glass; it looked utterly foul.

"What's that?" Simon asked, looking cautiously for Jenkins. "Why did you say we can't have that?" Sleep blurred his words.

"It's your medicine," Nanny said, pushing it at him and slopping some of the stuff on his pajamas. "And we can't let you sleep too much."

Simon sniffed at the purple liquid and put it down. "Why won't you let me sleep?" he asked.

She ignored him and walked to the door. "Jenkins!" she warbled. "He won't take his medicine!"

"No!" Simon said, and drank the stuff she held out. It was very nasty, just as he had thought. "Look, I'm all finished now." He handed the glass back to Nanny and looked up at her in mute appeal as Jenkins walked in the door.

"Are you a bad boy, Simon?" Jenkins growled, removing a thick belt from his trousers. He held up the thick leather, doubled it, and with a sudden movement, he cracked it against Simon's shin.

With a howl of pain, Simon doubled over his leg. Suddenly it was all too much. Incensed, he howled again – but with fury, and launched himself at Jenkins. "Get off you me, you great ugly git!!" Simon yelled, and with all his might, he punched Jenkins in the stomach.

The man just laughed, grabbed Simon's collar, and picked him up in the air. Simon struggled and tried to kick and hit the man, but Jenkins held him out in one hand with a chortle. "Hee hee hee! Simple Simon! Nyah nyah, doo doo!" the big man threw him down so that the boy landed with a slight splash in the chamber pot. Elaborately holding his nose, Jenkins left, saying "Stinky Simon! Peeeeee-yoooooo!"

With a brrrr of disgust, Simon bounded up and stripped off his pajamas. He looked for the dressing gown he had left in the corner, but someone had removed it at some point. Now, he reflected, he truly had nothing left. He wiped himself off as well as he could with his shirt, and he lay down on top of the sheet. A wave of total despair hit him, and he buried his face in his arms.

He had no idea how much time passed before the door opened again. Simon kept his head down and scuttled back against the headboard, holding the sheet over his head and legs.

"Sit up, you silly boy," a voice trilled. Barbara, wearing a green suit trimmed with peacock feathers, came into the room and looked around. "Oh, heavens," she said in her lilting voice. "You poor, poor thing. You have gotten yourself into a state, haven't you?" She leaned out of the doorway and beckoned to someone. Jenkins entered with a tray with a covered plate and a jug of hot water. A pair of clean pajamas hung over one arm. The huge man crossed his eyes and stuck his tongue out at Simon.

"No!" Simon gasped when he saw Jenkins, and he put up his arms in defense.

Barbara laughed. "Don't worry, my love. He won't dare hurt you while I'm here. Now, let's get you washed and dressed, shall we?"

Simon gaped at her. She appeared fuzzy; in fact, the room slid out of focus. "Do it myself," he managed to croak.

"Of course you can," she said, smiling, and turned to Jenkins. "Take that away, and get a mop," she ordered, pointing to the chamber pot. Jenkins scowled, but he scuttled to obey her with a murderous look at Simon. "Now," she continued, "we'll let you get dressed, and I'll be back in a moment."

Left alone, Simon stood up and wavered. Something in that purple potion that Nanny had given him made his head spin, and he grabbed the bed for support. He managed to make his way over to the plate and snatched up the cover, which revealed a roast chicken, stuffing, a mound of potatoes, and new peas with butter.

He nearly caught up the chicken in his bare hands, but he didn't want Barbara to find him naked, eating like a dog when she came back in. For some reason, it was suddenly very important what she thought of him. Instead, he picked up the hot water and managed to splash it onto his arms and legs without spilling too much on the floor. There was a clean towel with the pajamas, and he wiped himself off, promising to repeat the process after his meal. He hurriedly put on the new pajamas (they felt blessedly clean) and squatted in front of the plate.

He was on his second chicken leg when the key turned in the lock again. Getting up, he hastily swallowed and stood up. The room spun in front of him and he staggered and nearly fell. Barbara entered with a delighted smile when she saw him. "Well, you look much better!" she said. "Bring in a chair and table," she added, and Jenkins followed, bearing some small pieces of furniture. "Put his tray on the table, idiot," she snapped, "and mop the floor as I ordered."

"Now," she continued, "how do you feel, Simon? How are you treated here?"

To his horror, he felt tears in his eyes again. "'M all right," he said gruffly.

"No, you're not all right," she said, her eyes huge with pity. "Come on, sit on the bed and tell me all about it."

The medicine appeared to have completely sapped Simon's free will. He followed her to the bed and plumped down, and she settled beside him, put an arm around his shoulders, and gently pushed his head onto her shoulder. She smelled deliciously of water lilies and frangipani. "Now, tell me," she murmured in his ear.

"They, they won't let me sleep," Simon sobbed, filled with disgust at the way he was acting but somehow not able to stop it. "I'm so tired."

"Well, of course you are!" Barbara soothed. "Jenkins, finish cleaning and get out!" she suddenly snapped. "No, blockhead, leave the tray; Simon will want to eat more later. Won't you, my love?" He could only nod, guilt and shame curling in his chest.

"Now," she whispered, "why don't you lie down for a bit and sleep? You'll feel better, and we can talk some more. Would you like that? Hm?" Simon nodded again, and she pulled him down so that his head was cradled in the soft silk she was wearing. "There, now," she said softly. She bent over his ear and traced it with one finger. "Now, my love, go to sleep. That's it; close your eyes. Sleep."

CHAPTER 12
The New Employees

Kyoge and Neil stood at the back entrance to Pearson's factory. They were in line with a group of people who waited to apply for work. The other men and women coughed and shuffled their feet, probably trying to stay warm in the chill morning air.

Neil stole a look at Kyoge, who stood in the back, arms folded. The huge guard didn't move a muscle. He stood at least a head taller than even the biggest man in line, and his Lampalan training, or perhaps his own temperament, gave him an air of nobility that even the old clothes he had put on could not hide. Or so, at least, it seemed to Neil.

Mana had wanted them both to wear fine, tailored suits for the interviews, but Kyoge had scoffed at the idea. "I shall not be hired as a clerk, my queen," he had said, "or even as a worker on the main floor. I will be lucky if Pearson's takes me on at all. Better that they think I am a poor man from the islands than the Queen's royal guard." She had argued some more for form's sake, but at length she had given in, admitting his point.

It seemed that Mana and Kyoge had begun to enjoy their frequent battle of wills. When they had first met, Neil reckoned, the man had always listened to Mana, rather than argue with "His Queen." But now, whenever she voiced a complaint, a certain light that Neil recognized as the joy of battle came into Kyoge's eyes, and he argued with her readily and with great fervor. Neil had seen an answering glint in Mana's face on those occasions.

The door opened, and a thin, weedy fellow wearing pince-nez

stepped out. In his left arm he carried a large notebook, and as the line of people watched he scribbled something into it. "Right," he called out, not looking up from what he was writing. "Let's not take all day over this; *some* of us have work to do, don't we. Names, last and first in that order, and after you've been noted, file into the waiting room."

The small crowd shuffled forward as one, and Neil was pressed to the back with Kyoge, who held up his head with supreme unconcern. The line wound through the door slowly, as some of those waiting had either not paid attention to the clerk's directions.

"Look," the little man in glasses said to a woman with a shawl thrown over her head, "what is so difficult to understand? Last name first, and first name last, for heaven's sake."

"Begging your pardon, your honor, but I thought you meant first name first, do you see," she replied with spirit. "It's like what the fishwife said to the cabby, do you see, 'Move the baby out of the pram and let the lady see the fish-'"

"Just tell me your name, and go inside!" the man said, his visage reddening as he wrote furiously in the book.

Neil was next, and he said clearly, "Miles, Tom."

The man sniffed, and Kyoge stepped up behind Neil. "Whittle, Ezekiel," he said in his rich, booming voice.

The secretary looked up, gasped, and dropped his notebook. "Mother of all living creation! What in God's name-!" Neil bent down, picked up the notebook and handed it to him, and the fellow seemed to recover a bit. "Em, what was that that you said now?" He looked up at Kyoge again, and his pince-nez slid off his nose. "Dash it all!" he shouted.

Kyoge, or "Ezekiel," picked the lenses up, wiped the dirt off them with one rusty sleeve, and gravely handed them to the little man, who snatched them back and glared at Neil and Kyoge. "Go on, both of you," he blustered, "just get inside. Go!"

Neil quickly legged it through the door and saw that the group had reformed into another line standing in front of a window. There a sign was propped up: "CLOSED AT THIS TIME." The man with the pince-nez disappeared through a side door, and a moment later the same man reappeared behind the glass of the window. He removed the Closed sign, wiped his glasses, settled them firmly on his nose, smoothed his hair, opened his notebook, and called out, "Higgins, Bill!"

The first man in line stepped up to the window and began a whispered consultation with the secretary, who continued to take copious notes throughout. Neil shifted and looked around, preparing for a stretch of pure boredom. He turned to Kyoge, but the man stared over his head, waiting with all the patience of the world. Neil sighed and resigned himself, trying to think of a plan in case he shouldn't be hired. He preferred not to think of his parents and sisters. No one in his family had been found yet, despite Mr. Philips' inquiries into the matter. It was as though they had completely disappeared into thin air.

Bill Higgins was ushered into the factory, and the line shuffled forward. Some followed Bill inside after their interviews, and others were shown away; the woman with the shawl, surprisingly, was hired (perhaps just to make her stop talking, Neil thought) while some able-bodied men were directed away.

"Miles, Tom!" the little man called out. His stomach clenching with nervousness, Neil walked forward and put his hand limply on the counter.

"Yes, that's me. I mean that is I," he faltered, beginning to sweat.

The little man looked at him over his half lenses. "You may address me as Mr. Drake." He licked his finger, turned a page, and made a quick note. Looking up, he asked, "What experience have you had, Miles?"

"Tom" was prepared with his answer. "I worked abroad in Lampala," he said, "for one of the plantation owners there, Mr. Drake, sir," he responded. Well, that much was true, although a glorified nursemaid probably wasn't what Mr. Drake was looking for. "I'm good with numbers, and I can also-"

"Do you have a good hand?" Mr. Drake interrupted.

Neil looked at his own right hand, mystified. "I – I suppose so," he replied.

Mr. Drake heaved a loud, theatrical sigh. "Let's see." He twitched his brows together and shoved a pencil and a tiny scrap of paper through the slot at the bottom of the window.

Neil's brow cleared. As carefully as he could, he wrote 'Tom Miles' in script, added a flourish, and pushed it back through the slot. Drake frowned at the scrap for a minute and beckoned him to the inside door with his pen. "Report to the Accounts Department," he said. "Next!"

Neil walked reluctantly through the door, wishing he could stay and hear the results of Kyoge's interview. Of course, he hoped that the guard would get the job, but he was also certain that the dialogue between the guard and the little man with pince-nez would be entertaining, to say the least. Still, there was nothing for it but to enter the factory and look around for Accounts.

Inside, he had a confused impression of bright gaslights shining on brass parts that gleamed; mysterious machines that moved and hummed; and workers who walked quickly from place to place, intent on their own unknown tasks.

"Where you headed?" someone said in Neil's ear. He turned and saw a snub-nosed, brown-haired fellow of about his own age. The lad had a wide smile that revealed a large gap between his front teeth.

"Accounts," Neil said, smiling back. "Could you direct me to-"

"Do better than that," the boy said. "Take you there myself. Name's Jeremy," he added, as he headed off towards a series of large tubes and flywheels and threaded his way through them.

"Tom," Neil roared back, as the sound of the machinery increased. "What's that?" he asked. He pointed to a big spiral that hung from the ceiling, winding and rewinding endlessly.

Jeremy shrugged. "Don't know. It's where they process the sap from the bolemors, though, to make dye, you know."

Neil nodded. "Right, the bolemors. I'd forgotten them."

Jeremy turned, gave him another grin, and opened a door on the far wall of the factory. "Here you are. This is the office for Accounts. I'm headed to Developments, myself, but maybe we'll catch a cup of tea later – or something stronger, eh?" He winked outrageously at Neil and strolled away, whistling.

Wonder what he had meant by Developments, Neil thought. He walked into the office. The noise from the machines ceased as soon as the door swung closed with a click behind him.

The walls of the Accounts office were lined with new, wooden desks. About fifteen people, men and women sat in the office. They checked rows of figures and made copies of long reports. A large window revealed the busy street in front of the factory, and small lamps on each desk cast a bright glow over the clerks' work.

Neil looked around, feeling rather at a loss until someone said, "Hist!" One of the clerks was gesturing with a long pen at an empty desk. Neil nodded, approached the desk, and sat down.

His task was obvious. There was a pile of blank paper on one side and a letter on the other with a note attached that read, "Six copies."

Neil sat in the wooden chair and drew the letter forward. He copied the letter word for word, his pen nib scratching as he labored.

The work was boring, but it was peaceful in the office. The morning sunshine streamed in the yellow curtains at the large window, and the clerks wrote at the other desks, never looking up from their papers. After doing two of the copies, Neil found that he could let his mind wander while he wrote.

His hand had just begun to cramp up when the door opened and a coffee cart was pushed in. "And about time too!" the elderly man in the desk next to Neil's said, hopping off his chair. "Two lumps with mine, Charlie," he called to the boy pushing the cart.

The other clerks got up from their own desks and pushed forward, calling out orders, and Charlie, a thin, narrow young man, filled the cups quickly and passed them around. Accepting a thick, china cup, Neil took a grateful sip and looked around at his fellow workers, feeling a bit out of it. They began to talk as soon as the coffee had arrived.

"Hey, mates," one girl with ginger hair yelled, "we're forgetting our new partner in crime. What's your title, sonny?"

"Er, Tom Miles," Neil replied. He swallowed a large sip of scalding brown liquid.

"Tom!" everyone cheered.

"Let's sing him the song!" the ginger-haired girl said. "Come on, everyone, don't be shy-

Tom is the best,
We know it's true
When we're in danger
We'll look for you
You're one of us now
Through and through –
So don't be shy
Just because you're new!"

This was followed by three rousing hurrahs. Surprised, Neil held up his cup and pretended to toast them, a performance that was greeted by more cheers, as well as whistles.

The girl elbowed him in the ribs. "You're a one, aren't you? Eh? I'm Daisy, by the way, although everyone calls me Ginger. Can't think why," she added, bursting into a loud laugh.

The other clerks cheered again, and someone called out, "Go to it, Ginger! Friendly, aren't you?"

"Just introducing myself," Ginger screamed back, grinning widely. "How about you lot? Come on, be sociable!"

"I'm off," Charlie suddenly announced, pushing his coffee cart through the door.

Ginger's smile disappeared as if it had been wiped off her face. "Oh, right." Without another word or glance at Neil, she hopped back to her desk and began to write again. Looking around, Neil saw that everyone had followed her example.

Quickly, he sat back down and picked up his pen. The office was completely silent again, filled only with the sound of turning pages.

After a few more hours, Neil finished the letters. A clerk silently handed him a long list with the attached note, "Two copies." Just as he began working on the lists, the door opened again and Charlie reappeared, this time laden with sandwiches wrapped in thick greaseproof paper.

"Lunchtime, all!" the elderly clerk next to Neil said. Instantly the office was filled with loud conversation as everyone bustled forward to grab a sandwich.

"What's the fillings today, Charlie?" Ginger yelled.

"Ham," he replied, handing out bottles filled with a fizzy liquid. Neil accepted one as well as a sandwich, and went back to his desk to eat.

"Hey, Tom, did you meet your neighbor?" Ginger called out. She pointed to the elderly clerk at the desk next to Neil's. The older man bowed in her direction.

"Name's Jacky," the man said, proffering a hand. Neil stretched over his desk and shook it, and Jacky continued, "They got you roped in here, eh? Too bad, a nice young lad like you." He shook his head in quiet sympathy.

"We call him Jacky-Boy because of his young age," Ginger confided. "Says he hates the place. Been here thirty years, that's how much he hates it." She took a large bite of her sandwich, chewed with great energy, and washed it down with a large pull from the bottle of fizzy stuff.

Neil tried a sip and coughed; the bottles were full of lemonade, cold and tart. It was delicious, as was the ham sandwich. "How do you like working here?" he asked Ginger.

"He's started a conversation with me, lads! Get ready to be jealous!" she called out over her shoulder. A chorus of drawn-out 'Oooohs' greeted this sally. "It's not so bad," she continued in a somewhat normal tone. "I mean, the food and drink we get for nothing, and we can actually see what we're writing in here. It's not all cold and dark. Not like other places what I've heard tell of, believe me!" She bit into her sandwich again as if to punctuate her sentence.

Neil swallowed, and washed down a lump of bread with more of the lemonade. "How are the owners?" he asked.

"The owners?" She turned back to the clerks and asked, "What do we think of the new top brass, lads?" A chorus of boos, hisses and down-turned thumbs was the response.

"Eat up," she said, "because we don't know when the free tuck will stop. They already took away the Christmas party, and the summer outings," she added, in a lower voice. "These new owners are a right pip, if you ask me. They'll drive the place into rack and ruin, mark my words."

She popped the last of her sandwich into her mouth just as Charlie reappeared with the cart. Empty bottles were handed over, and when he left the office fell silent again. Neil turned to ask Ginger another question, but she had disappeared and was already at her desk, totting up on her fingers.

CHAPTER 13

A Desperate Bid

After a few hours of much-needed sleep, Simon woke refreshed. He bounded out of bed, stretched widely and yawned, an absurd feeling of expectation tickling the back of his neck. Why did he feel so happy? He began to bounce on the balls of his feet, and broke into a full run in place. Oh yes, Barbara. She had given him a good meal, and let him sleep, and allowed him to wash and dress in clean clothes.

At that thought, Simon stopped abruptly. Was he a dog or a pet to be given food and treats? What was next - a collar? He remembered that he had fallen asleep on her lap the night before, and his lips curled with disgust.

He started to run again, determined to pick up his strength. Now that he was allowed to have food and sleep again, he knew it wouldn't be long before he would be as vigorous as before, perhaps even more so. In a week he might even be able to square up to that goon Jenkins.

As if on cue, the door opened suddenly and the goon himself appeared, bearing the usual tray. Simon sat down abruptly and began to examine his toes, not looking at the man. Jenkins giggled to himself, picked the cover up from the food and waved it under Simon's nose. It was a large omelet reposing next to some roasted potatoes, and curls of steam escaped from the plate. "Yummy-yummy!" Jenkins said, waving it under Simon's nose.

"Very well," Simon said crossly, unable to bear the man in his room next to him. "Just put it on the bed, would you?" And *get out*, he added silently.

Jenkins grinned again, suddenly hawked his throat and spat loudly in the center of the plate. Replacing the cover, he put the plate on the bed, repeating, "Yum! Yum! Yummy-yum!"

Simon shot up from the bed. "You disgusting, filthy pig!" He made for Jenkins, who ran away and closed the door in Simon's face. A second later he opened it again, trilled his fingers, and slammed it with finality. "Get back here!" Simon bawled. "Take away this foul mess, and bring me some decent food! Where is Barbara? Wait until she hears about this – you great, dirty bastard!"

There was a snuffling snort by the door. Jenkins had heard Simon's shout and was amused by it. Simon banged on the door with his fist and yelled again, but Jenkins walked away, pounding his feet ostentatiously on the floor so Simon could hear him leaving.

Turning back to the plate, Simon's stomach heaved. He swallowed and moved the thing away from his bed so he wouldn't have to look at it. His head dropped into his hands. A feeling of utter despair overcame him, but he tried to shake it off. Very well, so he wouldn't have any breakfast. Trying not to remember the potatoes (they looked as though they had been roasted in butter) Simon began to run in place again, and got on the floor and did some sit-ups.

After exercise he was weary, and sweating, and his stomach complained with a steady hum of hunger. Since he had nothing else to do, Simon lay down and closed his eyes.

Instantly, the gramophone outside began blaring out a fugue, played with "molto allegro e vivace." Simon shot up, his eyes staring. Not this again! What on earth was going on? He put his pillow over his head, and the despair he had felt earlier washed over him again. "No," he moaned, unable to stop himself. "No. I'll do anything. Make it stop, Barbara. Make it stop. Barbara!"

He lost track of time, and fell into a sort of haze that wasn't sleep but a hideous grayness with the blaring music and the hunger as a constant background. Simon didn't know what he did during that time, or how long it lasted, or even where or who he was.

Suddenly the music stopped, and heavy silence descended on

the room like a blanket. Simon didn't move. He lay on the bed and clutched his stomach.

She came in, tiptoed up to him, and sat gently on the bed. "Are you all right?" she asked, in his ear.

Simon forgot that she had made him a prisoner or that she had ever threatened Miriam. He sat up, threw his arms around her, and held her tightly.

Barbara laughed softly and stroked his cheek. "And I'm pleased to see you, too!" she said. She wore a dress made of heather-blue wool, trimmed with ermine at the shoulders and cuffs. Simon sank his face into the soft wool and tried to control his sobs, He didn't want her to see him acting like a child.

"You really must eat something," she said.

He sat up and wiped his face with one forearm in a savage, quick movement. "Jenkins spat in it." He pointed at the discarded plate. At that moment he suddenly realized that he could have eaten the food on the plate, as foul as it was.

Barbara made a face. "Oh, no, really. He is just too horrible for words, isn't he? Let me take this away, and I'll bring you something else. What would you like? Some roast beef? Ham? Cold duck?"

Simon's head swam, and he dropped back into the pillows. "Yes, please," he gasped. "And could I possibly have some more hot water, please? For a wash?"

"Well, of course you may," she replied. She gave him a quick kiss on his forehead. When she bent over him he could smell her expensive scent. She stood up, smiling gently. "I'm very pleased with you, Simon," she whispered before she left.

He closed his eyes. Something in what she had just said was wrong, somehow, but he was too tired and hungry to work it out.

Over the next few days, Simon found the days were either cold and gray, or bright and happy. It all depended on whether Barbara visited him or not. When he was alone, the music continued to blast into his room, and Jenkins brought meals that were either not cooked or dirtied in some disgusting way. Once the man added a trowel full of manure on top of a perfectly good steak, and at other times he brought food as burnt and black as charcoal. After he left, the loud music would start up as soon as Simon lay down to sleep.

When Barbara came in, however, she brought delicious, well-prepared meals. As well, she directed Jenkins or Nanny to change the filthy linens or give Simon water for a bath. But, most importantly, she brought her own lovely self, which Simon began to watch for almost as much as the meals. Whenever the door opened and she stood there, his heart would give a queer kind of bound.

He began to flirt with her, as he had in the beginning when they had first met, and she encouraged him to kiss her hand, pay her extravagant complements, and sit next to her with one arm around her slim waist. He did all this happily, and he waited for her to reappear when she was gone.

Once he even caught himself kissing the hem of her dress. Getting up from the floor, he felt rather confused, and he couldn't remember getting on his knees. She looked delighted, however, and slipped a satin hand under his chin. "You are such a dear, good friend," she said, and kissed him lightly on the lips.

She left, and Simon sat on the bed. He gasped, and his heart thumped in his chest. Why had he ever thought that she was his enemy? That thought was nearly as foul as the food that Jenkins tried to give him.

He leaned back against the wall and crossed one leg over the other. Barbara now allowed him to have slippers, and he also could wear a robe that she had given him. Looking around at the small room, he sighed with happiness. He really couldn't imagine wanting to live anywhere else.

That night, the music ceased, and in the days that followed, it never reappeared. Soon Simon forgot that he had ever been kept awake by the gramophone. Jenkins didn't reappear, and only Nanny or Nurse served him with meals that were plain but good. Sometimes he had to take the purple medicine that they brought, but he didn't protest anymore. In fact, he looked forward to the floating feeling the tonic gave him.

When Barbara appeared, however, trays of paté, and caviar accompanied her, and she even had a bottle of champagne served one evening. That night Simon rather forgot himself after a few glasses, and before she left, he captured her against the door and kissed her firmly on her red lips.

"Well," she breathed, and she stared up into his eyes with her strange, orange stare. "That was a surprise."

He frowned. "A surprise? How so, Barbara? You must know how I feel about you."

She smiled, a delighted sparkle in her eyes. "But a few weeks ago-"

Simon stopped her. "A few weeks ago, I was a fool. I forgot what was important in my life – you, my darling, beautiful Barbara."

She smiled again. "I must go," she said, softly and with plain regret.

Simon put one arm on the door behind her head and looked down at her vivid face. "When will you be back?" he insisted, brushing the curls off her forehead with his fingertips.

"Soon," she replied. She closed her eyes like a cat as he stroked her brow.

"Very soon?" he whispered in her ear, moving closer.

"Perhaps even sooner than that," she responded. With a sudden motion she twisted out of his arms and left.

Simon laughed, standing back and putting his fists on his hips. She was a tease, the wild, beautiful girl!

There was a creak in the passageway. Simon's laugh stopped. A voice outside spoke, and he put his ear to the door.

"His parents want to know when we'll release him," someone was saying. "Becoming a bit of a bore, old girl."

"They'll have to wait." Barbara's voice was rather muffled by the door, but Simon could hear every word she spoke. "I am so very close," she continued in an exasperated tone. "I will not have all my work undone because of a pair of fools!"

"He is their son," the other voice replied. Simon recognized it; he could just picture Valiant next to Barbara, with a cigar in one hand.

"I suppose." she replied. "But he is my property now, and soon he will do whatever I say." The voices died as the pair walked down the hall. Their footsteps died away, and Simon couldn't hear any more.

Simon frowned. An instant earlier, he had been profoundly happy. He was in his safe room, and he had just kissed a beautiful woman. Now, he felt that something was terribly wrong, but he couldn't figure out what it was.

He turned back to his room slowly and began to change into new pajamas for bed. He had been given a chest of drawers and a simple jug and basin for washing. He rinsed his face and the back of his neck, still troubled. What the devil was the matter with him?

He got into bed and yawned. Nanny had given him a small draught of the dark liquid earlier that evening, and coupled with the champagne, it made him sleepy. He got into his bed (it was now spread with clean sheets and a fresh counterpane) and fell asleep.

He dreamed that he was in a dark room that was lit by a single lantern just outside. There was a cot in one corner, and a chamber pot in the other. In fact, it looked like a much more primitive version of his own room in the attic where he lay asleep.

A girl with dark curls sat on a small, dirty bed. She scratched quickly at the pages in front of her, and she stopped to read from time to time. Once she laughed at something she had written.

In his sleep, Simon smiled as well. He knew that girl. She had grown, however. In fact, you really couldn't call her a girl any longer. Her long legs were doubled up on the cot away from the cold stone floor, and the childish curves of her face had matured into sharp cheekbones and smooth skin.

She looked up and met his glance. With a shock, he saw that her eyes had never changed. They were just as black, and just as intelligent as ever. He gasped, and said her name, *Miriam*. The sound of his own voice woke him up.

His sat up in the bed and looked around wildly, panicking at the closeness of the four walls. He had almost forgotten how small his own room was until he had seen the narrow cell that Miriam inhabited.

Unless, of course, it was just a dream.

He shook his head. No. It was not a mere dream. And, at that thought, he remembered another dream that he had had ages ago, that first night in Miriam's own house. He remembered the small room, and the beautiful girl whose face was hidden shadow, carrying a tray with a bottle on it. He remembered the loud music, and the sense of overwhelming fear he had felt when he had the nightmare.

He jumped up from the bed and felt the walls with both hands, searching for – what? A crack? A gap? His hands pressed the bricks and stones and mortar, and he began to gasp as his fear and panic increased.

"Wait!" he sobbed to himself. "Stop it! Get control of yourself, Simon! Stop!"

He doubled over on the floor and covered his head with his arms. His gasps grew faster, but he couldn't control himself. He gulped for air like a fish out of water, but he was breathing in his own breath.

Somehow, it calmed him. The wild panting and sobbing eventually slowed, and he was able to breathe normally.

In the morning, Nurse brought in his medicine. Simon obediently drank it and waited until the woman left. As soon as the door closed, he spit it into his chamber pot and rinsed his mouth out with water from his washing jug.

After that he kicked the bed, stubbing his toe rather severely against the metal frame. *Scurvy! Pockmarks! Damn them all to the devil!* he cursed. Sitting down and nursing his toe, he gave full vent to his anger.

That bloody female thought that she had *tamed* him, like some kind of pet. Although, he mused, staring at the wall, that was exactly how he had acted. Like an animal. He ran to see her whenever she appeared. He waited for her at the door; he even kissed the hem of her dress. With a cough of self-hatred, Simon got up and paced the floor.

That was what had been wrong with what she said that night. "I'm very pleased with you, Simon." He might as well have been a baby or a dog. She had trained him, just like wild bears were trained to dance in street fairs. He had always found that spectacle sad and pathetic.

All right. All right. Simon forced himself to think. He had discovered her secret through some amazing luck, but she didn't have to know that. If he kept up the pretense of being her slave, perhaps she would drop her guard, or bring him out to see his parents, or something similar. That was whom Valiant had been referring to, Simon was certain, when he had overheard him and Barbara the night before.

Of course, Simon's own parents were involved with these villainous people too. It is never pleasant to realize that one's mother and father are in league with crooks, and that they might be crooks themselves. Still, Simon reasoned, they were his parents, after all. Maybe, if he could talk to his mother, or better yet, his dad, he could get them to look for Miriam. Perhaps they could find Neil. And his mother and father could drop all the nonsense associated with Miriam and Pearsons' Company.

Right, Simon determined, returning to the bed. He looked around again, as if some kind of membrane had been peeled from his eyes. Only a short time ago, he couldn't imagine living anywhere else. Now, he couldn't wait to get out of that room.

So, Barbara wanted to train him as her pet? Well, now she would be the beast, and he would be the lion tamer. First, he'd make her give him some decent lodgings and a pair of trousers, by God. And he'd convince her to take him on an expedition somewhere. One way or another he would get outside of that bloody room, anyway.

He lay on the bed, folded his arms under his head, and stared up at the ceiling. A few days more in the hellhole, and he'd really be on his way to rescue his friends.

CHAPTER 14

An Argument and Two Stories

With dreadful regularity, the days underground passed, one after the other. Miriam was awakened every morning by a large bowl of porridge being pushed into her cell. After she ate as much as she could and drank a mug of lukewarm, stewed tea, Miriam lined up with the other workers. Once Mrs. Siddons gave them the signal, Miriam marched down with the other women to the dark hole underground where she picked boles for hours.

She became good at the hot, monotonous work. Her fingers almost worked by themselves as she thought up characters and situations. The story of Thomasina was finished at last, written in a cramped script in the little copybook, and she had read the rest to Mack, who had nodded his head at the end. With a nudge to Bill, who had somehow joined them during the break times, he had said, "Right little author, ain't she? What's the next story about, eh?"

"I don't know," Miriam said slowly. "I've been thinking about a boy who is born with a key around his neck, and somehow he uses it to save his true love, years later."

"Bit young to be thinking about love, aincha?" Bill had grunted.

"I'm getting older," Miriam had responded. That answer surprised even her.

After Mrs. Siddons inspected her each day, Miriam went back to her cell and wrote another chapter of the new story, completely forgetting where she was. Now she lived in the boy's country, the boy with the key around his neck, and with him she searched for the gate to the huge maze where the princess was imprisoned. The lights were turned off abruptly, at nine on the dot night after night, which always gave her a shock, and she had become used to undressing and getting into bed in the dark.

One night, as she wrote on her bed, she had a strong feeling that someone was there with her, someone who watched her as she wrote. She looked up, expecting to see Mana, or Neil, or perhaps Simon. Yes, she had expected Simon, for some reason. She could almost hear his voice as he teased her and see the yellow curls on his neck.

Of course, she was alone in her cell, and no one was there at all.

The lights were put out, and she had to lie down in her narrow bed. And the next day arrived, and she had to march off down to the workroom and get pick boles again until lunch arrived.

"Come on, brainless, I'd like to have a bite to eat today, if you don't mind," Elsie said, prodding her. They were standing in line, mugs in hand, waiting for Minnie to dole out the noontime meal.

Without a reply, Miriam moved up in line and held out her mug, which was filled with water, and received a thick sandwich from Minnie, who gave her a big wink. "Can't wait to fill her belly, that one," she hissed, and she jerked her head in Elsie's direction. Startled by the girl's friendliness, Miriam smiled back and took her lunch back to the basket of bolemor twigs where she ate, as usual, all by herself.

She bit into the sandwich and prepared to mull over the problem of escape from Devil's Kitchen as well as the intricacies of trying to extract her hero from his predicament. At that moment, two girls drew up baskets and plumped down beside her. "Don't mind, do you?" one asked, her mouth already full of sandwich. Miriam recognized her as Joan, a worker with tight blonde curls and a loud voice.

"Of course not," she said, and she bit into her own sandwich. It was filled with roast beef today, but the meat was hard, and the bread was so dry that it clung to the roof of her mouth.

"Your story is lovely," Joan blurted, taking a sip from her mug. "Cor, this is like eating slabs of wood, isn't it, Win?" Her companion, a small, thin girl named Winifred, nodded. "I heard you talking to Mack and

Bill," Joan continued. "Hope you don't mind if Win and I listened in to a bit of it."

Win swallowed and tried to dislodge a hunk of meat from a back tooth with her tongue. "Mm," she agreed. "Gets a bit boring in here; we need something to liven us up a little bit."

"Oh," Miriam said, not quite sure of what to say. "Well, I'm glad you liked the story."

"Are you going to tell them some more today?" Joan asked.

"I'm starting a new story," Miriam said. "It's called The Princess in the Labyrinth."

"Oooh," Win said, impressed. "But we missed the end of the last one! It must have been when Mrs. Siddons called us aside to give us our earnings. Did that girl from the farm ever get the big marble back?"

"The Birthright?" Miriam said, smiling. "Tell you what. I'll tell you the end of it when we go into the yards."

"Yeah," Joan said, sitting back. "Yeah, that'll do. So, let us know, how did a toff like you ever end up down in Devil's Kitchen?"

"Just was unlucky, I suppose," Miriam replied. "Em, how about you?"

"Got caught when I skived a packet of sweets," Joan said, shaking her head. "Can you believe that? Down in this place, and all for a packet of jelly babies."

"Jelly babies!" Win repeated, with a loud hoot.

Despite herself, Miriam smiled. "Hope there were lots of blackcurrant ones in the bag, anyway," she commented.

Win and Joan looked at each other, and screamed with laughter. "Blackcurrant! You're not as serious as you look, are you?" Joan said, and she flapped her sandwich at Miriam.

"What's going on?" a suspicious voice behind Miriam said. She turned and saw Elsie, who stood with her fists on her wide hips.

"Just having a bit of a laugh," Win said.

"Yeah, can't hurt," Joan added.

"With *her*?!" Elsie directed a fat finger at Miriam.

"With me," Miriam replied. She threw down her mug and stood up. "It may surprise you, Elsie, to learn that I don't have the plague, I'm not deaf, and I am a real person. So stop talking about me as if I wasn't here."

Win and Joan looked at each other with wide, delighted eyes, and Win emitted another of her loud hoots. "Wooohooo! Watch out, Elsie!"

"Time, ladies," Mrs. Siddons called out. "Go on, you lot, get back to your baskets," she continued, coming over to where Elsie stood.

Elsie stared at Miriam for a moment, and when Mrs. Siddons had moved away, she jabbed a forefinger at her. "Right," she said, her eyes narrowed. "I've had it with you. This afternoon, my girl, in the yards."

Miriam lifted her chin. "I'll look forward to it," she replied, and she stared back.

With a long, suspicious look over her shoulder, Elsie moved away.

As they filed down to the yards, Elsie maneuvered herself behind Miriam and managed to step on the back of her boot. After the third time, Miriam swung around and hissed fiercely, "Lay off!"

"Lay off!" Elsie mimicked, causing Sally to scream with laughter.

Figuring that she was beaten anyway, Miriam whispered, "You sound like a pair of halfwits, the both of you. What were you put in Devil's Kitchen for, hopeless stupidity?"

Elsie stopped after that, as Mrs. Siddons hung back to find out what the all the whispers were about. The older woman moved away, however, to hand out the pay packets once they reached the yards, and Miriam was left alone with the two big, unfriendly girls.

"Right, you," Elsie said. "We've had just about enough of you, see?" She lunged forward suddenly and pushed Miriam backwards.

Miriam fell heavily onto the sand. Sally repeated, "Had enough of you!" She screeched with joy and added, "Fell right on her bottom, did you see, Elsie?"

"Pay packets," Elsie muttered in warning. "Here you are," she said to Miriam in a false, sweet voice as Mrs. Siddons approached, holding out her hand to help her up. Miriam ignored her and got onto her feet without assistance.

"One for you, and you," Mrs. Siddons said, handing something to Elsie and Sally, "and one for you, Miriam. 'Spose you've paid off your debts to the Headmistress. Don't spend it all in one place!" With a rich chuckle, she gave Miriam a square envelope. "Minnie!" she called out, walking away again. "Come and get it!"

"You can just hand that over to me," Elsie said, holding out a large, red palm. "Have to pay for your training anyway."

"What training – a push in the back and an empty basket?" Miriam said with anger. "Sorry, but if you want it you'll have to take it from me." She put her hands behind her back and, feeling rather like a bird that fluttered around a snake's head to protect a nest, she stuck out her tongue at the large girl.

Maddened, Elsie rushed forward. She was jerked back suddenly by a large fist that gripped her collar and hauled her backwards.

"What's going on here?" Mack asked, turning Elsie so he could see her. "Not interfering with my girl, are you?"

"Nothing to do with you, Mack," Elsie replied with spirit. "Ladies' matters. Shove off."

"We're ladies," another voice said. Joan walked up behind Mack and folded her plump arms. "Not messing with our friend, are you, Elsie?"

"It's story time," Bill rasped, with a rheumy cough. "Let her go, afore it's the worst for you."

Elsie looked around. A largish group had gathered around the girls, and there were mutters of "Shame!" and "Leave her alone!"

"Sally!" Elsie looked around wildly, but to no avail. Her friend had disappeared. With a pout, Elsie wrenched her collar out of Mack's grip. She turned and flounced away.

"Ah," Mack commented, sitting down and fishing for his customary cigarette. "Bill, got a fag? Ta. Now, what's the name of the new story?"

"We haven't heard the end of the old one yet!" Joan insisted, sitting beside Mack. "Move over a bit, can't you."

Mack stared at her mildly for a moment and nodded and inched over so Joan and Win could sit. "Right, repeat the end of the old one, and we want to hear about the boy with the key round his neck," he said.

"Yeah," Bill agreed.

"Well, all right," Miriam said, settling herself. "So. Thomasina entered the throne room of the foreign king, with the feeling as though she stood out in her dirty, ragged clothes. She felt as if all eyes were on her. The king, however, took one look at her and motioned for her to come to his side..." She was aware of all the eyes on her, but after a bit she forgot where she was as usual, and finished the story, embellishing it with some extra bits she thought of as she repeated the ending. Beside Mack, Joan smothered a tear in her gray smock as if she knew how Thomasina felt.

"...And there the Birthright sits to this day," she concluded after a bit.

Win sighed. "Oh, that was lovely. I can just see that foreign prince too, tall and strong, with black eyes."

"Just your type, eh, Winnie?" Bill guffawed, nudging her shoulder. She nudged him back, one corner of her mouth curving up.

"*Just* my type," she said with meaning. "Now, what about the – what's it called? The Princess in the Lavatory?"

"Labyrinth," Miriam said, laughing. "Are you sure you want to hear one more?"

"Come on, let's have it," someone said impatiently. Looking up, Miriam saw Frank, the joker from the train.

"Oh," she said. "All right. Well. Here goes. 'A man and his wife had always hoped for children, but many years passed and they gave up hope. One night, as they sat by their fire, feeling sad and alone, there was a knock at the door. A traveler had arrived, looking for a place to spend the night, out of the storm. Without a second thought, the kind couple showed him to their best room, which was still small and shabby.'"

"Like my cell," Frank said, but the audience hurriedly shushed him.

"The next morning when they awoke, the man and his wife found that the traveler had gone, leaving no trace. Nine months later, however, the woman gave birth to a son. But the strange thing was that the baby, who was as bright and bonny as anyone could wish for, had been born with a golden key on a golden chain around his neck."

Her gaze transfixed on Miriam, Joan sighed.

A tall shadow suddenly blocked the dim afternoon sunshine. "What is going on here?" the Headmistress said, looking at Miriam.

She scrambled to her feet and hurriedly brushed the yellow, clinging sand off the back of her dress. "Oh, em, sorry, Headmistress. I was just, you know, telling them a story."

"You were. I see." The Headmistress looked around at the assembled audience, who hastened to follow Miriam's example and stood up, discreetly tidying up different portions of their anatomy. The woman sniffed. "Gathering in groups, listening to fiction – all dangerous pastimes. I totally forbid it."

There was a general outcry, quickly stifled. Frank stepped forward and pulled his cap off his head. "Begging your pardon, your honor, I mean Miss, but we weren't doing nothing wrong. Nor was the girl."

Mack put one hand on Frank's shoulder. "And if we all sit here, we won't fight, or gamble, or steal things from one another at Break Time."

The Headmistress frowned, and her eyes swiveled over every person in the crowd. They stopped to rest on Miriam, and her cold gaze grew icier. "Not nearly good enough. I need more than that. What will I get in return?" she said.

With a start, Miriam remembered something. She handed back the envelope she had been given earlier. "Here," she said. "I don't need it. Keep my pay, and please let me tell them stories."

With a sudden motion, the Headmistress hooked the pay packet out of Miriam's hand. Her cold glance swept over the company once more, and she stalked away.

The group stood frozen for a moment, and Bill mumbled awkwardly, "Nay, you can't do that, miss. You can't give up your money for us."

Mack made an extremely rude gesture behind the Headmistress's back. "Bloodless old trout. And Bill's right, yer know; you can't give up your pay just to read us stories."

"Yer can't, Miriam," Win agreed. "What'll your family live on, eh?"

Miriam shrugged. "Haven't got a family. Look, they've started to line up. Come on." Without a backward look, she marched off and got into the row of girls.

Elsie got behind her in line again and seized the inner skin of Miriam's elbow in a tight, painful pinch, but Joan wedged herself between them.

"Drop it." She shoved her face into Elsie's. "Go on, leave go of her. Let her alone. Now, see? And don't touch my friend again, Elsie, or it'll be the worst for you."

CHAPTER 15

A Valiant Effort

N eil waved goodbye one last time to the group of clerks and trudged off into the dark night. He felt rather reluctant to leave his fellow workers. Their cheerfulness invigorated him after weeks of anxiety; for a few hours, he had even managed not to think about his family. Jeremy and Ginger had asked "Tom" to join them at a local pub, but he wanted to get back to the house instead and report to Mana.

As he walked back into the heart of the worst part of the city, it began to rain. Cold drops sluiced down the back of his jacket and trickled down his neck. Neil pulled his cap forward with a muttered curse, but it didn't do much good. He tried not to think of the crowd at the warm pub. Instead, he ran until he reached the street where they were living.

Inside the house, Mana and Kyoge stood in front of the fireplace in the sitting room. They were in the middle of a deep discussion. When Neil appeared, dripping onto the carpet, Mana came forward with a slight frown. "Neil!" she said. "You're positively drenched!"

"Began to rain," Neil said unnecessarily.

"Well, why didn't you hire a cab?" Mana asked. She pulled off his jacket and taking his hat. "Come and sit by the fire at once and warm up, and I'll make you a cup of tea."

"I shall make the tea for Neil, Your Majesty," Kyoge said. He bowed and walked out of the room in a manner that brooked no argument. Mana watched him leave and sat opposite Neil.

"Is something wrong?" Neil asked. He held his hands out to the fire.

"He didn't get the position at Pearson's."

"Really!" Neil exclaimed. "Oh. I'm sorry – er, that is-"

"Exactly so," Mana responded. "He wouldn't thank you for your sympathy."

"No," Neil agreed. Kyoge was so strong, and so elegant, that you could hardly say 'Sorry, old chap' to him and clap him on the shoulder. When the guard returned, bearing a tray, Neil took the cup and blurted out, "Where's Janet?"

"I sent her home," Mana said as she accepted a cup. She stared into the grate for a few moments. "I've been thinking," she said slowly, "that I might hire someone to go into Devil's Kitchen for us. A detective, or better yet, a spy."

"Devil's Kitchen!" Neil exclaimed. "But you can't. Mana, it's a dreadful place by all accounts." Quickly he related what he heard about it while he had been working.

Mana nodded, and looked up as Kyoge sat forward in his seat. The large guards clasped the arms of the chair he was in. "I have heard the same things, Neil, and some worse rumors as well, but we cannot leave any stone unturned. There is a distinct possibility that Miriam, and perhaps Simon as well, are held in that terrible place."

"I will go and work there," Kyoge announced.

Mana blinked. "No, not you; I mean to hire someone who would be sent there anyway. And as a Lampalan, the conditions would be very much worse for you in that place, I fear. No, I'll have to ask Philips to find me a man who is a thief, yet also trustworthy, if you get my meaning. If there is such a man to be had." She took another sip of tea and her forehead puckered.

"No need." Kyoge sat back with an air of finality. "I will do it."

Mana slapped her cup and saucer onto the tray. "It is too dangerous, Kyoge, did you hear what I said? I sometimes feel as though I'm talking to a statue when I converse with you! You could be imprisoned for months, perhaps years, and forced to take Copaiba –"

"Copaiba – what's that?" Neil asked, trying to forestall the argument brewing between them.

"-And you could be seriously hurt," Mana continued, as if Neil had never spoken.

"Do you think I am afraid of that, or of anything?" Kyoge said softly.

Mana turned to face him, the fire behind her deepening the shadows on her face. "No, you are not," she said. "And that is what makes me afraid. There is nothing wrong with a little fear at times, Kyoge. Sometimes it can keep people safe."

"And do you not think I am intelligent enough?"

"Oh, no." Mana leaned forward so that she unconsciously mirrored his attitude in her own chair. "No, Kyoge, I have every respect for your intelligence, believe me."

Neil began to feel awkward. Their conversation seemed to have reached a new stage of meaning, one that he didn't quite understand. He cleared his throat, stood up, and said, "Think I'll go and change out of these wet things." Mana merely nodded, and he walked out, trying not to clatter his boots on the wooden floor.

He could hear their voices as he clumped up the stairs, although he could not hear exactly what they said. Their tones were too low for eavesdropping. When he reached the door of his room, however, Mana suddenly cried out with exasperation, "I utterly forbid it, Kyoge, do you hear me?"

Dinner that night was a silent affair. Kyoge got out a plate of cold meats and cheeses that Janet had left in the press for them, and he and Mana pointedly ignored each other. The atmosphere in the small kitchen couldn't have been more uncomfortable, or tense. As soon as he could, Neil escaped from the dining room, and soon after he climbed into bed he heard Mana go up to her own room and slam the door.

He fell asleep, but strange sounds, hushed footsteps, little scrapings, and scratches punctuated his dreams. Did someone open the front door? He thought he heard a handle turn and the latch click, but he was trapped in a strange twilight world of waking dreams and was unable to move. He sat in a dining room and didn't know what to do with a bowl of warm water. He lay in a boat. He leaned over a tall cliff and looked down at Riki, who hung in a cage on the end of a long chain. He was at his desk at Pearson's, while Jacky crept about the office and filled everyone's mugs with a strange, purple liquid.

In the morning he woke up with a tight, grinding headache. He groaned, pushed his legs out from the blankets, and dressed quickly for work.

Mana was already up. Neil could hear her as she splashed water and opened drawers, but Kyoge's door was closed, and his room was silent.

Neil ran down stairs, grabbed a piece of cheese and a biscuit, and dashed out the door. On the steps outside he ran into Janet, who was just coming in. "Hullo!" she said with a wide smile. "Off somewhere, are you?"

"Got a job!" Neil yelled, and he clattered down the front steps. "Going to be late!" He dashed away.

In Pearson's, Neil found Accounts in an uproar. Ginger held court at her desk. She pointed at the door and said, "Didn't I say they'd be in to see what we was all up to? Didn't I? And now see!" When Neil entered with a guilty glance at the clock, she beckoned him over to her chair with huge gesticulations.

"What's going on?" he asked. He pulled off his cap and ran one hand over his hair.

"Tour of the factory," Ginger said. "The new owners. Oh Gawd, didn't I say it would be the end of the free meals? Eat up today, lads; we'll be on bread and water by tomorrow."

"The Marchpanes are coming here?" Neil had a queer, tight feeling in his chest.

"That's right," Jacky said. The old man turned and looked at him. "How'd you know their names?"

"Read it somewhere," Neil said, and he sat with a thump.

"Nine o' clock," Ginger intoned, and the room become as silent as always. Neil drew forward the report he had to copy and found he had also been given a list of figures to add up. Perhaps that meant that his work from the day before had been satisfactory.

He started to write. His thoughts turned to Simon's parents. What if they came in, saw him, and demanded that he tell them everything he knew? What if he got sent to that Devil's Kitchen? With an effort, he forced himself to concentrate on the report. He jumped with nerves, however, when Charlie came in with the coffee cart. Everyone leaped up and demanded a cup as well as extra biscuits. "Don't know when we'll see you again, Charlie!" Ginger sang out, as she slurped her coffee.

The boy nodded and disappeared. Neil sat back in his wooden chair to add up figures, and forgot everything else. Math had always been his strong point in school, and he quickly found some errors that required changes throughout the entire account on his desk.

He had just finished the first set of papers when the door opened again and Mr. Drake entered, waving in the Marchpanes. Neil ducked his head down over his report and prayed that they wouldn't notice him.

"Mr. and Mrs. Marchpane, I give you – Accounts!" Drake's fruity tones rang out through the office, and he waved one hand at the clerks. All fifteen of them were bent over reports and lists at their desks.

Theodosia's glance swept the room. "Do we really need so many clerks?" she asked, and she slapped a pair of puce gloves against her palm.

"Theodosia, my dear," Virgil spluttered. "Pearson's has many imports, and exports. We have a great deal of accounts to keep track of!"

Drake bowed. "Indeed, Mr. Marchpane. Correct, as always, sir. And now, if you wouldn't mind, we'd better go upstairs and view Developments." His voice died away as they exited the room.

Neil looked up, and saw the other clerks watching the door. "Whew!" Ginger breathed. Quickly, she bent back over her task.

With a lightened heart, Neil resumed his additions. He needn't have worried at all. He had forgotten that Marchpanes never noticed people they considered to be beneath them.

That evening, he was unable to evade Jeremy's iron will. "Tom" was dragged off to the pub by a large crowd of clerks and other workers. There he swallowed a small glass of cider and, under pretense of visiting the Gentleman's, he ducked out a side door and escaped to the headquarters.

Arriving at the front door, he ran in with an excited shout. "Mana! Kyoge! I've got news!"

Silence greeted this announcement. He popped his head in the sitting room, but it was empty. With another shout for someone to come, he made for the kitchen, but at that moment Mana's head appeared over the banisters.

"Neil!" She started down the stairs. "What happened at work today?"

"Oh, sorry. I didn't mean to shout so loudly. I just saw the Marchpanes today, that's all, and I thought you and Kyoge should know." Neil took off his cap and twisted it in his hands.

Mana reached the bottom and nodded, turning her head to look back up the stairs. The movement revealed the stretch of her long, beautiful neck. "Yes," she said. "I see. Well, I'm sorry, Neil, but you can't tell Kyoge. He's gone."

Neil stared. "Gone? What d'you mean?"

"When I arose this morning, I found that he had left without telling anyone. His room was untouched. In fact, he took only the clothes he wore and nothing else." She sat suddenly on the bottom step and leaned her forehead on both hands.

"I say," Neil sat beside her. "Oh, I suppose he's gone off to –"

"To the Devil's Kitchen," Mana supplied for him. "Yes, that's exactly what I think too."

"Gosh."

They sat for a few moments. Neil didn't know what else to say to her. When the front bell rang, loudly and insistently, they both jumped, and Mana got up from the stair.

Janet ran out of the kitchen, hurriedly tying her apron behind her, and Mana beckoned Neil into the sitting room. A moment later Janet came in with a pile of square envelopes and handed them to her. "The post, miss," she said with a wide grin. "Dinner will be ready in a moment."

Mana received the pile of notes. "Thank you, Janet." She put the pile on a little, glass-topped table. With a faraway look in her eyes, she moved to the window, pushed the faded curtain to one side and stared out into the street.

"Aren't you going to open them?" Neil waved at the envelopes.

"I know what they are," she replied. "Invitations, letters of introduction, and the like. I had Philips put out a notice that I was here in the City for the Social Season."

"So you can enter society, and discover how to rescue Kyoge," Neil reached for one gilt-edged envelope.

Mana turned and looked at him in the eyes. "Yes," she said. "Yes, of course. You're entirely right, Neil! You have both played your parts, you and Kyoge, and it is up to me now." With a little of her former energy, she sat down and picked up the first invitation. "From Mrs. Coope-Edgerton. With that name she is certain to be an encroaching female with a new fortune, wishing to make her way in Society. She's perfect."

"You're going to attend all of these parties?" Neil asked, appalled.

"Oh yes," Mana replied. "They'll want to show me off, as a new acquisition. Very well, I'll be their plaything, and I will use them at the same time."

"And what is it that you want to do?"

"Let's just say that I'll make a Valiant Effort." Mana opened another card.

CHAPTER 16
A Suspicious Game

When Barbara returned, Simon sat on the bed, his face in his hands. "Hello, my love!" she said brightly. "Do you like my new dress?" She put her hands on her hips and twisted her waist both ways so he could get a look.

Simon glanced up and grunted, "Very nice."

She frowned, and her white brow puckered. "What's the matter, Simon? You don't seem very happy to see me today."

"Well, how can I be happy," he exploded, "if I'm wearing nothing but blasted pajamas every time you come and see me? A chap doesn't want to meet a beautiful woman in his nightclothes, dash it."

"I would have thought that was exactly how-" She stopped. "Oh. Well, never mind. No matter."

"It does matter." He turned away. "I'm tired of these bloody slippers and dressing gowns. I've worn nothing else for weeks now."

"I see." She moved as if to sit next to him, but he made an impatient sound, got up, and walked over to the other side of the small garret. There he leaned his head against the wall and scratched at the plaster. "So," she continued slowly, "you're ready for a change, is that it?"

Simon didn't reply.

With a quick motion, she got up and stood right behind him. She said in a silky tone, "And just who are you to make demands on me?"

He turned and faced her. Her eyes were blazing, and her hair flamed against the dark stuff of her new dress; actually, she had never appeared more beautiful. He cleared his throat, and he forced himself to touch her wrist. "Who am I? I am someone who-" he swallowed, "someone who admires you with all my heart. That is all." At this point, he considered, he should have a gallant speech prepared, but he'd be damned if he could go on flirting with her. He just could not talk any longer with a woman who thought it was perfectly fine to imprison a person in a filthy room without a window.

However, she seemed content. She smiled and opened the door. "Good-bye, my admirer," she said, and was gone.

Simon breathed out slowly and sat on the chair. A few days earlier Nurse had brought up the seat for him and placed next to the bed. Who would be the next person to enter his room – Jenkins, bearing a leather whip and a tray of spew for him to eat, or Barbara, bringing in a suit of decent clothes for him to wear?

It was neither, as it turned out. A few hours later, Nanny entered the room, looked around with displeasure, and said with asperity, "Well, come on, and don't dawdle. We've got to move downstairs again, now, don't we?"

Simon bounded up, hardly believing what he had just heard, and quickly pushed his way onto the mean little hallway outside where, of course, Jenkins was waiting for him. The huge man contented himself with thrusting his tongue out to the roots at Simon; obviously he had been warned not to touch him. Nanny led the way downstairs, and Jenkins brought up the rear, his angry stare burning holes in Simon's back.

At the door of the room where Simon had first stayed in that huge house, Nanny took out a large ring of keys and searched through them. Simon waited while she opened the door and moved to hold it for her, but Jenkins gripped his arm. "No funny stuff, see," he growled.

Simon held up his hands and raised his eyebrows, oozing innocence, and Jenkins gave him a final shove into the room. The door was closed and, as usual, locked.

After being sequestered for weeks in the tiny attic room, the bedchamber felt large enough to stable a string of stallions. Simon wheeled around, waving his arms to taste the feeling of sheer space. He stopped when he saw what was on the bed. There, laid out, was a suit of clothes, complete with shirt, jacket, tie and a pair of trousers. A large hipbath had been brought up and it was filled with warm water.

One corner of his mouth curved up in a smile. His ruse had actually worked! Barbara, for whatever reason, seemed to care about what he thought, and she also cared enough to do what he asked. He wondered about it for a moment, but the bath was too enticing.

Quickly he stripped off his robe and pajamas and got into the tub. He gave a groan and closed his eyes with pleasure as the warm water covered his body. He felt as though he could stay in the bath for a year.

Miriam. Neil. His eyes flew open. Where were they at that moment? Was Miriam still on that dirty cot, in that tiny, dark room? At that very moment, did she think that everyone had forgotten her?

Sobered, he lathered himself up quickly, rinsed off and got out. A stack of thick towels had been placed to one side, and Simon wound one around his body and dried his hair in another with great energy. Blissfully clean and dry, he turned to the clothes on the bed and dressed quickly.

The sun's rays through the window were just starting to turn the brilliant shade of orange that proclaims late afternoon when he finished dressing. He sat on the chair by the door and looked around. There were books in the shelf. He could read if he wished. There was more hot water by the bed. He could have another wash later. Most important, there was loads of room in which to exercise. He grinned and looked up as the door opened.

Valiant and Barbara entered. The brother and sister were arm-in-arm. Barbara looked up at her brother, laughed at something he had said, and she addressed Simon. "Well, my dear, you certainly look as though you feel better. The clothes suit you."

Simon stood up and bowed. Valiant chuckled and added, "Quite a difference, hey, Barbara, my darling?"

"In many ways," she responded. They both looked at Simon, and he felt that he was supposed to say something.

"Why, thank you. Thank you both very much," he said, feeling a bit inadequate. "Thanks most awfully. Really!"

Valiant laughed. "Well, dear sister," he said in a low tone, "it looks as though you have won our bet." She hushed him with one finger on his lips, but she also smiled, evidently pleased. He cast another quizzical look at Simon and left the room.

Barbara watched him leave and with a glance at Simon, she walked over to the window. "It is a pleasant room, wouldn't you say?" she asked. The afternoon light slanted across her orange eyes.

"A very pleasant room," Simon said. He knew now what was expected; with a few strides he crossed the room and picked up her hand. "However," he added, turning her arm over and kissing her wrist, "it is still a prison."

"Still a prison!" She pulled her hand away from him. "What the devil? What on earth do you mean, Simon?"

"I am still inside this house, watched by a trio of guards, behind a locked door," Simon replied. He ducked his head to look into her eyes and began to kiss her fingertips.

"Well, of course! You can hardly blame us, can you? After all, a few weeks ago you tried to escape out the front door, in case you forgot!" However, she did not snatch her hand away.

So it had been several weeks that he had spent in that filthy room upstairs. Simon smiled and put one finger under her chin. He tilted her head up so he could look for a long moment in her eyes. "Barbara, I was a different person. Can't you see that? I have changed in many ways. Can't you trust me just a little bit more?"

She frowned. *She must know that her brow puckers prettily when she does that,* Simon reflected. "What do you mean, Simon? How exactly have you changed?"

"Well." Simon stepped back and waved a hand at her, indicating her rich costume, the lace at her throat, the gold leather of her shoes peeping out from her skirts, her heavy hair. "Obviously, you are someone who must go out a lot, I would say. You probably love to attend parties, and, you know, balls, and all that sort of thing. I would imagine that you ride like a wood nymph. And you probably go on hunts with all the local families. In fact, I would say that many gentlemen vie for the honor of your hand at dances. No?"

She tossed one long curl over her shoulder and pursed her lips. "What of it? I won't deny that Valiant and I move a great deal in Society, but what does that have to do with your room?"

"Barbara." Simon grew more confident in his approach. "I want to see you as you are in your own world, as it were. Ha ha!"

"Ha ha!" she echoed, beginning to smile. "So you want to attend soirees, and balls, and go hunting with me, and all that sort of thing?"

"If we are going to be together one day, as you hinted when we were in Miriam's house - rather, I mean to say my parent's house – I would think that we have to do the thing in the right manner."

"Well." She stepped away from the window and from him, and she wafted towards the door. "Clever, aren't you?"

He watched her move away from where he stood. "Barbara," he said, trying to keep the desperation out of his voice. "I just want you to trust me, can't you see that?"

She didn't say anything. With a slight grimace she opened the door and left, and locked it in what seemed a most pointed way.

Damnation! Simon swore, and he sat on the chair. He rubbed his upper lip with one hand and stared out of the window. He no longer saw the darkening sky. Had he gone too far and too fast? Perhaps Barbara would never trust him now.

The light faded, and Nurse came in and lit the lamp by his bed. She left a tray, and Simon, his spirits rising, saw that he had been given half a dozen oysters, a plate of coq au vin, and buttered parsnips for his dinner. At least it hadn't been Jenkins' manure special.

Suddenly hungry, he ate with vigor, sipping a little of the water he had been served. There was half a bottle of white wine on the tray as well, but he didn't drink any of it. He stared at it for a moment, and he poured most of it out into the ever-present chamber pot. Let them think that he was a lush as well as an idiot. After his dinner, he sat by the window, waiting for Barbara. He didn't know what else to do.

That night, however, she did not reappear.

Over the next few days Simon lived as he had before he had been dragged upstairs, except that he now was given clothes, all perfectly tailored in rich, luxurious wools and silks. There were socks, ties, and he had shoes made of the finest leather. He woke up each morning, took a leisurely bath, and fingered the razor that had been sent up. With regret, he decided that he didn't have enough whiskers on his chin yet to use it.

He read endless books and ate the meals that were sent up by Nurse and Nanny. Their only jobs seemed now to be to serve him. In the afternoons he stripped and exercised. His muscles grew hard and lean. He was able to move for longer periods of time, and he found he could run in place for half an hour before he even started to lose his breath.

He tried not to think about Miriam, still in that dark place, or about Neil, who was God knows where. He concentrated on getting stronger and tried to forget everything. At night he did his best to lose himself in another book. When he read he forgot his impossible planes for escape, and he was able to sleep. Long hours of rest, he thought, would give him more strength.

Like the prisoners he had read about, he began to keep a calendar, marking the days as they passed on the flyleaf of one of the novels on the shelf (it was an unlikely travelogue about a boy who traveled with his father's army.) Four, five days passed, and still there was no sign of his pretty jailer.

In a way, he was glad not to see Barbara, as it spared him the necessity of having to pay her the flattery she clearly expected. Still, even though the room was much bigger than the garret, it quickly seemed to become smaller to him, and he longed to go outside and smell fresh air, walk in the woods, ride a horse – anything but stay indoors another day.

Nanny and Nurse continued to be tightlipped in his presence. Simon thought that he might try to make friends with one of them, but they must have been warned not to talk to him. Nurse merely ignored him when he asked about events in the outside world – the weather, or whether there was any news worth mentioning. Nanny, when Simon addressed her, opened the door and allowed Jenkins to poke his huge head in and glare at Simon. He stopped trying after that.

On the evening of the sixth day he marked another line by his row of marks in *How Briggs Followed the Reveille* and closed the cover. He picked up another book he had started to read, part of a school series, but after a few minutes of midnight feasts and cricket games, he closed it as well and tossed it aside. Restlessly he got up and paced the room. He thought he understood how a tiger must feel in a cage at the zoological gardens.

He pried at the window, but it remained stubbornly shut as if it had been nailed down; in any case, there was the considerable height under his window to keep in mind. He turned to the door, tried the handle for the thousandth time, and flung himself back in the chair.

At that, the door opened, and Nurse entered with the usual dinner tray. Jenkins followed. The huge man carried a huge box. He plopped it on the silk counterpane in an unwilling manner. Simon got up, surprised. "What's this?" he asked.

Nurse sniffed, put the tray on a low table, and replied without a glance in his direction, "I would suggest that you open it if you want to find out." She swept out.

For once, Simon was able to ignore Jenkins. The man pulled grotesque faces at him but at length had to withdraw, defeated. Simon crossed over to the bed and picked up the lid of the box, which was embellished with a gold lion and unicorn, and bore the name of one of the most expensive tailors in London.

Inside, under layers of tissue paper, Simon found a suit of evening clothes. He picked up the jacket, and saw a large, square envelope that had slipped to one side.

He threw the jacket on the bed and opened the envelope. Inside was a large, thick card. He drew it out and read the words.

"Your presence is requested," it said, "at a gathering the tenth evening of this month. Dinner, dancing, games, and a full orchestra of musicians will be there for your pleasure."

With the card grasped in both hands, Simon brought it over to the window and stared at the words. His lips moved as he read them again, and again. He looked out of the window and at the trees. Beyond the woods, out there, somewhere, Miriam was held in a dark prison cell.

I'm on my way, Simon thought, and again his lips moved, as if he could say those words right in the girl's ear. *Hold on. I'm on my way for you.*

CHAPTER 17
Further Developments

N eil, have you seen my shawl?" Mana came out onto the landing and looked down at him where he stood, hat in hand, preparing to leave for Pearson's.

"No," he responded, surprised. "Didn't you leave it on the chair in the sitting room?"

"That is what I thought, too. Well, no matter. Are you headed out?"

"Off to the office." He waved to her, and she smiled, the lightness not quite reaching her eyes. "What are you doing today?"

"Oh, goodness." She began to descend the stairs. "Tea with Mrs. Coope-Edgerton, and she wishes to take me for a drive about the park. In other words, show me off. This evening there is a gathering for cards, and an outing to the opera, I believe." She stopped and consulted a small notebook, and nodded. "Yes, the opera, followed by burnt wine and shaved ham by the river..."

"Stop, stop," Neil said, holding his head. "No, really. Are you going to do all of that?"

She smiled, again with that tinge of sadness. "The more I am seen, the more I will become fashionable, and in that way maybe I might encounter the Marchpanes or the Cantwells at some point."

"And if you do encounter them?"

"Perhaps I can force their hand a bit."

"Do you really want to do that?" Neil started up the stairs, and stopped. "Mana, please be careful."

"I will, Neil. Thank you for your concern. But do you think that I do not know what is at stake? It is time for those four people, Barbara and Valiant, as well as the Marchpanes, to start to worry and wonder, as we have had to do the past few months."

Neil nodded. "All right," he said, as he retreated back down the stairs. "I must go to work. But be careful."

Mana nodded and turned back to her room. Maybe she still wanted to search for the missing shawl.

To tell the truth, Neil was rather glad to leave for the Accounts Office. The atmosphere in the house, after living with Riki's energy and laughter in the splendor and color of the tropics, was almost overwhelmingly oppressive. Mana was silent and sad. Even though she never spoke of him, she obviously thought about Kyoge all the time.

Moreover, the shawl was not the first item that had disappeared. Janet, usually so cheerful herself despite her delicate condition, reported food gone from the cupboards and the cold press. Two loaves of bread that she had baked were gone, and it made her cross and snappish. "What am I going to give you for tea, I should like to know?" she demanded.

Other items, pillows, linens, and clothes among them, also disappeared. Neil continued to dream at night as well; tired from the day's work, he did not wake up but lay in a stupor, hearing things move and creak, and was unable to get up to do anything about it, even if he had wanted to do so.

Thus, it was a relief to enter the Accounts office with the cheerful clerks, especially Ginger, who had decided that Neil was her property. A few evenings earlier, over a pint in the pub, she confided her attraction for Jeremy's wide, gap-toothed grin, and ever since Neil had become her confidant and somewhat of an unwilling accomplice in her schemes to "get her fellow."

At Pearsons' the free luncheons had stopped, as Ginger had predicted, but Charlie continued to visit with the coffee cart. However, the clerks had to hand over a few coins for their coffee, and biscuits cost extra.

Ginger, therefore, had started a plan whereby the clerks pooled their money and bought different types of foods in at the noon hour – pasties, pork pies, cheese and pickles, and ham sandwiches.

On top of that, anyone caught "being a misery," as Ginger put it had to fork over a small sum to the office kitty. There were other costly infractions, such as not saying "Good morning" upon anyone's arrival, forgetting to take one's hat off, or missing the paper-basket when firing in a wadded-up piece of paper.

Neil walked in, snatched off his hat, and quickly said, "Good morning!"

"Good morning," everyone in the office instantly responded.

"Meal collection," Ginger demanded, shaking an old biscuit tin under Neil's nose.

"Is that a joke in poor taste?" he shot back. "I'm certain I paid twice already this week."

"Not being a misery, are you?" Jacky said from his seat.

"No, no," Neil replied hastily, and he dug in his coat pocket. "Very well, how much is it this time, you blood-suckers?" Ginger held up two fingers, and Neil dropped a pair of coins into the tin.

"Thanks very much," she said. "I say, nine o' clock!"

Any talk or distraction once work hours began meant another fine. Neil sat down and began to tot up numbers. After his first week, he had been given nothing but actual accounts to do by the unknown "Upstairs," which was fine by him. Copying reports meant cramped fingers. Often he had to rewrite entire pages if he made a mistake, which usually occurred right at the top of a page, and were not discovered until he reached the bottom.

Neil was happy, therefore, to add up sums instead and keep running totals of deposits and sums paid out to various sources. He tried to puzzle out where the monies were going, but the sources named in the documents were given anonymous-sounding company names, such as "Amalgamated Ironworks" and "Boodleridge and Sons." He shook his head. It was impossible to glean any meaning from the information in the accounts.

When Charlie appeared with the coffee cart, Neil put down his pen at once. Work done during break time meant another fine.

"Jacky Boy's turn to pay," he sang out, echoed by Ginger.

"It's not!" Jacky protested. "It's Tom's turn to buy. I'm certain I bought the other day."

Ginger shook the box. "Misery?" she asked.

"Oh, very well," Jacky grumbled. He gave Charlie some money, and people lined up to get their coffees.

"Going to the pub tonight?" Neil asked Ginger.

"Rather," she said. "Not going to disappear in the bog, are you?"

"Ginger!" he said, shocked. "You pain me, really. A nice girl like you, using such language. Is Jeremy coming?" he added under his breath.

She pulled a face. "Yeah, him and that little bint from Developments."

"What, that blonde piece with the ribbons?"

She nodded. "That's her. He said he's had his eye on her for some time. Said he's glad he can talk to me about her; I'm a friend, see, according to him, even though I'm not a chap. Said he's glad he can get the 'female perspective' from me."

"Ooh," Neil said, pulling a sympathetic face. "Ouch. 'Female perspective' – tut, tut, that's bad."

Jacky cleared his throat loudly and pointed at them, and Neil suddenly realized that everyone in the office was sitting back at their desks, writing away. "Blast," Ginger swore. "Lend me some money, would you, Neil?" Dropping their pennies into the tin, she sat down and started to work.

Neil resumed adding up figures, as well as figuring the interest owed on some overdue payments. He found the work easy, but it did not stop him from worrying about Mana's entrance into Society and the pitfalls she might encounter there. However, if she were able to find those bloody Cantwells, especially that hellish woman with the red hair that Simon had been so taken with, it would be worthwhile. Barbara. Yes, that was her name.

And what about Kyoge? Where was he? Perhaps he should go and take a look at Devil's Kitchen some time. Yes, he would go that very evening, after he left the pub. Mana would be out until all hours, busy being someone's social "pet," and he did not particularly relish a night in the empty house alone with the disappearing items and the strange sounds. As much as he did not want to creep around a dark factory at night either, it would be better than staying by himself in a house that creaked and imagining who knows what.

Charlie delivered a huge pile of new reports and accounts and deposited them on the clerks' desks. "I'll be blowed," Ginger said, picking up some papers with distaste. "How do they expect us to get through this lot?"

"Work through lunch," Jacky replied gloomily. "Right, who's serving? Go on, dish it up, and we'll eat at our desks. No fair charging," he added hurriedly, seeing Ginger picking up her collecting tin with a gleam in her eye. "I'm not being a misery, just stating the truth."

"He's right," someone groaned. Edith, a small, elderly woman, got up and began to put slices of cold chicken on the thick white china plates Jacky had donated to the office. Neil received his share of chicken, new lettuce, and brown bread. He looked at the rows of numbers. If he increased his efforts he could just manage the pile by five. He chewed a mouthful of chicken and salad, wiped his fingers, and continued his work.

After one page of cramped figures, he turned it over and found a different kind of document altogether. Written in a fine, sloping hand on a thin piece of onionskin, it seemed to be a scientific treatise on the method of working an experiment. Neil looked at one passage before he realized what it was. The underlined words read: "...the mixture will become dark brown sherry color if the compounds be pure. Into this fluid thus obtained, insert a piece of palladium foil charged with occluded hydrogen. Add five drops of the tincture abstracted from the boles..."

Neil bent over the paper, frowning as he reread the strange document. The words reminded him of some of the more advanced lessons in Natural Sciences he had taken at Firbury College.

He covered the paper with one hand and glanced around the room. The other clerks were bent over their own tasks. Ginger's lips moved as she copied a report. Jacky sighed, cracked his knuckles, and resumed writing.

Neil coughed and brought his hand to his lips. He reached into his pocket for his handkerchief, dusted off his nose, and returned it to his pocket. Like Jacky, he sighed and resumed his work on the accounts. But the thin piece of paper was no longer on his desk.

At quarter past five, Neil put down his pen and looked up. The other clerks had also just finished, except for Jacky who had made a mistake and had to redo his last page.

"Overtime fines," Ginger said, holding up the tin. Coins were flung at her, and she expertly caught them and popped them in. "Good day for us," she said, peering at its contents. "We've got about eight and six extra – enough, say, for a round at the pub?"

"Yes please." Jacky put his pen down and stretched. "S'trewth, I could use a laugh! And a grand crack! And a pint! Who's in?"

There was a chorus of "Me!" "Me please!" Neil held up his hand to be included and went to get his coat.

The door opened and Jeremy popped in his head. "Neil my lad," he said, grinning. "Coming to the pub? I'd like you to meet Verity; she's coming too." He indicated a fluffy-looking girl with curly blonde hair. She nodded at him and moved off, followed by Jeremy who took her elbow and gazed down at her as if she were the only person in the world.

"Come on," Ginger sighed. "Might as well get it over with. Maybe he'll need my 'female perspective' again." Making horrible, mocking faces behind Verity's back, she headed down the rows of machinery that gleamed in the gaslight.

Neil caught up with her. "Ginger," he began.

"That's my name," she answered.

"What do you think all those extra reports were for that we got today?"

She frowned and looked around. "Shh," she said. "Come on outside. Here, hold a girl's coat, would you? Ta." She thrust her arms into the sleeves of her coat and stuck her arm though Neil's elbow. "Can't hurt," she whispered, making violent gestures at Jeremy's back. "Maybe he'll notice that I'm a girl, as well as a female, if you take my meaning."

"The reports," Neil prodded her.

She looked up at him, her sharp, inquisitive face screwed up with concentration. "They're covering something up," she said. "I've been at this too long not to know. But there is some sort of new business and not just because of the new owners. The factory has changed. They're trying to save money, which means they're spending it someplace else."

"Not at Pearson's," Neil mused.

"No, not here. Somewhere else."

"Yes," he mused. "Yes, that's what I thought too."

They walked on in silence for a few moments. Neil tasted frustration in the back of his throat. If nothing was going on at Pearson's, he had wasted his time, and he had accomplished nothing to help his friends. "What's the story with the Devil's Kitchen?" he asked.

"Devil's Kitchen?" Ginger repeated. "A nasty, dirty, place where they send prisoners to rot. I hope I never have the ill-luck to go there myself." She shivered. "Let's not talk about work any longer, hey? Come hold the door for us, Jeremy!" She entered the pub and pulled off her coat.

Over a small cider, Neil talked to Jacky and tried to prod him for information about what he had copied during the day, but the older man didn't have much to say. "Don't know," he said. "Don't want to know about that boring stuff. Fishing, now, that's interesting. Ever go fishing?"

Neil smiled. "All the time," he replied, thinking about his father's boat.

"Have you now!" Jacky sat up and began to tell a long story that involved a broken reel, a huge trout, and, somehow, a bottle of barley water. After a few minutes Neil managed to extricate himself but was claimed by Ginger, who indicated Jeremy and Verity with her head.

"Look at him," she said with great bitterness. "He's going on and on, and he doesn't realize that she doesn't want to hear any of it." Indeed Verity was looking at the glass panes of the window in the snug, the mirror on the wall, and the table in front of them; everywhere, in fact, except at Jeremy.

Neil shook his head. "A lost cause. Shame, really. Well, I should be off."

"Where are you off to?" Ginger demanded.

"Home," Neil said. He shrugged on his jacket and made his exit without too many jeers or friendly insults from the other clerks.

Outside a fine, misting rain was falling. Naturally, Neil swore to himself. Can't rain during the day, or after I get home; oh no, it always has to wait until I have to walk somewhere. He set out, and after a few minutes the drops increased.

He turned up the collar of his jacket and strode along, looking longingly down the street at the house where he and Mana were staying as he passed by. Still, inside would be the empty rooms and the strange sounds. Resolutely he wound his scarf tighter about his neck and walked on.

A woman selling old clothes from a barrow was just packing up for the day, and Neil asked her for directions to Devil's Kitchen. With a grunt, she jerked her thumb down a mean alleyway. Neil thanked her and started down the small, dark street with a great deal of nervousness. She didn't reply to his thanks, and when he glanced back at her, she still stared at him, as the rain fell unnoticed on her grizzled hair.

His footsteps echoed in the narrow street, and Neil stopped. I hear things everywhere, now, he thought, and he shook his head. He continued to the end of the alley, where another dark street jutted out, lined with buildings that were darker negatives against the dark sky.

"Hey," a voice said at his elbow. He jumped and turned around, his heart beating. Ginger stood beside him. She lifted one arm and pointed at one of the dark shapes. "It's that one there," she said.

He seized her arms. "Ginger! You little spy! What are you doing? You nearly made my heart stop!"

"Sorry," she said, pushing the wet hair off her face. "Followed you," she added in an offhand tone.

"Yes, I see that, but why?"

"Jeremy had begun to spout poetry to Her," she said. "I couldn't bear it, him making a huge fool of himself like that, so I left. What are you up to?"

He released her and stepped back. "I wanted to see Devil's Kitchen."

"Yes, but why?"

"I just wanted to see it, and besides, I had nothing else to do. That's it there?"

"Yeah," she said. She grabbed his hand. "Come on."

They crept towards the huge structure. There were no lights in the window; as far as they could see, the factory could have been deserted. "They live underground," Ginger hissed in his ear. "The prisoners do. They work underground too."

"How do you know?" Neil asked.

"Copied out the description on the bill of sale when the new partners purchased it, a year ago. Mr. Pearson had just passed on, and don't I wish he was still around."

"So you know what it's like in there?" Neil asked excitedly.

"'Course. There are several levels underground, and the building above is shaped like a cross, see. That wall surrounds the yards, where I imagine they let the prisoners outside once or twice a week."

"Gosh." Neil stared up at the building and wondered if Simon and Miriam both were locked up in that dark, forbidding place.

"Neil?" Ginger put a hand on his arm. "Neil, I'm wet through with rain. We need to push off."

"Just one more minute-" Neil stopped. The night had been punctuated suddenly by a gurgling scream from the huge factory. The cry reached a crescendo and was cut off suddenly.

They looked at each other, and Ginger grabbed his hand. "Don't need to hear any more," she said. "We're both going home, *now*." With his sleeve clutched in one firm fist, she marched off.

CHAPTER 18

A Large Party

I n his new suit of clothes, Simon was manhandled down the several flights of stairs by the odious Jenkins, who kept pretending to pick bits of fluff off the lapels of the new jacket. Simon wanted to turn and snarl at him to lay off, but he knew that would only give the goon great satisfaction.

It was with a sense of relief that he saw Barbara and Valiant in the hall, chatting in low tones. They looked up as Simon descended and Valiant said, "Good God, old man. Didn't know you had it in you." Jenkins instantly ceased his fooling about.

"Isn't he a picture?" Barbara smiled. She held out her hand to her brother, and Valiant put a small folded packet into it, with a loud, theatrical sigh.

"What was that?" Simon asked.

"A mere trifle, nothing for you to worry your head about. Come on, Cinderella's coach awaits. This way, old man, and, sorry to be a bore, but don't forget that Jenkins will come with us. Hey?"

Simon nodded. He had a feeling he knew what had just happened in the hall. Barbara had bet Valiant that she would enslave Simon as her own conquest. Rather, re-enslave him. He remembered the fool he had made of himself at Miriam's house, and the greater fool he had been upstairs in the attic room. The memories made his skin crawl.

On top of that, Valiant had just surreptitiously warned him not to try anything or else Jenkins would have his hide. Simon had no illusions as to who was the stronger of them; Jenkins could break his jaw easily.

However, in a contest of wits, things might well go his way. Everything about Jenkins was large, he mused, except for the man's brain.

He handed Barbara into the barouche and followed into the carriage, sitting opposite her. The seats were picked out in blue and cream velvet, the same colors of the trappings as well as the harnesses of the horses. Needless to say, the driver wore livery to match.

Valiant entered, sat beside his sister, and flashed his gleaming smile. "Well," he said, "we're off!"

The carriage began to move, and Simon asked, "Where's Jenkins?"

"Oh, he wouldn't ride in here with us," Barbara answered, amused. "I don't even like to be in the same room with that toad in human skin. I don't know how you stood it over the past few weeks, Simon. No, he'll follow in the cart behind us." She winked at her brother and continued, "You haven't noticed my dress."

"Very nice," Simon said. He felt as if that were a little inadequate and added, "Really, it's most awfully nice. It's ripping!" He gave an internal curse, hearing himself talk like a character from that schoolboy's serial he had been reading upstairs.

She seemed satisfied, however, and smiled at him. "It's the very latest stare of fashion, done in the manner of the islands; do you see? Apparently the tropics are all the thing nowadays."

"Why is that?" Valiant asked. "Lord, I could do with a cigar."

"Don't even think that I'll allow you to light one of those nasty things in here!" Barbara chided, as she laughed at him. "Everyone will think I'm wearing Eau de Tabac, instead of the most expensive continental perfume." Valiant reached over and pinched her arm, and she hit him with a fan of ostrich feathers dyed red and black to match her dress.

Feeling that he was unnaturally quiet, Simon cleared his throat and asked, "So, why is it that native dress is all the rage?"

"Oh, because of some island royalty or something. Some princess from some island. Simon, let me fix your collar button – there we are." She leaned forward, fiddled with his shirt, and sat back, satisfied with her handiwork. "Now, Valiant, I suppose we'd better lay down the rules."

Her brother stared out of the window at a group of women on a corner. They had left the countryside where the house was, and the barouche had reached the outskirts of London. He looked up, surprised, and said, "Oh, right, Babs. The rules. Well, now, look here, old man, we know you're with us and all that, but we can't have you pulling any of the funny stunts you tried before."

"Of course, we know you've changed at heart," Barbara added, and she leaned forward again to put one hand encased in red kid leather on Simon's knee.

"Of course," he replied. Again he cursed his inadequate answer. He cleared his throat, leaned forward towards her, and clasped her gloved hand in both of his. "Of course I've changed. I'm with you now, my darling."

"Hey, hey!" Valiant chuckled. "Getting a bit hot, now, aren't you old boy? But, just in case," he continued, "we have to have some insurance, you know."

"Insurance?" Simon frowned.

"Do you remember that little girl that you were so friendly with at the Marchpanes' home?"

Simon nodded.

"Well," Valiant said, "we happen to know where she is. Now, we'll take good care of her, don't you worry about that, but if anything did happen tonight, well..."

"Well, we just couldn't answer for the consequences," Barbara said, and she gave Simon's hand a light squeeze and sat back. "But, naturally, nothing will happen. You and I will dance, and you will fetch me champagne..."

"...And the other young bloods will tear their hair out in a fury," Valiant said. Barbara joined in his laughter. Her head tilted back a little, showing a fine expanse of white neck.

Simon eased himself back in his seat. He concentrated on the complicated embroidery sewn onto Barbara's red gloves so he wouldn't throttle that long, white neck. "Ha ha," he said. He swallowed and continued, "You have nothing to worry about. I said I just wanted to be with you in Society, Barbara. So, I'll do what you said, fetch you champagne, and dance, and all that kind of thing." He felt that more was needed, and he pressed on, "Thank you for this opportunity to show you that you can trust me. I think it's important if we are going to have any sort of a relationship."

"So serious!" The corners of her mouth dimpling, Barbara leaned back and, under pretense of rearranging her furs, she pressed the side of her satin shoe against his foot.

Simon turned his head away from her and looked out of the carriage window. He crushed his gloves together in one hand and forced himself not to jerk his leg away from the pressure of her slipper.

The smaller streets had given way to larger avenues, lined with trees and sparkling with lamps. "Isn't this a long way to come for a party?" he asked suddenly.

"Naturally we have rented a house in the City for the season," Valiant said. "We had to remain in the country much longer this year on your behalf, old chap."

"Oh, sorry."

"Our pleasure," Barbara answered, pressing his foot with hers again. Simon knew that some sort of mooncalf response was expected, but he just couldn't force himself to give her any more compliments. Luckily, at that moment the carriage drew up in front of one of the large houses behind a line of carriage.

Once Barbara had collected her furs and gloves, they stepped out and followed a crowd of guests parading up the front steps. Simon was so tightly squeezed in the throng that he couldn't have escaped, even if Jenkins hadn't walked right up behind him and looked at him with a meaningful glare.

"Is he going to breathe down my collar all night?" Simon said in an undertone to Barbara.

"Oh, I'm afraid so," she responded with a trill of laughter. "Don't worry, he'll allow us to dance and have dinner together. As long as you're with me, he'll leave you be."

With a stifled groan of frustration, Simon entered the house and handed his gloves, overcoat, and silk scarf to a waiting footman. They were bowed into a huge salon, which had festoons of silk over the ceiling and windows, creating a claustrophobic, tent-like atmosphere.

"Esmée has gone too far as usual," Barbara said in an aside to Simon and Valiant.

"Here she comes now," her brother murmured. A large, florid woman with too many diamonds wafted over to them. She uttered little cries of delight as she came forward.

"Valiant, my love! And Barbara! You look utterly ravishing!" The two women kissed the air by each other's cheeks.

"May I introduce Simon Marchpane, our good friend?" Barbara indicated Simon. "Simon, Esmée Coope-Edgerton." He bowed over the woman's tightly gloved hand and touched it to his lips, and she squealed again.

"Another handsome young man, Barbara! My heart will be broken if you and Valiant both don't dance with me later, Simon. Now, I must greet some more arrivals, but we will have a comfortable coze later, Barbara, my love." With a waggle of her fingers at them, she drifted off.

"Remind me why we go to her parties again?" Valiant asked, lazily amused.

"We don't," Barbara said, straightening his cravat. "We allow her the gift of our presence tonight because of the Arrival, and because everyone else is here to see it."

"What is the Arrival?" Simon asked, but he was cut off by a blare of trumpets.

"Oh, Valiant, look! It's just like a regal announcement from a play!" Barbara gurgled. The guests looked up in expectation, and the Coope-Edgerton woman appeared on a balcony above the dance floor. "She is taking advantage of her new acquisition," Barbara whispered to Simon.

"Honored guests," the large hostess intoned in a fruitcake voice, "it is my pleasure to present – the Island Princess!" She motioned with one gloved hand, and her diamond bracelets flashed in the candlelight.

Two pages came in. They scattered rose petals from small velvet baskets, and the throng parted. They were followed by a tall, veiled figure. Whoever it was wearing the veils entered without a sign that she noticed anyone in the crowd. A tall man with an effeminate air came up the steps towards her and reached for her hand with cries of, "Princess! Too delicious! What joy! Do say you'll have supper with us at my table!"

As if that were the signal, the crowd surged forward. Simon could no longer see the veiled princess. "Will we go and pay our complements?" Valiant asked.

"Oh, I think so," Barbara's eyes narrowed to slits. "But not now, Valiant. Something tells me that I want to talk to *this* particular princess in privacy."

From a hidden corner, a small orchestra struck up a light minuet, and in a moment the floor was filled with couples. Barbara turned to Simon, but he said, "Sorry, don't know this one."

With a light laugh, she put her hand on Valiant's arm, only to be claimed by another gallant who looked down at her with burning intensity. Her brother released her hand and said to Simon, "Looks like you'll lose your advantage over the other gents if you're not careful, old chap."

Simon nodded, suddenly filled with the desire to get away from them both. "Would you mind if I got something to drink?" he asked.

Valiant waved a finger, and Simon, turning, saw Jenkins behind a curtain, swinging something that looked like a pistol. Simon nodded wearily and went to one corner to be served a glass of champagne.

The man who had greeted the princess was there. Simon overheard him ask for two glasses of punch. As the footman hastened to pour the drinks, the gentleman flicked open a little turquoise box and scooped out a measure of bright yellow powder with one long fingernail. Casually he inhaled the powder, although he didn't sneeze; evidently, the stuff was not snuff. Instead, his face slackened, and a dreamy look came over his face. "Aaah," he breathed.

"What is that, Marquis?" a woman at his elbow asked, staring at the box with greed in her eyes. "Is it Copaiba?"

"It is," the marquis answered. "Most soothing for someone like myself, whose nerves are constantly jangled by the on-dits and pressures of the world." He waved one hand in the air, and his finger caught the edge of the cup the footman was handing him. Dark liquid and lemons cascaded onto the table, splashing his shirt.

"Damned idiot!" he shouted. "Look what you made me do!"

The footman was effuse in his apologies. "I am very sorry, sir," he gabbled, dabbing at the shirt. "I thought you had the cup in your grip, honest I did."

"You're a clumsy oaf! And stop pawing me!" The man raised both hands helplessly and stared down at his ruined shirtfront.

A grave butler appeared behind them, and offered, "If you would accept our apologies, sir, we have a spare shirt and cravat for you."

"Took me two hours to tie the thing. My own creation too," the man grumbled, but he allowed himself to be towed away.

Simon seized a glass of champagne and swallowed it in two gulps. He put the glass on the tray and took a cup of the punch. With a wink at the footman, he turned away and sipped it. It was too strong, and much too highly spiced, but he drank it. The longer he spent with the footmen was his excuse to stay on his own without the Cantwells for a few minutes.

"Don't like it?" a low voice said in his ear.

Simon looked up and saw the veiled, hidden face of the Island Princess. Quickly he put down his cup and stammered, "I'm sorry, Your Highness; I didn't see you there."

"How is your heart?" she asked.

He stared. "I beg your pardon?"

"Is it strong? Are you brave enough to see the truth?"

Feeling as though he had just slipped into a dream, Simon frowned and said, "Em, yes, I suppose I am."

"Be quiet for a moment. Promise me you won't say anything."

"I-"

"Not a word," she warned. Raising her hand, she drew back her veil. The Island Princess was Miriam's governess, Mana.

Simon nearly choked. She put her finger to her lips and breathed,

"Don't say a thing. They're watching you. Quick – where do the Cantwells keep you locked up?"

"Somewhere in the country," Simon answered. "I don't know where. It's a huge, tall house, though, and I'm on the floor second to the top."

She nodded. "Excellent. Now, move back quickly; leave your cup here, and dance with Barbara, for God's sake. Don't give them any suspicions." She put down her own glass of punch and moved away, not looking back at him.

Simon goggled at her for a moment, and her words sunk in. He put down his cup and wound back to the throng. Valiant had a cigar in one hand and Barbara tapped her fan against her wrist with displeasure.

As Simon approached, she demanded, "Where were you? How dare you just walk away from us?"

He smiled and bowed in front of her. "I am a disreputable villain indeed, madam. I must confess that the heat of being so close to you in the carriage gave me a terrible thirst!"

"What rot," a gentleman behind them said. "A likely story! Punish him, Barbara!"

"I intend to do so," she said, but her eyes smiled. "And no cup for me?"

"Unforgivable," the young man with the burning eyes murmured into her hair.

"You must earn it," Simon said, and he drew her suddenly into a tight grasp. "One dance, and I will fetch you drinks, diamonds, whatever it is that you require!"

"Damnable impudence!" the passionate young exquisite said, but he spoke to the empty air. Simon twirled Barbara onto the floor, and, with a smile, she followed his steps.

CHAPTER 19
The Infirmary

"At this point, Princess Harriet had worked herself into a fine temper," Miriam, as usual, forgot the workers who sat around her in the yellow sand and listened to the story. "'She shouted to the witch...'"

There was a sudden movement beside her, and she stopped. "Frank, what is it? Do you not feel well?"

Frank had put one hand over his face. When Miriam spoke, he looked up, and she saw that his skin had turned a pale gray, and drops of sweat stood out on his forehead. "Dunno what's the matter with me," he mumbled. "Be all right in a minute or two." As he spoke he swayed, and he fell over onto his side.

Mack got up with a curse, which he quickly cut off with a glance at the women. "Right, Frank my lad, it's bedtime for you and no mistake." He lifted up the small man easily and slung him over his shoulder. Miriam and some of the other workers got up as well.

"Do you need any help, Mack?" she asked.

The Headmaster noticed them and paced forward, his hands behind his back. "What has happened here?" he asked.

Mack turned, still holding Frank, turned. "If it's all the same to you, your honor, I'd like to get Frank here back to his cell," he said out of one corner of his mouth.

"What is the commotion, Headmaster?" The Headmistress came up behind them, and she loomed behind the two men. Miriam realized that she was nearly as tall as the Headmaster, and taller than Mack, who was not a short man.

145

"This worker seems to be sick," the Headmaster said.

"Thought I might take him to his cell," Mack announced.

"Not so fast. Put him down," the Headmistress said.

Mack stared. "He's in a fever – I can feel his bloody head! It's on fire! Have a heart, missus!"

"I said to put him down," she snapped.

"Put him down, Mack," Bill said in his mangled voice.

Unwillingly, Mack lowered Frank to the sand, where he half-stood, half-fell, supported on one side by Mack. "Guards!" the Headmistress called, adding two short blasts on her whistle. Two of the huge men Miriam had seen on the day of her arrival came towards them from where they had stood by the gates separating the men's and women's yards.

The Headmistress pointed a long finger at Frank. "Infirmary," she announced.

"Wait, no need for that," Mack said. "We can take care of him, can't we lads? Just needs a few days rest, don't you, Frank?"

The Headmistress stared at him for a moment, and repeated, "Infirmary." She raised one eyebrow, as if she dared Mack to say more, but he muttered something and fell silent. They all watched as Frank was dragged away by the huge men, his feet trailing in the sand. As he was pulled into the dark tunnel that led downstairs, Miriam could hear him begin to retch violently.

"Couldn't leave it alone, could you?" Mack suddenly shouted at the Headmaster.

"Mack, Stop it! What are you doing?" Miriam said, horrified.

"All of you, be quiet at once," the Headmaster announced.

Mack rounded on Miriam. "You think the Infirmary is full of soft beds and nice nurses, is that it? Think he'll be taken care of? That's where they do the experiments, my girl, with the stuff you pick off them twigs every day! And they do it on people – on us!"

"Your cane," the Headmistress said, looking at the Headmaster in a meaningful way. He raised a thin length of something that looked like whalebone.

"No, don't do that to Mack, please!" Miriam said, tears stinging her eyelids.

"I have heard enough," the Headmistress stated. "This ridiculous story-telling must cease from this very moment. Your fiction, girl, is causing dissent and disobedience, just as I thought. I absolutely forbid any stories from this moment. You –" she pointed at Miriam – "are fined a week's wages. And you are fined two," she continued, looking at Mack.

Everyone fell silent, and Miriam shook her head at the injustice of it. "Break time is over," the Headmaster said, swinging the cane. He took Mack by the arm and propelled him to the door, followed by the guard.

Soberly they lined up. Even Elsie didn't bother to torture Miriam, but instead she got quietly into her place.

As they started into the building, Miriam asked Joan in an undertone "Is that true about the infirmary?"

"Shh," Joan hissed. "Let's just say you do *not* want to end up there."

As they trooped down the stairs, Winifred spoke up in a woeful voice. "Joan, don't tell anyone, but – I don't feel so well either."

"Oh, gawd, that's all we need!" Joan exclaimed. Still, she exchanged places with Miriam and put out a hand to support her friend down the stairs.

Supper was late that evening, and when Minnie finally thrust bowls of cold stew into the cells, there were loud protests from the women.

"Going to turn the lights out on us!"

"It's a disgrace, making us wait so long!"

"Stone cold, this is!"

"Watcher thinking of, Min?"

"Sorry, everybody," Minnie called out, giving Miriam her bowl. "Lost two of 'em in the kitchens, and we're a bit short like."

As in the yards, a sudden silence descended. Finally, Joan spoke up. "What's happening to us, Min?"

"Looks like it's the Black Fever, and no mistake," Minnie said. She put a bowl into the next cell, where Winifred lay. Perhaps the girl smelled the stew, which didn't agree with her, as there was a sound of frantic scrambling, followed by loud vomiting. "Oh, lor," Minnie said. "Winifred, not you too?"

"Get her out!" It was Elsie's voice, frantic and hysterical. "Before she infects the lot of us!"

"Shut your hole," Joan said, "or you'll get what for tomorrow in the mines."

"Aw!" Elsie gave a cry of rage but quickly fell silent.

Minnie finished serving dinner, but she didn't call a cheery goodnight as she usually did; in fact, Miriam could hear her sniffles as she rattled the trays onto her cart and left.

She looked at the bowl of stew but didn't have the heart to eat it. For once, her stories held no attraction either, which was just as fortunate, for at that very moment, the lights were extinguished.

"Nine o'clock," someone said dolefully.

The only response was from Winifred, groaning in her cell.

By the next morning, everyone knew of the fever sweeping the Devil's Kitchen. Win was taken away, despite Joan's protests, as well as three others. Mrs. Siddons came down and directed Minnie to put slabs of bread through the doors, and she announced, "Work as usual, ladies. Come on, get out of it."

"We have to work on nothing but dry bread in our stomachs!" Joan said bitterly to Miriam as they came out of the cells, blinking in the light.

Miriam grimaced with sympathy but got into line. Mrs. Siddons, however, put one hand on her arm as the rest of them marched down to the mines.

"Not you," she said. "We need you in the kitchens today."

"Two cooks took sick last night," Minnie added. She winked, and added, "Mrs. Siddons said we could pick someone to help us, so I thought of you."

"Oh!" Miriam was surprised, and she felt very pleased. Following Mrs. Siddons, she thought, *Maybe I can search for an escape while I'm at it*. At that, she looked at Minnie. She couldn't just run out on her, and Mack, and the others. Not now. That was the problem with being in new places. You got involved, somehow, with the people you met. No, it wouldn't be as easy now to make a break for it. Still, there was no harm if she just looked around.

They made for the other side of the factory. Miriam supposed that they were somewhere near the room where she had been washed, her first night. It seemed very long ago now. That had been the last time she had seen Simon. She remembered his unexpected kindness to her on the train, when he put his arm around her shoulders, and tears prickled at her eyes again. Stop it, she thought. I'll start with the snuffles, and they'll think I have the Fever too!

"Here we are," Mrs. Siddons announced, coming to a huge metal door. Fetching a copper key from her apron pocket, she unlocked the door and waved at the room within. "The kitchens of the Devil's Kitchen, if you take my meaning."

"You are a caution, Mrs. Siddons!" Minnie said cheerfully. The large girl went in and took an apron from a hook. She had recovered her customary good humor, and she grinned as she handed the apron to Miriam. "Here you are, the latest fashion from the continent!"

"Lovely!" Miriam said, catching her mood. She put it over her head and twirled, saying, "Does Modom like?"

"Stop that now, the pair of you," Mrs. Siddons scolded, but a line which once might once have been a dimple appeared in her cheek. "We've got to serve these breakfasts here to the Infirmary."

Sobering, Miriam thrust her arms through the apron and tied it in the back. "Do we really have to go in there?" she asked.

"Hope you've got a strong stomach." Minnie fetched large loaves of brown bread from a cupboard in the wall. The kitchen was dark and narrow, but the floors were spotless, Miriam noticed, and the pots that hung from the ceiling, while old and scratched, gleamed dully. She had an idea who was responsible for the cleanliness of the place. Mrs. Siddons, her back to them, swept up crumbs and wiped shelves. When she finished, she slapped the damp cloth over one shoulder.

Minnie gave Miriam a loaf of bread to slice, while she took out a bowl of apples. "The one good thing about being in the infirmary is that you get apples every day," she said, slicing them into halves. "Supposed to be good for you." Miriam's mouth watered as she watched Min slice up the wrinkled, green fruit.

Mrs. Siddons opened a large, chipped crock, and she measured flour into a bowl. She shook her head. "Anything those poor wretches receive they deserve, believe me." She counted out two more scoops put the lid on the crock, and wiped the table with the cloth. "I shouldn't like to be in their shoes."

"Oh, Mrs. Siddons!" Minnie popped one hand over her mouth. "Do you think we'll catch the Fever by going in there?"

"We don't have a choice, do we? Have to go in any case. Besides, poor Winifred got it just by sleeping in her cell, so no need crying over milk that's not spilled yet. Come on, put that bread on a plate, and we'll start down."

Miriam hummed to herself, considerably cheered by being in the warm kitchen with the two women. For a moment, she almost felt normal again.

The Infirmary was upstairs, on a level where Miriam had never ventured before. The cart was put onto a large dumbwaiter, and it was hauled up on a rope once they climbed several flights of stairs. Minnie pushed the food cart down the hall, followed by Miriam and Mrs. Siddons.

"Through there," the older woman said, and she pointed at a set of swinging doors. "You all right, Min? Won't try anything funny, will you?" she added to Miriam. "Right, I'm off to start my baking. Ta-ra."

Minnie waited until the older woman left. She whispered to Miriam, "Try and keep quiet. We don't want to wake that lot in there." She pushed open the doors with the cart and walked through.

Although the infirmary was above ground, it was just as dark as the cells below. There were no windows, and only a few lamps sat on table in the center of the place. Rows of beds lined the huge room, and at the other end, the Headmaster stood with his cane, as he looked out over the patients.

The Infirmary

A tall, black man in a worker's smock pushed a broom in a shadowy far corner of the room. Several figures in white coats walked among the beds, as they scribbled notes and checked levels on medicines. Miriam nudged Minnie and looked questioningly at them, and Minnie whispered, "The doctors. Don't talk to them." Quickly she pushed her cart between the beds and began to put tin plates of bread and apples on stools by the patients' beds. One wheel on her cart squeaked, and it echoed in the vast silence of the place.

Miriam hastened to help her, and she caught sight of Frank, lying on one bed. He didn't notice her, however. His eyes were closed as if in great pain, and he mumbled something to himself. His lips were cracked, and one hand trembled on top of the covers.

The atmosphere was clean, despite the smells of human filth and the general feeling of horrible suffering. The doctors, to whom she must not speak, were all dressed alike and intent on their tasks.

They approached the Headmaster at the end of the row, but he stared out over their heads, and Minnie hastened away to the next line of beds. "Old effigy," she whispered to Miriam. "I think he's got embalming fluid in his veins."

Miriam smiled, but as she looked at the Headmaster, she could almost believe it. His skin was colorless and looked waxy, as if, when pressed by a finger, it would retain the indent of that pressure. With a shudder, she hastened to finish serving the last line of patients.

With a shock, she saw that everyone in the furthest row of beds were all as dark as if they came from Lampala, and they were also in a worse condition than anyone else in the room. Tubes snaked up from bowls on tables by their beds to incisions made in their arms, and one woman, her skin faded to an ashy color, tossed her head back and forth and murmured, "It's time, now. It's time. Help me; it's time. Time to go. It's time."

"Can't they do anything for her?" Miriam forgot to whisper.

"Miriam! Be quiet!" Minnie gave her a violent nudge. One doctor looked up from his papers. Minnie smiled and gave him a thumbs-up sign. He frowned but resumed writing. "Don't you get us in trouble,"

Minnie warned.

At the mention of her name, the lone, tall figure with the broom in the far corner looked at Miriam. Under his direct gaze, she looked back at him. He was also a native, but compared to the people lying in the beds, he was vibrantly healthy. Indeed, he was the very specimen of strong, vivid life.

Feeling uncomfortable, she looked away. "Sorry," she murmured to Minnie. They finished the rest of the breakfasts in silence and began to push the cart away. The black man stood still, both hands on his broom, and watched them leave.

Minnie pushed her way out of the room, and Miriam followed her. As soon as they left, Minnie rounded on her. "How could you? I worked my back off to get out of the boles mines and into the kitchen. Trying to put me back in the mines? Trying to get me in trouble? I'm sorry I chose you to help me out! I got you out of the mines for a day, didn't I?"

"Minnie, I'm terribly sorry," Miriam said miserably. "I just couldn't help it; when I saw those poor people. It reminds me of nightmares I used to have –"

Minnie blew one strand of hair out of her eyes with her lower lip and wiped her forehead. "Lord," she stated. "I didn't mean to screech at you, but you did give me a fright. Should have given you more warning of what things are like in there, I suppose."

She headed towards the dumbwaiter and Miriam followed, but she couldn't help looking back. The large man with the broom had followed them into the hall. On impulse, Miriam raised one hand to him, as a salute. Gravely, he raised his hand in return.

CHAPTER 20
A Night Rescue

Valiant handed Barbara into the hall of the house and brushed past the yawning butler without a single glance at the man. "As usual, my lovely, beautiful sister, you were the center of all attention." He raised her fingertips to his mustache.

She laughed and twirled under his arm. "I must confess it went better than expected."

Simon entered behind them more soberly, his hands clasped behind his back. "Did you have a nice time?" she asked softly, and she stopped in mid-twirl in front of him.

"How could I not?" he answered. "I was with the eye of the hurricane."

Valiant barked a short laugh. "Very good!" He clapped Simon on the back. "I will have to use that quip, with your permission, of course, old man. Eye of the hurricane, eh?" With a chuckle, he disappeared down a hallway, and Barbara beckoned to Simon.

"Come on," she whispered. "We'll have one last glass of something before we retire."

Although his eyes burned with weariness, Simon followed her to a large, ornate study where Valiant had already poured out brandy. As usual, he puffed away on a lit cigar. "Here you are, my love." He handed a balloon glass to Barbara. "You're rather young, but it's good for the blood," he added, and he gave Simon a smaller measure.

Barbara laughed without humor. "Just because he is young doesn't mean he can't handle certain things," she snapped.

Valiant looked up, and his fox's eyes gleamed. "Of course not, my darling girl. And anyone looking at you, furthermore, would think that you were barely out of the schoolroom."

Simon received the glass in silence, and ignored this exchange. He wondered about the effeminate man at the party who had spilled the punch. "Have my parents manufactured something called Copaiba?" he blurted. "Something that people take in powdered form, like snuff?"

Barbara stared for a moment. She put down her glass and lay a hand on Simon's sleeve. "It is our new line of medicinals, and it is what will make us all rich," she said in dulcet tones.

"Seems that you're rather rich already," Simon raised the brandy snifter, which was crystal, and so antique that the glass had attained a bluish tone.

Valiant's smile grew broader. "A philosopher, by God." He puffed on the cigar.

Barbara, however, darted out one hand, grabbed a fistful of Simon's shirtfront, and pulled him close to her. "How dare you ask about our plans?" she hissed. She rose on tiptoe and moved her face an inch from Simon's. "And, if it comes to that, just how did you find out about Copaiba?"

Simon pretended to bluster. "Barbara!" he protested. "Em, my, er, love. I saw someone at the party using some powder, and someone mentioned the name. And I thought I had heard the word before, at Miriam's – at my parents' house. I just want to know what my parents are involved with, if I'm to be your partner." He brushed the wrinkles out of the shirt as she released him.

"And what are your thoughts on the subject?"

Simon took a deep breath. "None at all." He washed the words out of his mouth with a sip of brandy. "As long as we can be together, Barbara, nothing else matters."

Valiant whistled through his teeth, and waved the decanter of brandy at him. "Did I say earlier you were a boy? You've grown older by the minute tonight."

Simon held out his glass to be refilled and winced at the huge measure that Valiant sloshed into his glass. "I suppose that there is no such thing as being too rich," he said, as he held the glass to his lips. The dark liquid burned his mouth. He wished he could exchange the disgusting brandy for a glass of pure water and a bed. How did people drink it night after night?

"How right you are!" Barbara laughed. Her brow puckered again as she grew serious. "It is not just the money, Simon. It is power that matters. With such extreme wealth, you can forget ever having to go back to that sordid little school, and no one will dare to question us when you and I do get married. And we can go anywhere we want, and do whatever we want." She licked a drop of brandy off her pink lips.

"Hear, hear!" Valiant cheered, waving his cigar. "Here's to the happy couple, eh?" He proffered his glass.

Barbara chinked hers against his, and they drank. Simon wanted to say, 'Hold on, just a second, don't I have a say in this?' He forced the corners of his mouth upwards and sipped his brandy, trying not to shudder at the taste.

"Must say, it makes me rather sentimental. We'll increase the family ties, and all that." Valiant swallowed the last of his wine.

Barbara slipped her arm through Simon's. "We have the rest of our lives together, Simon."

This is too sudden, he thought, but it sounded like a line from a fainting heroine in a romance novel. He nodded and buried his nose in the brandy glass.

Much later, Barbara brought him up to the room, and she kissed his cheek at his door. "Darling Simon," she whispered, "I know we have to wait for some years, but I am so happy."

He laughed in an embarrassed way and stretched. "Oohh, gosh; wine went to my head, better get some sleep." He yawned and covered his mouth theatrically. Barbara laughed again and pushed him into his room; Simon noticed that her newly found happiness did not extend to leaving his door open. Once again the key was turned in the lock once the door closed.

She won't leave anything to chance, he thought, as he stripped off his new clothes and flung them with dislike in one corner. Let the filthy Jenkins pick them up in the morning. He remembered Barbara's shapely hand on his arm and splashed water onto his chest violently. He dried off as if he could scrub off the memory of her touch with the towel.

Feeling somewhat better, he got into bed. Although he expected to toss for hours as he considered the events that had just unfolded, he fell asleep in an instant.

He sat up suddenly and looked around. It was still dark, and although it had felt like he had closed his eyes only for a few seconds, the clock by the bed showed he had slept for several hours.

There it was again. He heard a scratch at the door. The hinges squeaked quietly as it opened, and a figure in a nurse's uniform entered. Simon yawned and fell back. "Nurse, is that you?" he murmured.

"Shh," the figure warned. It approached the bed, and Simon sat up again. The person bent over him and whispered in his ear, "Hello, Simon."

"Is it – Miss Postulate?" He bounded out from under the sheets and flung his arms around her. "Gosh, I'm so glad to see you!"

"Be quiet at once," she cautioned, and he sobered.

"You're right. Sorry."

"You'll need something to wear," she added in a low tone.

Simon nodded and looked at the wadded-up party clothes that he had flung in the corner. He refused to touch those. He rummaged in a chest and found a pair of wool trousers. His hear beat faster with joy as he thrust his legs into them. Grabbing a thick pullover, he hissed, "I'm ready."

Mana motioned to him, and they approached the door cautiously, Simon still pulling the jumper over his head. Mana held one finger to her lips and looked up and down the hallway. It seemed deserted. One lamp guttered, its wick curling, and somewhere downstairs, a large pendulum clock bonged slowly.

Silently she stepped out, and Simon tried to imitate her soundless manner of walking. They approached the stairs and began to descend, slowing at each landing to listen for any noise.

They reached the kitchen on the bottom floor, and Simon breathed out a noiseless sigh of relief. Still, this was close to where he had been apprehended before; they weren't safe quite yet.

Mana tiptoed across the flagged floor, but suddenly one of the doors in the kitchen opened. Jenkins, his huge chest bare, came out from the pantry holding a cold chicken leg. Mana and Simon froze, and as they watched him he bit into it. He looked up and saw them standing in the middle of the room and his eyes bulged.

"Hey –" he tried to say. A bit of chicken must have gone down the wrong pipe, and he began to choke.

Mana watched him, her brow clearing, and as he wheezed, she caught his chin in one hand and forced him to look at her. "You haven't seen a thing," she said, and she looked directly into his eyes.

"Haven't seen a thing," he choked, and swallowed.

"You're going to tell us if anyone else is up."

"Else is up – no, no one up. Nurse is sick with some fever. Nanny is visiting a friend. I hate him!" he burst out. He squeezed the chicken leg so violently that the bone snapped. Grease dripped between his fingers.

"It's all right," Mana soothed. "You like her, is that it?"

Jenkins nodded.

"If you let us go, she'll like you too."

"Let you go."

"And not say a word. If you can remember that, she'll like you too," Mana finished.

Jenkins shook his head, and he watched as she waved Simon forward and crept out of the kitchen. He continued to watch, his mouth open, until the door swung shut.

Simon breathed, "That was fantastic! Miriam said you could do some sort of mind control, but I never believed it myself until just now."

"Shh." She reached into a pocket in the nurse's uniform and withdrew a long feather and a small vial of oil. Approaching the front door, she dipped the feather into the oil and applied it to the handle and the lock, and opened it.

The door swung open, and they left, Mana closing the door silently behind them. Simon breathed in huge lungfuls of fresh air. The grass swayed under his feet and he bent over suddenly.

"Simon! What is it?" Mana asked him.

He straightened. "I'm sorry. It just - I just can't take it in – that I'm away from them. From her."

She put one hand on his sleeve, and he didn't mind it at all. It was not in the slightest like Barbara's touch. "I know, Simon. Believe me, I understand what sudden freedom feels like. But we must go *now*, or you'll be recaptured. Can you ride?"

Simon nodded, reflecting on the days he took riding lessons at school. It seemed like another age.

Mana headed down the long avenue that wound in front of the house. She stayed close to the hedges that lined it. Simon did likewise, and he prayed that Valiant or his bloody sister wouldn't take it into their heads to look out of the bedroom window or, worse, go for a night-time stroll.

They reached the bottom of the avenue after some minutes, and Mana straightened. "We can talk now," she said. "Still, we must hurry, Simon! You'll have to ride on my saddle behind me. I hired a big horse; will you be able to climb on?"

Simon nodded, and they neared a tall shadow, one that snorted and cropped a bit of grass, in the larger avenue Simon had traveled earlier to go to the party. Mana approached the horse, put her foot into the stirrup, and swung herself up easily.

She held out one hand for Simon, and he mounted behind her, surprised at how fluidly his muscles worked. "Where did you get the horse?" he whispered as she gathered up the reins in one hand.

"Come on, beauty," she said in a normal tone to the animal. "Everyone of quality keeps a horse in town, don't you know that? Even foreign princesses." She touched the horse's belly lightly with one foot, and they began to move.

He laughed as the horse broke into a canter, and a gallop. "A princess!" He held his head back to feel the wind rush past him. "That's a good ruse!"

"Better than you know," she called over one shoulder. "And Simon – Neil will be so glad to see you!"

"Neil is with you?" he asked, leaning forward. "How about Miriam? Did you rescue her from that terrible place?"

Mana half-turned. "What terrible place?"

"You know, that Devil's Kitchen."

Since he clasped her waist with both hands, Simon could feel her intake of breath as she faced the road and bent over the horse's neck, urging him to go a bit faster. "Watch for loose stones, beauty," she said, "but carry us like the wind! Devil's Kitchen, you say? I've found Miriam. At last!"

CHAPTER 21
A Dark Encounter

S eems that Verity told him she's not interested in him; he's not serious enough." Ginger took a huge bite of her sandwich and chewed ferociously.

"Jeremy's far better off, if you ask me," Neil looked at the hard lump of cheese he had brought for his meal with disgust.

Ginger cackled, and gave him a hard shove. "Isn't it the truth? Here, have a bit of mine; that moldy cheese is only fit for the bin. Of course, he doesn't see it that way. Thinks his heart is broken, and his life is over, and so forth."

Neil frowned. "Sounds completely boring. Remind me never to fall in love."

Ginger sighed with a dramatic air, placing one hand on the pocket of her shirtfront. "Alas, my boy, there's no escape from that dire fate for any of us."

"Stop it," Neil said. He remembered a pair of long, dark arms, skinny and flexible as ropes, and black hair that was always coming out of neat braids, and he sobered.

Ginger peered into his face. "You've gone all solemn. Could it be – that the untouchable Tom Miles has own affaire of the heart going on? Who's the lucky lady, Tom?"

"Get away," Neil shoved her again. He didn't want to become like Jeremy, who had completely lost his cheerful grin over the past few weeks and who trailed between the huge cogs and wheels in the factory in a lost way, sighing at intervals. *No thanks.* "Let's change the subject," he said determinedly. "Where's Jacky today, do you think?"

"Don't know. Wasn't going out on holidays, or I'd have known."

The door opened and Jeremy, with a ghost of his former grin, announced, "Watcher. The big man's coming by this afternoon."

"Jeremy, my lad!" Ginger squealed. She rushed over to him with a packet of biscuits and offered them to him. He waved them away with none of his usual jokes.

Neil wiped his mouth and went back to his desk. The big man? That could only mean Mr. Marchpane. With a sick feeling in his chest, Neil went back to work. However, a moment after Jeremy left, Ginger wandered over to his chair and draped one arm over the back of it. "He wants me to have a meal with him," she announced casually.

Neil turned and grinned. "Does he really? Well done!"

She pulled a wry face. "Says I'm the only one he can talk to about Verity. Suppose I'm his chum now, more like."

"Still, you never know. Dazzle him with your wit, and soon he'll forget that Verity ever existed. Besides, there's nothing better than a bit of friendship." He smiled and put one hand on her arm before she could go back to her own desk. "Stop a bit. Who's coming in this afternoon? The one that your boyfriend mentioned just now?"

"Old fish-face Marchpane," she answered promptly.

"Why?"

"Wants to discover why so many employees have been out this week. It seems Jacky-Boy isn't the only one out today."

Neil nodded and bent back over his accounts. So it *was* Miriam's guardian who was expected after all. Somehow he would have to lay low while the man walked through Pearson's.

However, several hours passed and nothing untoward occurred. Neil finished a large stack of accounts. He had discovered three errors that would save the company hundreds of guineas. He turned to a long list of supplies and began to check them.

While he added up the amounts of string, sealing wax, and paper the different offices had purchased, the door opened. Drake, as usual, showed the new owner around, and his affected voice announced, "Mr. Marchpane, our owner! Mr. Marchpane, sir, this is Accounts –"

Drake was pushed to one side. "Yes, yes, you already showed me," Virgil said with some irritation. "What I want to know is, why are so many workers not at their desks? That one there, for instance."

He pointed to Jacky's desk; as it was right beside his own place, Neil bent lower over the list he was checking. He held his breath and peered closely at the distribution of ink and parchment in Developments. Over his shoulder, he heard Drake as he muttered something about rampant disease, infectious influenza, and not wanting to get the entire office sick.

"Infections!" Mr. Marchpane echoed. Removing a handkerchief from his breast pocket, he dusted off his hands and frowned, holding the hankie over his nose. "Well, er, time for me to be going. Really must be off." With great haste, he backed out of the office, followed by Drake. Beside him, Neil could hear Ginger's snorts through her nose.

"Pay the fine," a girl at her elbow said. "No snorts during work hours."

"Dash it." Ginger pushed a few coins into the box.

As they got ready to leave, Ginger tied back her hair with a ribbon. A moment later she undid it again and combed it back with her fingers. She put her head on one side and began to braid it. Giving up, she wailed to Neil, "What should I do?"

"Just do what you normally do," Neil advised, grabbing her ribbon. "It looks very nice. Here, that's it." He tied her hair back and knotted a bow, and turned her to the room of clerks for approval. "What do you think?" A chorus of whistles, stamping, and applause was the response.

Ginger flashed a huge grin. "Right! Thanks, lads! And a *special* thanks to Tom," she added, and kissed Neil loudly on the cheek and left.

"Ooooh," everyone said. "And a special thanks for Tom."

Neil turned his back on them in disgust, but he couldn't smother a large grin. He picked up his coat and headed out to the back door, putting his hat on as he went.

Except for one carriage at the corner, the narrow street was deserted. As always, a fine rain had started to descend. Neil blew out a frustrated breath. He thrust his hands deep into his pockets and began to walk, but as he neared the main throughway the driver of the carriage chucked to the horse and the equipage began to move slowly.

Neil slouched along. He didn't notice the vehicle that followed him. Out of the company of the noisy, cheerful clerks, he started to worry about his family. Where the devil could they be?

Mana had asked Philips to make several inquiries, but so far his research had turned up nothing. And how about his friends? After a few months of investigations, all their work had been fruitless, and they had even lost all contact with one of their own group. Where was Kyoge tonight? Was he a prisoner as well, in the Devil's Kitchen? Neil thought he might go back there, to see if he could find the large man, but first he should tell Mana what he was doing, if she wasn't at another large party.

On the doorstep of the house, he fished out his key and opened the door. He didn't see the carriage had stopped on the pavement some yards behind him. He opened the door, but suddenly a cloth was thrust over his mouth, and someone who was large, and strong, picked him up and brought him to the waiting vehicle.

"In here," the occupant hissed. Neil was tossed inside, and the passenger moved her mustard colored skirts away from him. After a few moments, the vehicle began to move again.

Neil lunged for the door, but the woman pushed him back and showed him a tiny pistol that was pointed at his chest. She lifted her head, and he knew who it was.

"Mrs. Marchpane!" he said. "What – what a surprise! I didn't know you were in the vicinity. Have you taken lodgings nearby?" he gabbled, one eye on the revolver.

"Stop that nonsense." She twitched her skirts again. "We know that you are working for Pearson's Company under the ridiculous name of Tom Miles. Did you think that we were utterly stupid?"

"Of course not," Neil swallowed. "I was just afraid that my family would be charged for Simon's disappearance – hold on a moment!" He forgot about the gun and sat forward, excited. "You know where

Simon is! You *must* know, or that would have been the first thing you would have asked me. Where was he taken? Is he well?"

Her eyes narrowed. "You're not exactly in the position to ask me questions," she said. "What were you doing in Pearson's? Don't give me any nonsense, now. Is that Postulate woman with you?"

"Who?" Neil blustered, taking refuge in stupidity.

"That governess, blockhead! The black islander woman that Virgil hired to take care of the Pearson brat!" Her hands tightened on the gun. "I knew it was a huge mistake to employ her," she said, as if to herself. "That's when it all began to unravel."

Neil lowered his voice and, with great caution, he edged forward on the seat. "Why do you say that?"

"She made me sign that paper, the contract to employ her as Miriam's governess. Somehow she made me sign it, along with Virgil. I still don't know how she did it. And now our sources say she escaped from Atol, and now what is to be done? Barbara says that Simon's change of heart is complete, and I do hope so, for the dear boy's sake, so he can be rich and have all the things that Pearson brat has now. I *do* miss Simon *so* much. He is very stubborn, though. He is like my family in that regard. Virgil hasn't the will of a fly-"

She seemed to be talking to herself. Neil kept an eye on the pistol in her hand. So she had known about Atol, and the events on Lampala, and she and her husband had probably ordered Mana to be captured.

He remembered Cantwell's dark form, holding a cigar and talking to the deposed king. It felt like an age ago, that night on Lampala. He had crouched next to Riki, in the forest, while Atol chatted with that partner of theirs.

"Where is Miriam?" He moved still nearer.

"The girl is safe." A smile twisted her thin lips. "She is fed, and clothed, and she has much to occupy her time." The smile disappeared, and she continued, "Production has fallen off there, as well. This nasty influenza - it will ruin our second quarter. I do hope Simon hasn't caught it. The poor boy will go out without his woolens."

Neil couldn't help smirking to himself. His 'woolens!' As soon as he saw Simon again, he'd have to remind him to wear his 'woolens.'

Mrs. Marchpane stared out of the carriage window and muttered something about Simon. Gathering all his courage, Neil launched himself forward and reached for the gun.

She looked up in surprise and tried to jerk the pistol back just as his hand closed on it. He got it out of her grasp, but one long finger closed over the trigger and squeezed, causing the gun to go off with a deafening report. The pistol jerked out of their combined grip and fell in one corner of the carriage.

Neil flung himself to one side and grabbed the gun. He pointed the gun at her and said, "Now, Mrs. Marchpane, take me to where Miriam is." She screeched and lunged, but he waved the pistol at her. "And I want to see Simon, too," he added, "and my family." *I've done it!* he exulted. *I've solved the case!*

At that moment, just when Neil felt victorious, the door to the carriage opened. A tall, thin man with hair combed across his bald skull poked his head inside. Without a word, he put one hand over Neil's. His grip felt like his hand was made of cold chicken bones. Neil was forced to let go of the pistol. The man jerked his head to the outside.

They had stopped at the factory, the Devil's Kitchen. The tall, thin man gripped Neil by the neck and flung him out of the carriage in front of the gates. A guard at the gate hauled him to his feet.

"Misbehavior," the man said. "We know how to take care of violent youths in here, Mrs. Marchpane."

She leaned out of the carriage. "I leave him in your very capable hands, Headmaster."

"Stop! Mrs. Marchpane!" Neil shouted. "What about Simon? If the Cantwells put me in here, what have they done with Simon?" She hesitated for an instant before she leaned back into the shadowy interior of the carriage. "It's people's lives that you are playing with here!" he cried, and he wrested his head away from the guard's fingers. "You're killing your own son! Do you even know where Simon is?"

"Inside immediately," the Headmaster said in his cold voice. "We don't want anyone to get wind of this." He covered Neil's mouth again with his large hand.

Neil looked after the carriage with despair as he was propelled inside the forbidding factory. The driver slapped the reins on the horse's back, and it whinnied and moved off. The wheels crunched on the stones, and the coach disappeared around a corner. Had Mrs. Marchpane even heard him at all? As the tall gates closed behind him, Neil could only hope his words had been heard.

CHAPTER 22
A Secret Letter

P rincess Minnie found the hidden treasure, and saved her kingdom," Miriam read. Minnie leaned against the hot press where the kitchen linens were dried and heaved a huge breath.

"What's all this?" Mrs. Siddons turned from the huge oven and shut the door with a bang. "Enough foolery. Get those trays ready for downstairs, and be sharp about it."

Miriam hopped down from the counter where she was perched and folded the pages lengthwise. "Here, Min," she said, handing them to the girl. "You keep them."

Min accepted the story. "Gosh, thanks ever so much. I'll hide them under my mattress. Can't remember the last time they turned the bed."

Mrs. Siddons tutted. "Disgusting, I call it. The state of the ticking in those cells is shameful. Whole place needs a good turn out so it's fit for decent human beings. And what those blacks have to put up with in that infirmary upstairs, I shouldn't like to think."

"Islanders, you mean." Miriam loaded thick bowls onto the meal cart.

Mrs. Siddons looked up, a ladle paused at her lips. "What's that now?" she asked through the steam curling around her face.

"They're islanders, not blacks," Miriam said. "If you look, their skin isn't even black."

"Aren't we fancy." Minnie crashed a pile of spoons onto the tray beside the bowls.

"Now, Min," Mrs. Siddons said. "Islanders it is, although I never met one that could talk like a Christian."

"That's because the doctors up there load them up with that drug, just to see what happens to them. Like they're animals or something." Miriam picked up a pile of folded napkins.

Minnie paused. "You're not going to make a protest again, are you, up there in the Infirmary? And make me lose my place?"

"Oh, no, Min, I promise. Don't worry." Miriam's tone was fervent enough to make Minnie's worried brow clear.

"Miriam's right, however." Mrs. Siddons dropped her voice to a whisper. "It just isn't right what's done to those poor people here in this place, and those what do it will get their punishment soon enough, mark my words."

The girls looked at each other in astonishment, but they didn't comment. Mrs. Siddons put the huge pot of soup on the cart and waved them out of the room.

The first stop was the mines, this time, where Miriam used to work. They pushed the cart onto the dumbwaiter, lowered it, and ran down the stairs.

Somewhat out of breath, they retrieved the cart on the bottom level and hefted the huge pot to the final descent. "Grab some of those bowls," Minnie ordered. "I can lift this great, heavy thing myself." The sleeves on her shift tightened as she lifted the iron cauldron.

"Thanks, Princess Min," Miriam couldn't help saying. Minnie laughed but saved her breath and didn't reply.

In the mines, the workers dropped their baskets and lined up readily as soon as they smelt the soup. "Duck pressé today, Min?" one of them asked.

"Pressé's off," she responded, doling out bowls of soup. "'Fraid you'll have to settle with lobster patties this once."

"You did all right for yourself, didn't you," Sally said to Miriam as she approached, staring at her accusingly through the tangled strings of light hair that hung down over her face. "Two, please, Min."

"Where's Elsie?" Miriam asked.

"Over there," Sally snapped. Miriam looked and saw Elsie huddled by the wall, holding her stomach with a miserable look on her face. "No need to raise the alarm, though, see? I'll take care of her."

"I wouldn't tell those butchers upstairs about her even if my worst enemy was sick," Miriam replied with spirit. "Min, didn't Mrs. Siddons send down a jug of water on that cart? She probably wants something to drink, instead of soup." Handing the bowls to Sally, who received them without knowing what else to do, Miriam fetched the huge pitcher of cool water, and bore it back down.

"Fetch her mug," she said as she set the large jug down.

"I'll get it," one of the workers said. She got Elsie's tin mug, and Miriam filled it. Elsie ignored her, or perhaps she felt so poorly that she couldn't open her eyes.

"Ta," Sally said grudgingly, taking the water.

"Hide her between those packing crates over there, see," Min suggested. "Wouldn't want one of those Heads to see her in that state."

"They never come down here," Sally held the cup of water in front of Elsie. The girl drank weakly, and she pushed it away.

"Poor thing," Miriam said to Minnie as they climbed back up, looking back.

"She really should be taken away," Minnie whispered. "Spreading the disease to the lot of us by staying there. Still..."

Thinking of the dreadful Infirmary, Miriam nodded with silent understanding.

"Processing room's next," Minnie said, heading to the large room with the strange machinery. The huge spiral in the center still twisted endlessly. However, fewer workers stood in front of the machines, and those that were there had to work between two stations to cover for those who had been taken ill. As Minnie pushed the cart in, one of them looked up and gave a faint cheer.

"Time to rest a bit, girls," she said. They lined up in the customary manner and Miriam doled out the rest of the soup, while Minnie poured water into the outstretched mugs.

"One more stop," she warned, filling the last woman's cup. "Think you can handle it?"

"I said I could," Miriam replied with some irritation. The heat and the dark of the factory were depressing, after the shining, cheerful kitchen.

Minnie held up her hands and pulled a mock grimace of surrender. "All right, all right, just making certain," she said.

Miriam laughed. "Come on, you." They pushed the cart to the dumbwaiter and hauled it up, and dashed up the stairs.

"Cor, my belly's emptier than a trumpeter's balloon," Minnie complained. "Don't say a word, but Mrs. Siddons made Welsh rarebits for the two Heads, and she promised to save some for us."

The thought of melted cheese sauce on toast made Miriam's mouth water so much that she had to swallow. "Gosh," she replied. "Let's hurry."

After they reloaded the tray in the kitchen, they went up to the hallway where the Infirmary was. Miriam could hear the muffled groans before they opened the doors with the cart, but she tried to close her ears to the sound. Instead, she passed out the food without any comment.

Almost all the beds were filled now, she saw. The Headmaster stood at the back of the room in his usual spot. He swung his cane in an idle manner, flanked by two guards. Except for the increase of patients, the scene was the same as the day before. Even the large fellow from Lampala was still there, the broom still in his large hands.

As Miriam wound down the row of beds where those from the islands lay, the big man looked up again and stared at her. Miriam served the last patient, a young girl, whose mouth was covered in weeping sores. When she finished, she looked at the huge man.

He beckoned to her in such a regal manner that she found she had to obey. She walked over to him with the tray of bowls. "Let me help you with those, Miss," he said in a low, rich tone. He held the tray as she put some dirty cups on it; as she took it back, he slid something flat and square under the cloth covering the tray.

"Thank you very much," she stammered. He merely nodded in the manner of a king. His head held high, he turned back to his broom.

Miriam tightened her grip on the tray and walked out of the Infirmary. She tried not to look at the Headmaster in a guilty way to see if he had noticed the exchange. In the hallway, while Minnie was bent over the cart, she extracted the large square object from the tray. It was an envelope, she saw. She pushed it down her front.

"Can't wait to tuck in; how about you?" Minnie asked, as she straightened up from the dishes.

"Tuck in?" Miriam asked, praying that the square of paper wouldn't fall onto the dark, cracked floor.

"Woo-hoo! Hello! Bell's ringing, answer the door! Welsh rarebit, remember?"

"Oh, rarebit. Right."

"And how about a bit of help with the cart?" Minnie asked, and she gave Miriam a shove.

"Oh, sorry, Min! I must be so hungry I'm losing my wits." Miriam grabbed the other side.

As they ate their rarebit, Minnie and Mrs. Siddons talked in dramatic fashion about the influenza in the factory. "Heard some of the workers coughed up blood, they were that ill," Mrs. Siddons said.

Minnie took a huge bite. "'Ow! How disgusting! Gives me a right turn, that does. And I heard some goes into fits if their fever goes high enough."

"Shouldn't be surprised," the cook said, wiping her mouth. "My eldest was always subject to fits."

"Can't you write a story about the Fever, Miriam?" Minnie asked.

Miriam looked up. "A story? I hadn't thought about it, but yes, that's a great idea, Min! Thanks!"

Minnie sat back, pleased. "Gosh, I'm full, Mrs. Siddons. Hit the spot, that did. Carting those trays around really works up an appetite."

"Too full for apple tart?" Mrs. Siddons said, getting up and taking the plates.

"Not really! Apple tart?"

"And custard," the cook said, with a wink at Miriam.

"You sit down, Mrs. Siddons; I'll get it," Miriam said, struck by a thought. "Is it in the pantry?"

"Don't mind if I do," the cook said, and she lowered herself back into her chair and crossed her thick legs at the ankles. Miriam picked up the soup bowls, brought them to the deep sink, and went into the pantry.

With a quick glance at the other two, Miriam quickly fished the envelope out of the front of her dress and tore it open with her thumb. A creased sheet of paper was inside. A note was written on it in large, looped handwriting:

Dear Esteemed Miss Pearson:

Mana is near.
With the most sincere wishes for
Your Continued Very Good Health,
I hereby remain –

Your servant, Kyoge Seminary, Esq.

Miriam closed her eyes for a moment. Mana was near.

She wouldn't allow herself to cry, she vowed. Miriam scooped up the pie and a jug of yellow, creamy custard and hurried back to the kitchen.

Before the lights were turned out that night, Miriam dug her notebook and Mana's comb out of their hiding place behind the brick. She held the comb against her cheek and thought, *She's near. Mana is near.* After all that time she had spent slaving away in the Mines, wearing dirty smocks, eating the disgusting food and avoiding the Heads and their guards, at last her own governess was near.

Tears pricked her eyelids. What would Mana think of her now? With a watery grin, she sat on her bed, neatly tore a page out of her copybook and composed an answer.

Dear Mr. Seminary, Esquire (it read,)

Gosh, thanks so much for writing to me! So you must know Mana. Is she safe? How did she discover where I was? You're both so clever to have found me.

Is it true that the Marchpanes own this factory? My father never ran this place, did he? It just couldn't be possible. Do they really intend to sell that horrid stuff that they give to the Islanders in the Infirmary? Or to people in England? We must stop them, somehow.

I hope I can get this message to you. I'll hold onto it until it's safe.

Thanks again, ever so much, and all my love to Mana,

Miriam

She folded the square of paper. At that moment, someone marched up outside her cell and thrust a key in the door. Quickly she jabbed both letters, the copybook, and Mana's comb down her shirt. Miriam looked up, the picture of innocence, as the Headmistress entered.

"You will come with me." The woman seized Miriam's wrist with a grip like steel pincers.

Miriam pulled back. "Wait a bit. Where are you taking me? What did I do?"

"No questions," the woman said, as she shoved Miriam out the door to where two of her guards waited.

"Just let me know what I did wrong!" Miriam shouted.

"Miriam, is that you?" Sally yelled from her cell. "Shame, let her go, Missus!"

The other occupants began to shout as well. "She hasn't done nothing to you! Let her go!"

"Silence!" the Head shouted, her face turning red. "All of you are fined a week's wages, and you lose yard privileges as well!" Silence greeted this announcement.

"But, just tell me what I did," Miriam begged. The Head didn't reply. She motioned to a guard.

CHAPTER 23
Out of Hiding

At a small stables right on the outskirts of the city, Mana handed the reins to a grumpy, sleepy stable hand. There Mana and Simon got into a little carriage that she hired from the stables and headed back to what she called the Headquarters. "It's just a house, Simon, so that makes it sound much grander than it really is!" she added with a smile. She leaned back against the cushions.

Simon sat up and stared out of the window as if he could make the vehicle go faster by looking at the buildings they passed on their way. "I don't care. Where's Miriam been this whole time? And I just want to see Neil again. Hope he's held up well during my imprisonment. Has he been with you?"

"Well, yes and no. He managed to make his way to Lampala, where Atol had me chained in a cage. And he also managed to free me, so he is a true hero."

"Atol!" Simon sat forward. "Who on earth is that?"

"The king of Lampala, while I was gone. He is no longer the ruler there. He was involved with your hosts, Barbara and Valiant Cantwell."

"Ugh," Simon said. "I can't believe I – Miss Postulate, did you ever think you liked someone, and later you discovered how loathsome they really were? What an idiot I am! I could kick myself for the things I said to that Miss Cantwell."

She sat forward and took one of his hands. "Oh, no, Simon, don't do that," she advised. "I highly doubt that you're the first one to find yourself in that particular situation, you know. And Miss Cantwell is extremely attractive, with a great deal of charm. It would have been very unusual indeed if you hadn't fallen for her."

Simon cleared his throat and said, "Neil is the true hero, if he was able to get to Lampala. How did he rescue you?"

Briefly she gave him an account of the events on the island, and the adventures she and Neil had encountered in town, ending with Kyoge's disappearance. At that, she fell silent and dropped Simon's hand.

He, however, was troubled by a new thought. "So Neil hasn't been in touch with his parents, nor his sisters, since we left Miriam's house? His parents must be out of their minds! Shouldn't we get in touch with them? I've a good mind to write them a letter, this very day, and tell them it's all my fault."

"I haven't been able to find his parents," Mana said. "And it's not all your fault, Simon. Nor was everything your responsibility. I have the idea that we all played our parts. You were rather heroic, yourself – I don't know what you went through in that house, but I'm sure it wasn't the easiest thing in the world."

"And that's another thing!" He waved one hand in the air. "All of this needn't have happened if it hadn't been for my own parents! When I think of that room I was in for weeks, and when I had to put up with Jenkins' spit, and kicks, and punches, and insults, and when I had to give Barbara compliments and dance attendance on her... I don't ever want to see them again, after this."

"Look, I don't think you're alone in that, either. Your parents have made some mistakes, but I hope that they might see reason eventually. Actually I plan to visit them today." She looked at the brightening sky. "Care to come with me?"

His eyes bulged with horror at the thought, but he swallowed once or twice and uttered thickly, "Very well."

"Well, that's all settled. I see we're close to the house. It is right around that corner there."

"I can't wait to see old Neil again," Simon said. "And do you know something, Miss Postulate? I want to tell Mother exactly what I think of her and her plots with the Cantwells." As soon as the carriage stopped, he bounded out onto the pavement.

Mana stopped to pay the driver and followed more slowly. Simon nearly burst with impatience on the pavement when she turned to him. "That house there," she pointed, her face just visible in the gray light of the early morning.

He didn't reply but dashed up the steps, pounded on the door and let loose a volley of rings on the doorbell. "Neil won't mind," he confided to Mana as she reached his side. "He'll just have to wake a little earlier than usual, that's all."

"Why don't we just use my key?" Her eyes narrowed with amusement. She opened the door, and stood aside as Simon raced inside and up the steps.

"Neil!" he shouted. "Come on, professor, stir your lazy stumps! It's the returning soldier, home from the wars. Neil! Hi, Neil! Which room is he in, anyway?" Simon turned to Mana.

"That one." She pointed, and Simon threw open the door.

The room was deserted. The bed was made and Janet had turned down the covers the night before, but no one had slept in it.

"Well, that's strange," Mana said. "No, it's no use looking in the drawers, Simon; he wouldn't be in there. Maybe he fell asleep on the sofa, or is in the kitchen, although one would think he'd have heard your yells."

Without hesitation Simon pushed past her and ran back downstairs. Mana could hear him as he threw doors open and shouted for Neil.

"Not here either?" Mana caught up with him in the kitchen. The table was laid for breakfast, but the room was deserted. "Oh, this is ridiculous. He's got to be here somewhere. Let's start again upstairs and go through each room systematically."

With a backward glance, Simon followed her and stubbed his toe on the stairs, since he wasn't looking. He cursed and swept through the rooms where Mana and Neil slept, but they were still empty.

"This," she stopped in front of a closed door, "was where Kyoge slept."

"Oh," Simon said. Without hesitation he plunged into the room, which was almost painfully clean, and vacant. A clock ticked in that quiet way that emphasizes the emptiness of a house.

"Well!" Mana said brightly. "Not here, is he? Let's go back downstairs and try again." She closed the door behind them carefully and they went back to the sitting room. Simon actually looked underneath the sofa and chairs but found nothing.

The tiny kitchen garden was empty as well when they went outside. "I suppose we could check the cellar," Mana said in an uncertain voice. "The entrance is inside the kitchen. Still, there's just the coal down there, and some old boxes and things." Simon didn't wait to hear the rest but ran back inside.

She caught up with him just as he was diving down the cellar steps. "Be careful," she said in her governess voice. "Let me get a light."

"Here he is!" Simon called out triumphantly. "He's sleeping down here!" His cry of triumph was cut off by a scream from the person he had grabbed in the dark, only it wasn't Neil. The person was not a boy at all.

"Simon!" Mana said. "Who on earth have you got there? It certainly isn't Neil, at any rate. Wait, let me get a candle, for heaven's sake."

"No need, I've got her," Simon said, coming up the stairs and dragging at someone who scratched and clawed. "Who are you, little hell-cat? And what have you done with Neil? Tell me!"

"Simon, let go of her at once," Mana ordered. "And you, miss, what are you doing in our cellar?"

"Not up to any good, that's certain," Simon answered, as he reached the top of the stairs with the intruder fast in his grip. The girl looked up at them through her filthy, matted hair, and Mana gasped.

"Riki! Riki, is that you?"

"Yup." Riki sniffled. She jerked her arm away from Simon's grip and folded her arms in front of her. Her face was dirty. The smell hit them in that moment.

"Oh, my," Mana said. "Riki, we need to get you into a bath at once. And what your parents must have thought these past few weeks! Between you and Neil, I don't know what to do first; not to mention Miriam."

"Stop a moment," Simon held his nose. "This is the girl that you told me about? Who helped Neil on the island?"

"What of it?" Riki demanded.

"How on earth did you get here?" Mana said. "Wait, that's not important now. I'm going to run you a bath this instant. Simon, heat some water, and see if Janet left us any bread and eggs."

"Just listen!" Riki shouted. "Forget all that! Neil has been kidnapped!"

Simon ignored her stench. He grabbed her arm again. "What was that? Neil? What happened to him?"

Riki pulled her arm away from him. "You're rude," she decided.

"You must tell us!" Simon insisted.

"Stop, both of you. Riki will tell her story in the tub," Mana announced.

"Not in front of him." Riki folded her arms in front of her chest.

"No. Just tell it to me as I give you a thorough wash. Come upstairs this minute."

Riki looked mutinous, but Mana gave her a push towards the stairs. For a wonder, Riki obeyed.

Fuming with frustration, Simon went to put some water to boil. He wanted to call someone for help, or ride out himself in search of his friend. To come this close to Neil and have him disappear under his nose was sickening! Unable to contain himself, he went to the stairs and yelled, "Shouldn't I call for a policeman?"

"No," Mana called back without further explanation.

Feeling grumpy and gritty from lack of sleep, Simon went back and waited for the pot to boil. After a few minutes his frustration increased. Just how long did it take water to heat up, anyway?

He remembered that Mana had mentioned bread and eggs. Simon went in search of them. It was when he began to break the eggs in a bowl that the kettle decided to boil, naturally, so he had to wipe white-of-egg slime off his fingers before he got the water.

He hefted the pot up the stairs and knocked on the door. There was a shrill scream, a soothing murmur, and Mana opened the door a crack, looking a bit worried. "Is that the water? Oh, thanks so much, Simon." She hesitated. "The thing is, Riki's forehead is very hot, and she says she doesn't feel well. Of course, it's no wonder with her living in a coal cellar for so long. She probably scrounged food and blankets from us at night, but there are reports of some kind of influenza going about the city. I think she might have become ill."

"Oh," Simon said. He tried to feel sorry, but he hardly knew the girl, and he was more worried about his friend. "What does she say about Neil?"

"Only that he was taken by a woman in a puce and gold carriage. I'm afraid-"

"Puce and gold," Simon interrupted. "Puce. That must be Mother. I bet the driver was wearing a coat to match the carriage, too. My God!"

Mana stopped him and took the kettle. "We'll talk about it later."

Simon scrambled the eggs and had actually cut some rather thick slices of bread for toast when Mana came down, looking rather weary. "I put her to bed," she said, and she dropped into a chair.

Simon handed her a plate. "Have some eggs," he said in an offhand tone.

"Simon! What a surprise! I didn't know you could cook."

"Used to make eggs over the oil stove at school during the middle of the night," he explained, and he sat opposite her and handed her a thick slice of toast. "Sorry, it didn't fit in the toast rack."

With a twinkle, Mana accepted the huge slice of bread and scraped a little butter onto it. "Listen, Simon," she said, "someone has to stay with Riki. I'm going to go and see your parents today, if I can, but I'd like you to be in the house in case she needs anything."

He sat up. "But I thought you had a maid in once a day. Couldn't she look after the wretched girl?"

"Janet's in a delicate condition," Mana said carefully. "Do you know what that means?"

He coughed, waved his piece of toast and showered the kitchen with crumbs. "You mean she's having a baby, I suppose. So she can't get too near someone who's sick – oh, blow. But I wanted to tell my mother just what I think of her." He put down his toast. "When I think of that little room I lived in, held prisoner by those Cantwell fiends, and it was all because of them – my own parents! - I would like to have it out with her as soon as possible."

"We don't know what the Cantwells told your parents," Mana said. "I'm sure your mother and father thought you were well tended to all along, and that your best interests were in their minds. Your parents just wanted to make money for themselves *and* for you, which isn't such a bad motive, Simon."

His jaw set. "I don't care. I'll never forgive them."

"Well, if you're in that mood, it's certainly better that you don't see them today," Mana responded as she stood up. "By the time I'm dressed and ready, your parents should be awake. I don't think they'll thank me for disturbing their breakfast, but so it must be."

"I don't have to sit by the girl's bed and hold her hand or anything, do I?" Simon pointed at the ceiling above him.

"No," Mana laughed. "Didn't you have a holiday task for Firbury? Why don't you work on that?"

Simon was appalled. "Prep? For school?! I've been away for ages. I can't go back there again and listen to boys talk about cricket and maths after I've been a prisoner. And I can't do rotten prep work right now, not with Neil and Miriam still missing!"

"Yes, you can. And you might as well start as soon as you've had a rest. I think I have some schoolbooks in the house. It used to belong to a schoolmaster, I believe. You can write to Neil's parents as well, just in case we do find them. Now, move along, Simon."

Looking thunderstruck, Simon went upstairs.

If Miss Postulate was tired after she attended a party as the main guest, rescued a boy from a villain's clutches, and discovered another child hidden in her coal-cellar, she did not betray it when she was shown into the Marchpanes' rooms in the City. The pert maid who had answered the door had been disinclined to let her in, but after Mana murmured Simon's name, she was allowed to enter. Inside the house she was shown to a garishly furnished parlor room, although she wasn't offered a seat.

After a few minutes, Theodosia burst into the room. One finger was raised, and she shook it under Mana's nose. "How dare you!" she started. "How you can stand there in our home! Ah, and by the by, do you happen to know where Simon is?" Virgil entered at that moment, wiped his lips, and threw his napkin onto a table shaped like an elephant's head.

"Mrs. Marchpane, why don't we sit down and talk about this predicament?" Mana said.

Theodosia looked at her up and down. "As if I would ask a creature like you to sit in my sitting room!"

Virgil stopped her and put one hand on her arm. "My dear, let us at least listen to what Miss Postulate has to say."

"Thank you," Mana said. Slowly, Theodosia sat, and Mana perched on the very edge of a hard-backed chair. "I know where Simon is; in fact, I saw him this very morning. However," she added, as Theodosia opened her mouth to rant, "I'm afraid that he is very angry with you."

"With us?" Virgil's eyes started out of his head.

Mana nodded. "He went through a very difficult time in the Cantwells' house. In fact, I would classify it as torture."

"Nonsense! I spoke to dear Barbara often over the past few weeks, and she said that she and Valiant took the best possible care of our only son." Theodosia sniffed.

Mana leaned forward, and when she spoke, it was with severity. "He was kept awake and hungry most of the night. He was threatened with physical harm at all times. He was kept in a small attic without hot water nor proper clothes."

Virgil propped himself on the arm of Theodosia's chair. "I find that very hard to believe, Miss Hm-Ha."

"Mr. Marchpane, every word of what I say is true. But beyond that, we must discuss your business, or rather, Miriam's father's business. Your sale of the copaiba tincture is not only criminal in nature, it also endangers the lives of countless people including the people from my homeland. It must not continue. In fact, the entire copaiba business must shut down, now." She fixed Virgil and Theodosia with a steady gaze.

The woman stood up. "Stop that!" Her voice was shrill with fear. "You're trying to influence us to do your wishes! Oh, you can't fool me. I know what you did when you forced us to hire you. Barbara explained your voodoo magic to me!"

Mana shook her head. "I would not dream of using any form of thought control or hypnosis in such a serious matter. You need to decide this on your own, in order to maintain Pearson's future, and in order to keep your own family together. Simon knows what you have done, you know, and he will not stand for it."

"I've heard enough!" Theodosia screamed. "Virgil, throw this creature out at once!"

Mana stood up and looked down at her. "I am not a creature," she said. "My name is Queen Manapalata, and I govern Lampala. That means, of course, that I control all the island's exports. Shipments of the bolemors will stop this instant if you do not heed what I say." She moved to the door but turned back with one hand on the frame. Her back was perfectly straight, and her head was held high on her long neck. "You should know that Simon will not call himself your son unless you stop the production of the drug and sever all ties with the Cantwells." She removed something from her glove and put it on the elephant's head table. "This is the address of my house in London, in case you change your minds."

Queen Manapalata nodded in their direction. With a swish of her skirts, she left the room.

CHAPTER 24

In The Devil's Kitchen Again

Y ou mean you couldn't find Neil?" Simon asked, his mouth open in a tragic O. The effect was spoiled by the huge slice of cake he held in one hand.

"I know exactly where Neil is, and I shouldn't be surprised if we see him today." Mana took off her gloves.

"And Miriam?"

"And Miriam as well." She sat at the kitchen table and removed a long pearl-studded pin from her hat. "Janet, is there any more tea in that pot?"

"Not a drop, Miss Postulate, but I'll boil the kettle in a minute."

"She will, too," Simon confided. "It took ages when I tried to heat that bath water myself, but Janet can make tea and set the table and cut up sandwiches in less time than that."

Janet was delighted. "Get away with you!" she said, and she flicked a tea cloth at him. Simon dodged.

"I'm going to lie down for a bit," Mana suddenly announced. "Simon, maybe you should have a rest, too."

"Sleep! I couldn't possibly sleep. And besides, I rested for ages when you left."

Mana noticed that he hadn't mentioned his parents. "How's the patient?"

"That girl is a fright," Simon said. "She argues with anything you say, and she's as thin as a lizard."

"I meant to ask, how is she feeling?"

Janet turned from the oven holding a loaf of bread. "She still has a fever, and she's getting worse. Simon's right, though, she refuses to take medicine or stay in bed."

"You didn't go into her room, did you Janet?" Mana got up and picked up her gloves and hat.

"No, but I could hear the howls each time Simon here tried to give her a dose."

"I'll go and see her," Mana said. An instant later, Simon could hear her deliberate footsteps going up the steps and into Neil's room. He winked at Janet and gave her a thumbs-up. There was silence for a long time, followed by a muffled cry, which was cut off instantly. Simon waited, but nothing else occurred.

"I'm going to see what happened," he whispered, and Janet nodded, agog. Simon crept up to the Room of Terror, as he had begun to call the place where Riki stayed, and cautiously opened the door. Mana sat by the bed, and Riki was asleep. The girl's thin chest rose and fell as she slept.

"Don't wake her." Mana came out and closed the door.

"How did you do that?" Simon was astonished.

"Just a little trick I know. Now I really must lie down." At that moment, there was a loud, insistent knock on the front door.

Simon frowned. "If that little demon in the bed wakes because of some tradesman..." He didn't finish his statement but ran down the stairs and flung open the door, ready to give someone a piece of his mind.

Instead of a salesperson, however, his parents stood on the top step. "Simon!" his mother said in a loud voice. She launched forward and threw her arms around his neck. "I've missed you so much, my darling boy!"

"Hasn't been the same without you, Simon, old top," Virgil breathed awkwardly and patted Simon on the back.

"Be quiet!" Simon whispered, waving frantically at the stairs. "Come on, into the sitting room, before you wake up the hellcat upstairs – oh, never mind. Just get inside."

Mana came down the stairs with a stately tread. "Simon, those are your parents, and I expect you to use a more respectful form of address, please."

"More respectful-" Simon goggled at her, as he shut the sitting room door behind them. The room was rather chilly by the light of day. The fire hadn't been lit, and the open windows revealed the mean street outside. "They allowed me to be held by the Cantwells. They imprisoned you on the island, or at least knew about it, it seems to me, and they sold this drug on the street, and they've made both of my friends disappear."

"Now, now," Theodosia began, "you simply don't understand these things. Perhaps all of this might seem, in this light, a bit extreme, but we're doing it for our fortune, and your own future, dear boy."

"Factory doing better than expected," Virgil grunted, getting out a cigar. He put it to his lips, but Mana gave him a straight look, and he quickly removed it to a breast pocket. "Making scads of money, enough to support you in luxury for the rest of your life, Simon, if things keeps going as they are."

"It's not my money," Simon said. His fury made his nostrils flare. "It's Miriam's. And do you know something, Father? If you sold that drug to innocent people, she'd rather not have it. Nor more would I. Not to mention the fact that she's missing, and so is Neil – abducted by you, mother, I'll be bound - and I was tortured for weeks on end, as was Miss Postulate."

Mana held up one hand. "I have one statement to make. Mrs. Marchpane, you are a greedy woman and you have broken some laws to get what you want, but I do see that you are devoted to your son. I suggest that you discover what it is that he really wants before you do anything else. Mr. Marchpane, you are a spineless fool, but you seem to have some affection for your wife and son. You need to abandon all thoughts of selling the copaiba tincture, *now*."

Theodosia, who had begun to bridle at this speech, deflated and turned to Simon. "Very well," she said in an odd, defeated tone that was completely out of character. "What is it you want us to do, Simon?"

"Rescue Miriam and Neil," he said promptly.

She sighed.

Simon looked at Mana with suspicion. "Did you just do that mind control thing on them?"

"Honestly, I didn't, Simon," she said. "I think your mother just saw sense, perhaps for the first time in her life. Mr. and Mrs. Marchpane, I take it that we need to go to the Devil's Kitchen to rescue Simon's friends. Is that correct?"

Theodosia clamped her mouth shut and nodded.

Mana rose, and continued, "I'll assume you have your carriage here with you. We'll use that, if you don't mind." Without waiting for an answer, she walked out of the room. Simon stalked after her, ignoring the pleading glance his mother gave him.

He continued to ignore them on the journey, looking out of the window and humming loudly whenever Virgil or Theodosia tried to talk to him. His mother actually looked to Mana for support. Mana, however, had her eyes closed with exhaustion as she leaned back against the cushions.

The carriage rolled into the dark alley that bordered the Devil's Kitchen, and Simon leaped out as soon as it stopped. There were no bells or knockers on the huge, dirty doors, but he began to hammer on them.

The gate was opened, and a guard, a plug of tobacco in his mouth, poked his head out and spat on the ground by Simon's feet. "Ain't acceptin' no trade terday," he began, but he caught sight of the Marchpanes. "Oh," he said, and opened the gate a few inches.

Simon pushed his way in and looked around. "I remember this filthy place," he said, turning the corners of his mouth down. "You might enjoy hearing that I was hit by one of these goons they employ here, *mother*," he finished. "Come on, Miss Postulate. Let's find the bony old hag who runs the place."

"You mean the Headmistress." The guard recognized the description. "This all right with you?" he asked the Marchpanes. When Virgil nodded, the guard shrugged as if to say, *All the same to me,* and he trudged off.

They followed him through the sandy yard into the dark factory. The guard walked down a long hallway, through several sets of doors, and down another hall. The interior was lit by lanterns that flickered in the gloom.

He stopped at a painted door that was somewhat cleaner than the rest of them and knocked. A low voice intoned something from inside, and the guard lifted his shoulders and said, "She says to wait a bit."

"Aren't these your employees?" Simon said to his father, incensed. "I've waited long enough, thank you very much." He twisted the knob, opened the door, and marched in.

Both of the Heads were in a large chamber that seemed to be used as an office. Simon's footsteps echoed as he clumped inside. Dark portraits of old men flanked a large fireplace with a liver-colored marble mantel, and a long, heavy desk sat in front of the dreary hearth. Simon thought that it looked like a much dirtier version of his own Head's office at Firbury.

The Headmaster was at a sidewall. He had just finished locking a large cupboard there. The Headmistress looked up, and anger flared in her cold eyes. "How dare you?" she began, but she stopped as Virgil entered the room. "Mr. Marchpane. I didn't see you there."

"'Know you didn't," Virgil said, puffing on the cigar he had previously put away. "Would have opened the door straight away if you had. Thing is, you need to release two of the workers here. Neil Gillsworth and Miriam Pearson."

"I hadn't been made aware of this," the Headmistress replied, twitching her brows together. "This violates our agreement, much as I would wish to cooperate with you on the matter, of course."

"Just send that guard to get Miriam and Neil at once, you frozen old trout," Simon burst out. Behind him, there was a sound of a loud snigger, hastily cut off as the guard clapped one hand over his mouth.

"What do the Cantwells have to say about this?" The Headmistress ignored Simon. "You gave them power of attorney, so I will need their agreement in this matter."

"You did what?" Simon rounded on his father.

"Well, I sort of – it seems that I – I might have done something like –" Virgil blustered.

The Headmistress sniffed and her eyelids closed a little over the icy eyes. "Get their approval, and come back within a week. I utterly refuse to rush into anything."

Taxed beyond forbearance, Simon shouted, "This factory is closed as of this moment, you withered prune!"

"No, it is not." The Headmaster dangled his keys and stood beside the Headmistress. "It has become a much bigger and more profitable proposition than you realize, Mr. Marchpane."

Virgil opened his mouth, and his cigar dropped to the carpet. "Look here, you can't talk to me in that way!" he said.

The Headmistress raised her whistle and blew a long, loud blast on it. "My guards will escort you out," she said, looking down her nose at the group.

Simon looked at Mana for help, but her eyes were closed, one hand pressed to one temple. He bunched both hands into fists and glared at the Headmistress. "Give it up, haddock face," he spat. "Your little reign as Headmistress of the Devil's Kitchen is over." There was a faint cheer from the guard, who quickly straightened his face, turned, and examined the dismal portraits on the wall as the Headmistress raised her eyebrows at him.

"Here are the rest of my guards now," she said. The heavy tread came nearer, and she pointed to the door. "Open it."

The guard with the tobacco-plug turned from the dismal portraits, shrugged again and flung the door open. Instead of more goons, however, a tall man with a stately bearing and rich, dark skin stood in the entrance. He had someone else behind him.

"Kyoge." Mana whispered. "You heard me."

"My queen," he replied, with a bow. "Of course I heard you."

"Hey, is that Neil?" Simon shouted. Kyoge pulled the figure forward, and Neil fell into the room.

"Simon! Hey, Simon! You should have seen it – he was great! They were just about to inject me with copaiba in that place they call the

Infirmary, and Kyoge simply appeared out of nowhere, picked me up, and walked out with me! He says he was there the whole time!" While Neil yelled this explanation at the top of his lungs, the two boys began to punch each other as a form of affectionate greeting.

The Headmistress began to swell with fury. "Get them out of here!" she suddenly shouted to the guard with the tobacco plug.

"No fear." The man folded his arms and jerked his chin in Simon's direction. "I like his spirit. 'Frozen old trout,'" he repeated, and he sniggered again.

"But where's Miriam?" Simon looked around.

"Not in her cell," Kyoge replied. "I made inquiries."

"She's in the cupboard." Mana pointed to the door the Headmaster had just locked up when they had entered the study. "I should imagine they were just about to interrogate her when we walked in."

"Give us the keys." Simon looked at the Headmaster.

"That will require a writ signed by all four of the owners," the Headmaster began, "and as there are only two here, I'm afraid-"

"I'm tired of this," Kyoge growled, coming forward. He picked up the Headmaster by the scruff of his neck with one huge hand. As the man dangled helplessly in his grip, Kyoge abstracted the ring of keys and tossed them to Mana. "There you are, my queen."

"I really do wish you would stop calling me your queen," she said, as she caught the keys and unlocked the lock. She opened the door and Miriam lay there, bundled and trussed up, a thick gag over her mouth. Mana reached into the closet to pick her up, but Kyoge forestalled her. He dropped the Headmaster, who crashed to the floor and strode forward. With surprising gentleness, the large man pulled Miriam out. "Knife," he said.

The Headmaster, who had picked himself up, breathed in and said, "In the desk, but you'll need written permission-"

"Here." The guard filched an old pocketknife from a hidden recess of his trousers. "Will that do?" He leaned forward and watched in an interested way as Kyoge ripped through Miriam's bonds with the rusty blade. As soon as she could, the girl tossed away the gag and spat.

"Ugh!" she said. "That was foul – someone's moldy socks, I think." She stood up, rubbed one ankle, and hopped over to Mana, who clasped her in a huge hug.

"Er, hello, Miriam," Simon said.

She looked up. "Simon! I thought I heard your voice! And Neil as well. Fantastic! But how did you both get here?"

"How did you-" Neil began.

"We'll catch up on all the events later," Mana said firmly. "Let's give these two Heads a taste of their own medicine, and we have a sick little girl at the Headquarters to attend to."

"We do?" Neil asked.

"Riki." Mana smiled at him. "She followed us here from Lampala." At this piece of news, Neil clapped one hand to his forehead, aghast.

"Bad luck, old son," Simon said to him with heavy sympathy.

Kyoge pulled the Headmaster and Headmistress into a death grip. "How about a hand?" he asked the interested guard.

"Don't mind if I do," the man replied without hesitation. He picked up the ropes that had held Miriam in the closet, and wrapped them around the ankles of both Heads. The Headmistress struggled, and mouthed threats, insisting that proper protocol must be observed, but Kyoge's large hand wrapped firmly around her neck, and she subsided.

Once the Headmistress and the Headmaster were securely tied up, Kyoge and the guard shook hands. "If yeh ever needs a job, come and see me," the man said. "Ask for Rog at the train station. I never seen a better grip in all my born days."

Kyoge bowed. "I give you my thanks, Rog," he said.

"We really must go." Mana put her hand to her temples again. In an instant, Kyoge was at her side. He wrapped his arm around her waist.

"You need a rest, my queen." He propelled her out of the room.

"They really are quite something, aren't they?" Miriam watched the pair leave together.

Simon reflected that Miriam had grown taller, thinner, and paler, in the last few months. And her curls, which used to fly all over the place, had been chopped off. "Yes, indeed they are," he said.

"Um, come on." Neil dragged at Simon's sleeve. When the other boy protested, he apologized. "There's someone I really want to see."

"Riki, he means. She's a proper hellspawn, too. Just wait until you meet her," Simon whispered to Miriam as they followed everyone else downstairs. "Poor fellow," he added.

CHAPTER 25
The End of the Adventure

J anet met them at the door of The Headquarters with a worried look on her face. "Sorry, Miss Postulate, but they pushed their way in," she began.

A silky voice interrupted her. "So sorry to intrude on the party." Barbara, in one of her fashionable gowns, came out of the sitting room. Valiant lounged behind her, his usual cigar in one hand.

"How do you do, Mr. and Miss Cantwell," Mana murmured. "I'm so sorry, but I don't allow anyone to smoke in this house."

Valiant widened his eyes. "No?" he asked. Deliberately he puffed on the cheroot and released a long stream of smoke in Mana's direction.

Miriam could feel her temper rising, and beside her Simon muttered, "Why, that bloody bastard. Just you wait!" Kyoge said nothing, but he stiffened.

Mana merely ignored him. "Why don't we go into the sitting room, instead of standing out here in the hall. Janet, a large pot of tea, please." She moved past Barbara and Valiant into the room, her head held high. Miriam saw Neil nip up the stairs when he thought no one was watching.

Inside Mana sat and waved a hand at the settee, indicating that the 'guests' should sit down. Theodosia and Virgil plumped themselves on the cushions, but Barbara walked up to Mana, bent right into her face, and said, "I've worked too hard to make this thing come off to stop now because of some idiots with some sort of island mentality. First off, you can't dissolve the pharmaceutical division without my consent, do you hear?"

"My, word gets around quickly," Miriam said.

"Ah." Mana sat up straighter. "Yes, Miss Cantwell, you managed to maneuver yourselves into a partnership with the Marchpanes. I suppose that attorney, Fortescue, had something to do with that. How much did you pay him, I wonder?"

Janet entered with a large tray, and Kyoge, with his slow grace, took it from her and put it on a low table. The girl closed the door very slowly, and Miriam could hear her breathe at the keyhole.

"So, we really must demand that the production of copaiba continues uninterrupted, you know," Valiant said to Virgil. "Sorry, and all that, old chap."

"But that is completely impossible." Mana reached for the teapot. "Cream, Miss Cantwell?"

Barbara waved the question away with impatience. "Why is it impossible? I'd love to hear what an ignorant savage like you has to say." At that, Kyoge turned, a growl rising in his throat, but Mana stopped him.

"The answer is simple. You cannot produce the drug without the bolemor trees, and I will stop all exports from Mixiamani as the present ruler of Lampala."

Barbara laughed. Her nose wrinkled in the attractive way she had. "But you're not the present ruler," she said. "That person is Atol, who has returned here to the City under my protection. It seems you cannot be proclaimed Queen without that ridiculous crown, and that has gone missing."

Mana smiled. "Miriam?" she asked.

Miriam, who was considering various ways of smashing in Barbara's face, looked up. "Huh?" she said.

"I believe you have something of mine that I left you in trust."

Miriam frowned, and light dawned. "Of course! I'm so stupid, honestly, what a thick idiot I can be at times." She fished down the front of the smock she still wore. "Sorry," she apologized, "no pockets." With triumph, she produced a handful of objects – two letters, a worn notebook, a stubby pencil worn to a nub, and the wooden comb.

Mana stood and, approaching the girl, put her arms around her and gave her a kiss. "Good job, Miriam. You really are a worthy heir to Pearson's Company." She held up the dark, wooden comb and announced, "This, Miss Cantwell, is the Glorious Corona."

For a moment the scene froze. Everyone in the room looked at the carved object. The dark wood curved in a delicate arc. It was covered with intricate carvings and inlaid pearls that gleamed.

Valiant made an amused sound in his throat and relit his cigar. "That's the thing Atol stripped the islands for, eh? Doesn't look like much to me."

His sister laughed with him, but Kyoge had had enough. With one stride, he crossed the distance between himself and snatched the cheroot from Valiant's mouth. Throwing it in the fireplace, he snarled, "You will do as the Queen requests and not smoke in her presence. And you will address her with respect. Is this how you treat royalty in England? That-" he jabbed one finger at the Corona – "is a sacred object of my country and you will treat it as such."

"And this," Barbara said, "is a pistol. And it is pointed at your Queen." A deadly little weapon had appeared in her hand, and she held it steadily in Mana's direction. "Now," she continued, "perhaps we can talk some sense. You will not stop the exports of bolemors. In fact, you will increase the numbers of trees coming into the factories. You and your friend will stay in the Devil's Kitchen, I believe they call it, along with those two brats. Simon will come back with me."

"Wait just a moment, old girl," Virgil protested, who had been watching the proceedings with bewilderment. "You can hardly think that Theodosia and I will allow that."

"Be quiet, you fool," Barbara snapped. "Tyoge, or whatever your name is, take 'your queen', that dreadful girl, and that fisher boy to my carriage. We're returning to the Devil's Factory."

"No," Miriam moaned. "I simply can't go back there."

The door suddenly opened, and Riki, looking even thinner than usual, stood in the hall. "Can't sleep," she complained.

Everyone looked up, startled, including Barbara. Miriam gasped as

Simon launched himself at the Cantwell woman and butted her in the stomach with his head. Surprised, she let the gun go and it skittered on the ground, where Kyoge, with a lightning reflex, picked it up and held it at Valiant's head.

"Simon!" Miriam screamed. "Gosh! What a hero you are. I could kiss you!"

"Why don't you?" he said with a broad grin. Miriam turned bright red and mumbled something.

"How dare you, you stupid boy!" Barbara raged, but Kyoge waved the pistol at her.

"I have decided that I do not particularly care for you, or for your brother. Shut your mouths, both of you, or I will shoot you. Do not believe that I won't." He held his head up and looked down his nose at her, and she grew quiet.

"Excuse me," Valiant said. Kyoge looked at him and gripped the pistol tighter.

"Well?" the big man asked. "What is it?"

"Effectively, none of you can stop the sale of copaiba," Valiant continued. "There is no record of its manufacture, nor even of how it is made. By this time the factory at the Devil's Kitchen will be dismantled. There is nothing to say that it was ever produced, nor that it was even harmful in any way. All records of its production and even of its formulaic nature have been destroyed by now." He smiled affably at the group.

"Go," Riki said. She coughed and pushed someone forward.

Neil stumbled in to the room. "Ah, that's not quite true," he said, holding up a thin document. "While I was working at Pearson's, I came across this. I believe it's the formula for producing copaiba, isn't it?" He looked at the paper in his hand and read, "'Into this fluid thus obtained, insert a piece of palladium foil charged with occluded hydrogen. Add five drops of the tincture obtained from the boles...'"

Barbara turned, and her eyes widened as she saw the paper. "Where on earth did you get that?" she screeched.

"Neil, you brick!" Simon yelled.

"Kyoge, I agree with you," Riki said. "I don't like that man either. Or that woman," she added, and swayed. Neil hurriedly put an arm around her shoulders, and Mana got up.

"Up to bed, Riki," she said. "Janet," she called, "come in. I know quite well you've listened in on the entire conversation in the kitchen; go and fetch the police at once. As for you, Neil, get some belts and cravats and things from upstairs, as it seems we have to tie up yet another set of criminals today."

Half an hour later, a sergeant arrived with two more policemen in tow. Valiant went quietly enough, asking if he could smoke on the way, but Barbara still cursed and shouted when she was bundled out of the door.

Simon suddenly made a noise in his throat and ran after her. "Stop!" he shouted. The two policemen, engaged in making certain she didn't twist away from them, didn't look up, but Barbara turned her head to him. "What did you do with Neil's parents?" he called.

A slow smile spread across her face and she began to laugh. She continued to gurgle with mirth as the police pushed her into the black carriage.

Valiant, however, had the last word. As the Maria rounded the corner, he shouted, "Don't forget this!"

Something fell onto the cobblestones with a huge smash. Neil frowned, and Simon said, "What the blazes was that?"

He dashed to the end of the street, accompanied by Miriam and Neil. There they found, strewn in spectacular fashion, the bits and pieces of what had once been Miriam's Crown Phoenix.

"Oh, no," she whispered, picking up some of the keys. She let a Q drop through her fingers onto the street.

"Sorry, Miriam." Simon put one arm around her shoulders.

Neil looked at the pieces, and with a grunt of decision, he began to pick them up. "Here, give me a hand, Simon," he said.

Reluctantly, Simon let go of Miriam and helped to pick up the broken machine. "It can't be repaired," he protested.

"No," Miriam said. "No, it can't."

"Too bad," Neil said. "It must be unique. Where did you get it, Miriam?"

"It was Dad's," she said, squatting beside the two boys. "Here, chuck those letters into the skirt of my smock."

They returned with the pieces of the machine, and Theodosia gasped as she saw it. "The Passage!" she said.

"Suppose we're going to be bankrupt, old man," Virgil said as Simon handed his bits to Neil, who popped them in a bag. "We'll have to pay for real ships and long sea voyages now."

"Bankrupt?" Mana descended the stairs, a cloth folded over one arm. "Nonsense."

"Well, if we give up this Devil's Kitchen, we're done for. Sank all our funds into production and research of the copaiba stuff. That is, unless Miriam can hand over some of her money to us." He raised his eyebrows at her in a hopeful way.

Simon interrupted. "No fear, Dad," he said. "You're not going to mismanage her inheritance like you did with the company. And I'm not going to marry her just so you can get at her money, do you hear?"

Virgil turned bright red and spluttered. "Why, I never heard such a thing! Where on earth did you ever get that idea?"

Mana slapped the cloth over the banister. "No one will marry anyone, not at the moment at least, and Miriam's funds will stay where they are. Pearson's will continue to manufacture pharmaceuticals, but they will be actual medicines, Mr. Marchpane, and not opiates."

Virgil looked at her, interested. "Go on," he said.

"The boles are raw products. If they are processed differently, they can be manufactured as the cure for this current influenza fever, which is currently ravaging the county. I am going to give some medicine to Riki now, and she'll finally be able to get a good, natural sleep. You can borrow against Miriam's funds to test and produce it, and in a few months Pearson's will be on its feet again." Mana closed her mouth and swayed. She grasped the banister with one hand.

Kyoge frowned and strode forward. "No more talk," he said.

"Administer your medicine to that little one, and you must rest." Ignoring Mana's protests, he guided her upstairs, one hand on her waist.

"Cure for influenza, eh?" Virgil stuck out his bottom lip and nodded to himself. "Could do well, could do very well indeed. I'd have to smooth out the business details, of course."

"Dad," Simon said. "Dad, do *you* know where Neil's family is?"

"Afraid I don't, old son. That Cantwell woman took care of that whole business."

Simon's shoulders drooped again, and he watched his father disappear into the sitting room to talk to Theodosia. He sighed and plopped onto the bottom stair.

Miriam sat beside him on the step. "What will happen to Neil?" she asked. "Suppose I have to go back to live with Old Walking Stick. That is, I mean your father. Sorry."

Simon bumped her shoulder with his in acknowledgement, and, heartened by this, she confided, "I must say I don't like the idea, but perhaps I can come to Lampala in the summertime, and maybe I can go away to school next year. And it will be lovely to see Furnace, and Mrs. Williams, and Nelly, and everybody again."

"I'll have to go back to Firbury," Simon replied. "Wonder what all the chaps are saying about my and Neil's disappearance? Gosh, I'll have to repeat the year, I suppose."

"How about Neil?" Miriam demanded. Simon looked at her. "Are you listening to me?" she pressed. "Neil must have lost his scholarship; he told me upstairs that he won't be able to go back to Firbury. And if he can't find his family, he'll be out on the streets."

"Oh, that," Simon said. "I'll get Dad to give him a scholarship through Pearson's, and he can go back to the Company to work when he graduates. Not as a clerk, though, but something higher up, of course. And we'll keep up the search for his parents."

"And how about you?" Miriam asked.

"What about me?"

"Won't you miss that Cantwell woman?" Miriam blurted out the question, and she dropped her gaze onto her hands in her lap. How ridiculous of her to blush!

"Well, Miriam," Simon said, "as a matter of fact, no, I won't. I won't miss that dreadful woman one bit. In fact, when she had me in prison up there, in that dreadful room, and I felt like I had lost my mind, it was *you* that I saw. I saw you in a dream, and that's what saved me from losing my mind."

"Oh," Miriam said. Suddenly the house got very still and very quiet. Simon's gaze was intent upon hers, and for some strange reason, she couldn't look away. And she found she couldn't breathe, either. Her heart began to hammer in her chest, and her mouth opened in a slight gasp.

Simon's grin disappeared. He opened his mouth to say something, closed it again, and edged a bit closer to her on the step.

At that moment, Neil appeared at the top of the stairs and trailed down, dragging his feet on the worn treads of the stair carpet. "What are you two talking about?" he asked.

Miriam jumped, and she and Simon moved apart.

"What? What did you say, Neil?" Simon cleared his throat.

"I wanted to know what you were talking about," Neil repeated.

"You, among other things," Miriam said. Simon shifted.

"You don't always have to tell the exact truth to everybody when they ask you a question, you know, Miriam," he said.

Neil sat on the step behind them and dragged his face down with his hands, making his spectacles pop off. He balanced them back on his nose. "Mana told me that she will hire Philips to search for them. My family, I mean. What am I to do? Now I'm even more in debt to you both than ever," he burst out.

"Neil, stop it," Miriam ordered. "If it weren't for you, I'd still be in the Mines in the Devil's Kitchen, and Simon would still be held by that ghastly Cantwell female."

"And you *are* going back to school," Simon said, "with me."

"And I'm going back to my house," Miriam said, "but we'll all see each other on holidays and things. And Neil, you can come to Lampala with me in the summer."

"What about me?" Simon asked.

"Oh, you can come too," Miriam said.

"Generous of you," He gave her a shove.

"Well, of course I meant both of you." She shoved him back.

Kyoge interrupted this battle by coming down the stairs with a small tray, and they stood up to let him pass. "Sir, how is Riki?" Neil asked.

"Still sleeping, but she's not as feverish as she was."

"And Mana?" Miriam asked.

Kyoge smiled. "She is sleeping too. I want her to get as much rest as she can, for we must return to Lampala by the next boat. She has much to do there, now that you have saved the Glorious Corona, Miss Miriam." He bowed, and continued his stately journey to the kitchen.

"I think they will get married one day, don't you?" Miriam whispered loudly. The two boys didn't bother to answer her but instead made horrible faces at each other.

'Well." Miriam stood up. "I suppose I'd better get ready to go back to the house with your parents, although I don't have anything to pack. I do need a bath, though."

Miriam went upstairs, and Simon watched her go.

He wouldn't see much of her in the year to come, he thought with a pang. Still, there was something to look forward to, which was always good. "Lampala this summer," he said.

"Can't wait," Neil agreed.

It would happen a year from now, and she would be that much older, and so would he. You could do a lot of growing in a year. Whistling, he stretched out his legs, and Neil hit him.

"Still tuneless, I see."

"Speak for yourself, professor," Simon retorted, and he made room for Neil on the bottom step. The two boys sat back and listened to the chimes of the clock in the hall.

EPILOGUE
A Strange Ending

Miriam lay in bed, her hands clasped around her legs. She was back in the little room that Mana had moved her into, ages and ages ago. As strange as it seemed, Uncle Virgil and Aunt Theodosia slept downstairs, in her father's old bedroom.

There was a snuffling snore from the person in the bed next to hers. Miriam looked at the cot that had been moved into her room until something more permanent could be arranged. Riki lay there, one skinny arm flung over her head. She and Miriam, although they quarreled in mighty style from time to time, had become close friends. It had been decided that she would stay on the mainland and learn her lessons with Miriam's new governess, Miss Thompson.

Mana had gone. Miriam knew that her governess would have to return to her own country, eventually, but the sorrow of saying goodbye was still with her. She closed her eyes, as she recalled a conversation between Mana and her guardians that she, Riki, Neil and Simon had shamelessly eavesdropped on a few months ago.

"You plotted with Fortescue, Henry's lawyer to gain access to the Company and the Pearson holdings," Mana had stated. It was not a question.

"Ah, well, yes, that is so," Uncle Virgil had admitted. Aunt Theodosia had merely sniffed and looked out of the window.

"You were willing to use Miriam as your own pawn, but I don't think you will try that in the future." She stopped speaking and looked at them.

"No." Theodosia spoke bitterly. "Simon has seen to that. It's ridiculous, really, how much the dear boy worries about that girl!" At that point Neil, his face pressed to the wall of the adjoining room, had nudged Simon, who rolled his eyes at him. Riki had poked Miriam with one bony finger.

"No, we'll take good care of her, Miss Postulate," Virgil promised, "if you can let her stay here. And I'll run the factory under your conditions."

Mana's response had been cool. "My only concern is for Miriam. I could take her to Lampala, but I think it best that she remains here on the mainland for a few years, and she can decide for herself." Her voice acquired a steely edge. "Be assured, however, that if I hear of the tiniest wrong-doing, or if Miriam suffers in any way, I will shut down all imports from my country and close the Company."

"Hurrah!" Simon had whispered, but at this point Furnace had entered and discovered them crouching by the fireplace. All four of them had been hustled out of the room.

Miriam sighed and pulled the blankets up around her waist. So many things had happened since. It was hard to keep track of them all. The Company had closed down the Devil's Kitchen, and the workers had been given either positions in Pearson's or had been pensioned out with favorable recommendations. Mack, she had heard, was working on the machines that processed the influenza medicine, as were Mrs. Siddons and Minnie.

Riki, once she had recovered from the influenza, was adamant about staying on the mainland and having lessons with Miriam. She had really wanted to go to Firbury College with Neil and Simon, but she had been told that it just wouldn't do.

And Mana had left, along with Kyoge. That had been terrible, especially when Miriam had watched the boat disappear in the distance, heading towards the island that no longer appeared to float over the waves. The Passage had closed, thanks to Valiant. The Crown Phoenix was still in pieces, waiting in a vault in the city, so the voyage to the island now would take weeks instead of days.

Of course, some bad things had happened as well. The Cantwells had left the prison where they were held, helped out by a series of large bribes brought about by Fortescue, the crooked attorney. They had subsequently disappeared, and no one had heard of them since. Atol, who was supposed to have escaped to the mainland, had disappeared as well, if he had ever been there at all.

But the worst was Neil – he had never found his family, although Philips, who was now the lawyer for Pearson's, had hired detectives and plainclothes policemen, all to no avail. The house near the docks had been discovered, locked and boarded up. His family had apparently disappeared one night, and that was the last anyone ever heard from them.

And there was Simon. Miriam wrote letters to him at Firbury, and he wrote back in great length. He always demanded more stories and told her what was wrong with the last ones she sent. It always infuriated her, but he was usually right.

She would see him and Neil in the summer. She would see Mana in Lampala, and meet Riki's parents and brothers. It was a strange ending, although a wholly satisfactory one.

There was a distant hoot, followed by a faraway, lonely whistle as the Night Watchman Express rounded the turn near the grounds of the house. The train still ran late at night past Miriam's house. Only a few farmers rode on it now, home from the market or off to the shops.

Miriam yawned and lay down on her pillow. The sound of the train no longer gave her nightmares. After all, she had faced much worse things. She closed her eyes, and slept.

THE END

CROWN PHOENIX:

Lamplighter's Special

Bonus Chapters

PROLOGUE
The Lamplighter's Special

M ana!"

The girl's cry caused most of the sailors to turn and stare. Miss Miriam had been a good passenger, unlike that little imp Riki. The girl with black curls was almost a young lady now, after all. The crew of The Lamplighter had grown accustomed to seeing her scribble away in the copybook she always kept with her. She was polite, clean, and quiet, in direct contrast to Riki, who tangled the ropes, climbed the riggings, and punctuated her talk with what the cook called some "very warm language."

Mrs. Marchpane, Miss Miriam's guardian, wore an ill-advised dress of liver-colored satin and a sour look of disapproval. Miriam ignored her and dashed down the length of the ship to wave at a group of royal Lampalans in bright silks on the sands. "The Queen of the island 'erself, so they say," Tom Nugget said to the bunting tosser, who had just raised the flag hoist. Tom, a seasoned sailor who fancied himself an expert on Lampala and their trade with the Pearson company, jerked his thumb at a tall, beautifully dressed woman who stood at the front of the crowd, waving.

Miriam arrived with a jolt at the end of the ship. Unable to contain herself, she jumped up and down as the gangway was prepared for their arrival. Riki joined her by the rail in short order and began shrieking to her parents, "*Mami!* Mami! Papi! Did you miss me? Where's Neil?"

"Riki, you are shouting directly into my ear." Miriam couldn't help smiling at her friend's excitement, though.

"Sorry, Miriam!" Riki shouted again. "Mami, *where is Neil?*"

"Ouch! You can ask about him when we get off the ship." Miriam planted an elbow in Riki's ribs. She waved again to Mana and wondered if she would ever get used to the idea of her former governess as Queen Manapalata of Lampala.

Riki jumped off The Lamplighter's railing and tugged on Miriam's hand. "Come on; we'd better make certain that terrible lot who man the Lamplighter won't leave behind our bags in our cabins."

Miriam gave one last wave to Mana and followed Riki. The Marchpanes were already surrounded by a huge mound of trunks, valises, and hatboxes. Riki pounced on a smart bag with leather and brass handles and cried with triumph, "Here's mine! Where's your luggage, Miriam?"

"Miriam's things are all here." Aunt Theodosia frowned. "And a little more decorum would not go amiss."

"Sorry, Mrs. Marchpane," Riki said instantly.

"Wonder if they have a decent cellar where we're staying?" Uncle Virgil inserted one finger into the space between his neck and his collar. "Deuced hot here in the tropics, isn't it?"

The gangway was secured in place, and the sailors moved the ropes aside, directed by Tom Nugget. As soon as she could, Miriam tumbled down the planks onto the wooden pier that led to the soft, warm sand. Behind her, unheeded, Aunt Theodosia called, "Miriam! Virgil, did you see that girl? Really!"

Riki was close behind Miriam. They ran over the sand, feeling it sift under their city boots, right up to the group of people with Mana.

"Hello!" Mana said, her face bright with a big smile. "Miriam, it's so good to – oof!" She stopped as Miriam ran right into her and grabbed her around her waist, ignoring the various dignitaries and guards behind the queen.

"Remember decorum, Miss Miriam." Kyoge bent to pat the girl's arm.

"You sound like Aunt Theodosia," Miriam giggled. "Gosh, must I call you Queen now, Mana?"

"Indeed you must," Kyoge began, but Mana stopped him with a hand on the heavily embroidered sleeve of his jacket.

"Time enough for all that state business later, Kyoge, for heaven's sake. Let's get everyone into the shade as soon as possible."

By this time, Riki had bounced over to the group and had been enveloped by Chichilia and Weko, her parents. Her brothers, Jirili and Kakujife, stood behind the trio with broad smiles on their faces.

Miriam gave Mana one last hug and stepped back. "Goodness, you look beautiful, Mana! Goodness, your dress is amazing! Goodness, how are things on the Big Star Island? And on Mixiamani, the other island? Goodness, did Atol ever reappear?"

"And where is Neil?" Riki said. She planted herself on the sand beside Miriam and grabbed her hand. "You're saying 'goodness' a lot, Miriam."

"Neil and Simon are at your parent's house, Riki, where you and Miriam will be staying," Mana said. "I thought that would be nicer for you both than rooms at the Palace, since your house is so close to the sea. It is my understanding that the young men are preparing a surprise for you both."

Miriam's heart gave a strange stutter. She had written to Simon quite often since school had started at Firbury College, but she hadn't seen him since then. His letters were long and filled with stories from his school. He also kept up his demands for more letters from her, and he continued to complain that she didn't tell him enough about her writing, or about Riki, nor her lessons. And had she heard from Mana, he added, and how was she getting along with Riki and his parents?

Miriam herself could have filled pages with long stories about her new governess, hired after Mana returned to Lampala, and how she and Aunt Theodosia managed to be civil to each other. She found that she held herself back, however, when it came to Simon. How, for example, would she ask in a letter if he ever still thought about Barbara, the beautiful woman who had caused Miriam to be kidnapped, and who had imprisoned Simon himself? And could she question him about his broad shoulders and his dark gold hair and whether it still curled up at the back of his neck? No, of course she couldn't.

The last time she had seen him, there had been something, a moment.

Yes, a moment. She supposed that was the best way to describe it. She and Simon had been exhausted from everything they had gone through last summer. For one minute on the steps, in the house that Mana had rented in a poor section of London, they had finally stopped their arguments.

And, Miriam thought, blushing a bit as she remembered it, what then? Nothing, really. They had stared at each other for a long, silent minute until Neil had barged in and sat between them. No, she told herself, it had been nothing at all. Only, sometimes at night, just before going to sleep, she wondered what Simon would have done next if Neil had not clumped down the stairs at that particular instant.

Miriam put her free hand on her cheek as if to push the redness back. By this time the group had turned away from the ship, followed by a troop of sailors and guards carrying the load of luggage.

Riki tugged at her other hand. Feeling her heart beat a bit faster, Miriam walked towards a grove of lime trees, pointed out by Riki.

"This is the path to the sea," Riki said. "It goes right to my house. Gosh, what wouldn't I give for one of Odjo's meals right now? Hope he made crab fritters and mango sauce and coconut patties."

"Is that where you live?" Miriam stopped. The house and the surrounding gardens were lovelier than anything she could have imagined. Riki, when she had described it to her in England, had called it "a decent-sized home, not as big as yours."

"Riki, this is incredible! Did you really grow up here?"

Riki shrugged, but Miriam could see she was pleased. "Look, Chichilia put out my parrot!" she said. "See that whacking huge cage for one silly bird? I have to clean it out, though. Wonder if I'll still have to do that since we are on holidays. And d'you like our garden?"

Miriam nodded, a bit dazed. The lawn was bright green, punctuated with red and yellow and pink and blue flowers, and a small pool was in one corner, fed by a tiny stream. "I've never seen a more beautiful place in my life," she said.

One of the windows in the upstairs part of the house shot open. Two heads emerged, one gold, one dark. Both boys wore huge grins. Neil's glasses flashed in the bright sunlight and he let loose with a loud whoop. Riki cupped both hands around her mouth and yelled, "Neil! Simon!"

The faces disappeared from the window, and some seconds later the girls could hear loud thumps as Simon and Neil bowled down the steps. Miriam began to laugh.

The front door was thrown back, and the boys shot out of it and jumped off the porch. Simon ran right up to Miriam, grabbed her into a huge hug, and swung her around in a circle.

"Simon!" Aunt Theodosia said in a scandalized tone. "Put her down at once! What are you thinking – an English boy never does that to a young lady! Remember your manners at once!"

Neil, who had done much the same thing with Riki, put her down on the grass and said, "Sorry, Mrs. Marchpane."

"Sorry, Mother." Simon still wore a huge grin. He wrung his father's hand and submitted to a hard peck on the cheek from his mother, rolling his eyes at Miriam as he did so.

"Oh, and wait until you see what we've got for you and Miriam!" Neil poked Riki's shoulder.

"Food first," Chichilia said. "Odjo has been cooking all day."

"Oh, food," Neil said. "'Spose you're all hungry after the food on the Lamplighter. Right."

Aunt Theodosia frowned and pointed at the carvings on the wooden pillars surrounding the porch. "Are those heathen gods or idols of some sort? Really, I don't know if I can sleep here with such things..."

"I thought you might like to stay in the Palace instead, Mr. and Mrs. Marchpane," Mana said. "The children can stay here with Chichilia and swim and fish during the day, and you can have the finest set of rooms we have to offer on the island."

"Without Simon? Certainly not!" By this time Theodosia had swept into the dining room.

"The French ambassador stayed in those rooms at the Palace, did he not?" Kyoge followed and rushed to push Aunt Theodosia's chair in before taking a seat beside Mana.

"Indeed he did," Mana murmured. "What a very convenient memory you have, Kyoge."

"I have my moments," the large man said. Miriam thought that she detected the hint of a smile on his face. As for Mana, she definitely was amused. Miriam began to wonder about the relationship between the two of them.

"What about it, Mrs. Marchpane?" Mana said, taking a seat next to the older woman. "No, *you* sit at the head of the table, Weko; I am fine here."

"Well, I don't know…" Theodosia hesitated. She was obviously dying to see the French Ambassador's suite of rooms.

"The bed chambers have just been redone in silk and the finest pearl fittings," Mana said. "And the French ambassador brought in a large store of fine cognac during his last visit."

"Cognac? We'll stay at the Palace." Uncle Virgil sat down next to his wife. Odjo handed him a large platter filled with all manner of sandwiches, pasties, and fritters. "What's this, hey? Crab? Don't mind if I do. Plantain? Not really my sort of thing – but is that lobster?" He mounded a huge pile of delicacies on his plate.

Riki waited until her mother signaled to everyone to begin, and she took a huge bite. "Oh, mango – delicious! You just can't get this kind of thing in England! Too bad that old Passage can't be opened anymore; we could import Odjo's food…" She stopped and realized that everyone was staring at her. "Well, you could," she added.

"May we go to the sea?" Simon asked. "We can eat anytime." He was obviously bursting with some sort of secret; he kept nudging Neil with one elbow.

"Simon!" his mother said again, but Chichilia laughed.

"Of course you can," she said. "In fact, Odjo has prepared a basket to take with you. Just don't be too late, Riki. The grownups can chat while you all -"

"Don't say it!" Neil begged. "Don't give away the secret!"

"Fantastic!" Riki yelled, and popped up from her seat. "Sorry, I meant to say – may we please be excused from the table, Papi?"

Weko nodded. "Indeed you may, Riki. Don't forget to be back by early evening for dinner."

Miriam followed the three others outside. She couldn't wait to take her shoes off and feel the sand.

Riki walked next to Simon. She chatted to him in a confiding tone. "My mother used to say my name like that all the time too. 'Riki! *Riki!*' Just like yours did, just now."

Simon nodded. "I thought it would get better after last year, but I think she's grown worse. How do you both put up with her?"

"Oh, Aunt Theodosia isn't *that* bad," Miriam said. "We've grown accustomed to her; haven't we, Riki? And she's always off to the shops, for one thing."

"I can just imagine," Simon said. "Remember that puce dress she used to sport at dinner parties? Hideous. Look, we'll go right through here. There's the sand. And look at that! Neil and I helped build it!"

The two girls stopped and stared. There, on the beach, some distance down from where the Lamplighter was docked, a tall, very narrow building stood. It had two wheels in the front, as well as bright flags that hung from the pointed roof and down the sides.

"What is it?" Riki finally asked.

"It's a bathing machine, silly," Neil said. "You go in and get changed into swim things in there. If you really want to, someone can tow you and the machine right into the water, if you're feeling modest and all that."

"But we haven't got bathing things with us," Miriam objected.

"Mana sent some for you from the Palace," Simon said, grinning again. "Got them in some fancy shop in Paris or some such place. They're already hanging up in that machine. Why don't you two go and get changed, and we'll dive in to the water after you're ready?"

Without hesitation, Riki shot into the strange structure. Miriam frowned. "But I can't swim," she said.

"Oh, nonsense. We'll teach you," Simon said. "Go on, hurry up! I'm dying of the heat."

"I see you are just as used to ordering people about as ever," Miriam said, sniffing. However, she approached the "Bathing Machine" and entered the tall, rather rickety door.

Inside, Riki was already in a state of undress. She took down a green striped pair of pants that were hanging on a hook and put them on. "Gosh, am I supposed to wear these in the water? And that shirt – and is that a hat?" She plopped a frilled cap on her head and crossed her eyes.

Miriam began to laugh. "Well, this should be interesting," she said. She climbed into a red version of what Riki had on and hung her clothes on a hook.

When they emerged, the boys were already in the water, splashing each other and yelling at the tops of their lungs. "Come on in!" Simon shouted, as soon as he saw the girls. "It's great!"

"Where did you change?" Riki asked, unabashed, after she had darted into the water.

"In the trees," Simon said. "We don't need a silly Bathing Machine, but we knew Mother would insist on it for you girls if we all wanted to go into the water for a plunge. Do you like it? Isn't the sea warm?"

"It's fantastic," Miriam said. "The water's so clear! Not like the sea at home. This is blue – bluer than anything I've ever seen!" She hopped out of the way as Simon splashed her.

"You won't get very far if you jump around like that," he said. "Try and lie back; here, I'll support you." He pressed her shoulders back in the waves and wound one long arm underneath her waist.

Miriam closed her eyes, shrieked, and found that with his support she was able to float on top of the waves. Her body, held up by the salty water and Simon's forearm, moved with the waves.

"Open your eyes," he said in her ear. She looked up at the sky, as blue as the water, and couldn't help laughing again.

"What's so funny?" Riki asked. She was on Neil's shoulders, clinging on with long, slender fingers.

"I never thought I'd be here a year ago," Miriam said. "Here, let go of me, Simon." She stood up and shook some water out of one ear. "You know, when I was in that awful underground factory, I never thought that one day I'd be on an island, in – in Paradise!" She gestured at the blue water, so clear that they could see their feet, the white sand, and the young bolemor trees, shading the Bathing Machine on the beach.

"It really is perfect here," Simon said. "We've been on Lampala for - what is it, two weeks now, Neil? And I'm already getting brown, see?" He pushed his arm next to Miriam's, which was indeed quite pale in comparison.

"I'm browner than any of you," Riki said, with a chuckle.

Neil eased Riki off his back. "It really would be perfect, if it weren't for..."

"Has there been any word at all about your family, Neil?" Miriam asked.

He shook his head and got drops of seawater on his glasses. "Mana engaged another London detective to look for them," he said. "He's the third one, now. Still – nothing. It is as if they disappeared from our house. No one saw anything happen to them, either. The last chap said the place was completely deserted. There were dishes on the table, as if they were just about to sit down for a meal."

Riki twined one arm around his waist and leaned her head on his chest. Simon clapped one hand on Neil's shoulder. The four of them moved through the water so that they stood close together, feeling the movement of the waves against their legs and the warm breeze in their hair.

"Oh, I *wish* I knew where they were at this very minute!" Miriam cried.

PART ONE
Grimstead Compound

CHAPTER 1
Dirty Hands and Clean Hands

L izzie stuck her hoe into the hard soil, stepped on it with the toe of her boot to press it into the earth, and wrenched another clod of mud out. Her arms already ached, and it was barely mid morning.

Ahead of her in the row they were working, her eldest sister, Ninna, wiped her forehead with the back of one gloved hand. "Do I have dirt on my face?" Ninna asked.

Lizzie leaned on her hoe and stretched her back to ease some of the pressure on her spine. "No, you don't." She thought how pretty her sister looked, even in her ancient dress and worsted jacket. It never occurred to her to tell her so.

For her part, Lizzie didn't bother to wear gloves. Her last pair had finally fallen to shreds a few days ago, and she certainly didn't care if she had dirt on her face or not.

Ninna smiled, satisfied. She dug her hoe into the earth, and Lizzie sighed as she resumed her own work. The ground they worked was rocky and hard, although the soil itself was dark and moist.

Grimstead Compound had been their home for several weeks, now. Ever since they had lost their house, and their parents had become what they were.

Less than a year earlier, they had been a poor but well-respected family living at the docks. Da owned his fishing boat and had a share in another ship. He paid rent regularly on their house. Most importantly, Neil, their brother, had earned the chance to go to Firbury College, a real, proper, upper-crust school.

Then Neil had disappeared, along with two of the children in the house where he had been staying. Once he had gone missing, all their lives had changed.

Lizzie frowned. Back on the docks, her mother had been quick with a story, a hug, or a slap, whatever the situation merited, and she had a loud laugh that made other people chuckle just by hearing it. Da was always busy with his boats and his fishing. When he came home, however, he was willing to play a game of chess with Neil or give them all a tune on his fiddle.

Now, when Lizzie and Ninna came in from the fields for a noontime meal or at the end of the day, their parents were always sitting, sitting, sitting in the same chairs. The girls left in the morning when it was still dark out. Mam was silent in an old stiff backed kitchen chair, and Father was slumped in the only padded seat, staring in front of him with red-rimmed eyes.

"Lizzie! Ninna! Have a drink?" Matilda, their youngest sister, grinned up as she ran up to the two girls working in the field and offered them a jug of cool water.

"That's fantastic, love; thanks," Ninna said, grabbing the jug. "Just what we need. But, what's this?" She peered into the water. "Why are there stones in the jug, love?"

"They are clean." Matilda screwed up her eyes and peered up at her oldest sister. "I washed them for ever so long at the pump. And they'll keep the water cold longer for you and Lizzie."

"I'm certain they are clean, knowing you." Ninna tipped her head back, drank, and handed the jug to Lizzie.

Lizzie was desperately thirsty after the morning's work. She drank until her stomach felt swollen and handed the jug back to Matilda. "Thanks, Matilda." Despite worrying about her parents, she couldn't help smiling when she saw her little sister's gap-toothed grin. "All well at the house?"

"I have the spuds scrubbed for supper, and I think I've managed to make some bread. I had to clean the stove and the table and floor after, though."

"Not too much scrubbing, now, Matilda." Ninna touched her sister's hand. It was already reddened from all the cleaning it had endured that morning.

The hand was snatched away and hidden behind her back. Lizzie's youngest sister washed her hands and scrubbed the floors whenever she could, ever since they had been forced to move away from their old house.

"Actually, I wondered about Mam and Da," Lizzie blurted. Ninna poked her in her back with one impatient finger.

"Sounds like you're doing grand, love," Ninna said, giving Matilda a hug. "Near broke our teeth on that last bun you made; didn't we, Lizzie? We'd look like you, now, Matilda, and our teeth would break if we eat more loaves like that!"

Matilda laughed, showing her missing front teeth. Lizzie saw her sister rub her hands before she ran back to the tiny house where they now lived. She knew her youngest sister had already planned to visit the well and wash her hands again.

Ninna wheeled on Lizzie and drew in a long breath. "Haven't I told you to shut your gob about that when the young one is around? I'm deeved enough as it is by the way she washes things all the time. Her skin will be coming off her fingers, soon."

Lizzie scowled. "Well, if you don't mind what has happened to Mam, then I do," she shot back. She put one fist on her hip and hefted the hoe, willing herself to stop from boxing her sister's ears.

Ninna's lovely face seemed to crumple. Without a word, she turned around and resumed her work, yanking at the matted grass and tough roots with extra vigor.

Lizzie opened her mouth to say that she was sorry. She shut it again after a moment. What would be the use? They would only end up in a quarrel over something else. Ever since Neil had left for that upper crust school and subsequently disappeared, she and Ninna had been like two cats that spit and hissed at each other for no reason.

And when they had all been brought to the cold, harsh farm on

Grimstead Compound with an offer of work and a place to sleep, things had steadily gotten worse between them. And Mam and Da seemed to grow steadily more dependent on that nasty syrup they drank. And Matilda was obsessed with unseen dirt on the floor.

Lizzie decided to keep quiet. Instead, she was writing an account of what had happened to her family over the year. At night, after they had dinner, she would flex her tired fingers and scratch out an account, as if she were able to write a letter to her brother, Neil. She told him about the farm, and her parents, and their new life at Grimstead Compound.

Her fear was that if she didn't write what happened every day down somewhere, she would forget her brother altogether. What if – and the thought made the breath catch in her throat – what if she and Ninna had to live on the Compound forever? What would happen to them if they were forced to work that blasted soil and watch their parents grow more and more withdrawn? When she wrote things in her old journal, it was the only way she had of making sense of it all. She would write an account of how she and Ninna always argued, she decided, and perhaps she could think of a way to make it all better again between them.

She dug her hoe in again. A clod flew up and hit her cheek, and she smacked away the dust with her arm. Neil was the one who understood her. He liked to read, too, just like she did, and he had supplied her with his used books and papers from his school.

Of course, as a girl, there had been no chance for her to go. Still, Neil had written to her, and she had written back, when they were still living by the docks.

Now, there was no more news of Neil, and there were no more docks. All they had to do day and night was to till the cold, silent farm, and work the huge clods out of the dirt.

"Lizzie," Ninna said. "Lizzie, do you hear that?"

Lizzie put one hand on the small of her back and stood up. She squinted across the long, dark field they were working. It was divided from the next farm by a narrow lane and a low scrub hedge.

From far away there came the sound of a job-carriage bowling down the lane. "Squire Bisselthwaite," Lizzie said.

Ninna nodded. "Aye. Wonder how his horse feels, pulling the Squire's fat self around the Compound?"

Lizzie giggled. "I think he stole Mam's side of bacon when we were first moved here," she said.

"He *is* a side of bacon," Ninna said. Lizzie giggled again and scanned the lane.

"Do you see anything, Ninna?" she asked. To her, the world was continually blurred around the edges; it only went into sharp focus when Neil used to let her wear his spectacles, before he left for holidays with that friend of his and disappeared. When she had to take the spectacles off and give them back to her brother, the world went fuzzy again.

For an answer, Ninna pointed to the road. "I can't see, Ninna," Lizzie said, exasperated. "You know I can't."

"I think he has Priam on the cart with him." Ninna tucked a long glossy ringlet behind one ear.

"Oh, Lord bless us and save us; not that blowhard," Lizzie retorted.

Ninna ignored her. She waved in the direction of the carriage and the deep dimple in her cheek reappeared. Lizzie thought that the Squire's son must have waved back at her.

"Is the Squire's other son with them?" Lizzie asked. "The one that no one ever sees? Mags from the next farm over was telling me about him the other day."

"Lizzie! I think they will arrive at our cottage!" Ninna dropped her hoe in the ground and straightened her gloves. "Should we walk back down there, d'you think?"

Lizzie groaned. "'Spose we'd better," she said. "Who else is going to deal with the Squire, Mam and Da?"

Ninna's dimple disappeared. "You're right," she said. She picked her hoe up and shouldered it. "Let's go and rescue Matilda."

The sisters walked to the small, squat house. As they approached it, Ninna grabbed Lizzie's arm. "Priam *is* with him! Look!" she hissed.

"Where?" Lizzie blurted. "I can't see a blessed thing, Ninna, and you know it! Are they over there?" She flung out an arm in the direction of the house.

Ninna grabbed her wrist. "Stop it! They'll see you! Just follow, and stay behind me. I don't want to be mortified."

Lizzie did as she was told, but she made a horrible face at Ninna's back. They went in the small divided door, and Lizzie could make out the figures inside. Squire Bisselthwaite stood in front of the cold fireplace. His son was indeed beside him, and the tall young man looked around at the tiny, dark room.

"Why, it's the Squire!" Ninna said as soon as she and Lizzie entered the front room. "What a delightful surprise! How are you today, Squire?"

"Humph," the Squire grunted. "Cold in here. Need to keep a fire going in case of guests."

Lizzie bit her tongue on her retort that they had precious little fuel, and what they had they saved for the cooking. She glanced at Ninna, who kept a gracious smile on her face while she frantically motioned to Matilda to put on a pot of tea. "Will you have tea with us, Squire?" she asked.

"Tea?" Mam said, sitting up in her chair. "Oh, no, no, no. Time for tonic. Tonic, girls! Tonic! Where's the tonic?"

Squire Bisselthwaite and Priam both frowned. Lizzie hurried over to her mother's side, knelt by the hard chair, and said, "Wait a minute, now, Mam. I'll have your tonic for you in a minute."

Her mother continued to struggle and protest, but she grew quiet when Lizzie took a brown bottle out of her pocket. "Tonic," Mam muttered.

"Just a few short minutes and you can have some, if you're quiet." Lizzie felt a bit frantic.

"Can't stay, Miss Er." The Squire's frown deepened. "Need you and your sister at the Manor. Got some guests arriving in a week. Need extra hands in the kitchen and some people to attend to the tables, and all that sort of thing. Might as well get your things ready at once to come with me."

"Oh!" Ninna said, stepping back a bit. "But we can't leave Matilda and Mam, nor Da either."

Priam interrupted. "Sorry to push in and all that. Forgot about your sister, didn't we, Father? Don't worry," he said to her. "We'll have the people from the next farm over come and give a hand."

There was a long silence. Lizzie felt her temper boil over. Did the Squire really think that she and Ninna could just waltz out of their house, and leave little Matilda to take care of two sick parents and mind the house all at the same time?

"But the farm-" Ninna began to twist the hem of one cuff with her long fingers.

"Oh, stow the bloody farm," Priam said. "You would be much more comfortable at the Manor, and we really need some help. Unexpected guests and all that. And, I'd wager you'd like to take a holiday away from the fields, eh?"

Lizzie dropped her eyes to her blistered palms. To not have to wield that blasted hoe for a week, maybe two – the thought was heaven.

She shook her head. Matilda, in the corner of the room, looked anxiously up at one face, and then the other. "We couldn't possibly leave our sister alone for such a long time," she said. "Even with the help from the Thornycrofts. Matilda is too young to deal with such a thing, and she would have to give our parents their tonic every day."

"Tonic!" Mam said, getting up from her chair. "Is it time for tonic?" There was a rustle beside her as Da struggled to stand as well.

"Lizzie!" Ninna hissed. Lizzie didn't care. She would rather work her hands to the bone than abandon Matilda, the way that they had all been abandoned on the cold farm, months ago.

The Squire opened his mouth, but Priam put his hand on his father's sleeve. He said something in the large man's ear and smiled again at Ninna. "Tell you what. Father and I will step out and have a bit of a discussion," he said. He and the Squire walked just outside the door and began to argue in low tones.

"I'd better give Mam and Da their medicine," Lizzie said. "Matilda, have you got a spoon?"

"Here you are, Lizzie! I just cleaned them all again, this morning. Lizzie, Ninna, are you going to have to leave me behind here?" Matilda puckered up her brow, under the neat parting in her smooth, brown hair.

"Nonsense," Lizzie said, taking the spoon. "Ninna and I will stay with you; won't we, Ninna?" She measured out a spoonful of the dark brown liquid and held it to Mam's lips. Her mother opened her eyes and grabbed Lizzie's wrist. She swallowed and spilled a few drops in her eagerness.

"I suppose so." Ninna looked at the open door. "But wouldn't it have been lovely, not to have to scrabble away at that hard ground for a few days?"

"Ninna." Lizzie pointed to Matilda. Their sister twisted a rag in her hands, and as they watched, she bent down and began to clean the floor.

Ninna sighed, and she bent down and put her arms around Matilda. "Of course we won't leave you, sweetheart," she said. "No need to wash that floor again. It's already clean from this morning, see?"

Lizzie poured a second dose of tonic and was about to give a spoonful to Da when Priam walked back into the house. "I say, I think I may have hit on a solution," he said. "How about if you bring your parents and your little sister with you to the Manor? We'll have rooms for you all. Nothing fancy, mind."

Ninna gasped and clasped her hands under her chin, just like a character in a penny-dreadful novel, Lizzie thought. "Really?" she said. "Oh, Lizzie! Did you hear that? How kind of the Squire! And how kind of you, too, Master Priam," she added, her eyelashes fluttering down on her cheeks.

"But, Ninna-" Lizzie objected.

Priam interrupted, looking relieved. "That's good news! It's all settled then. I'll send a cart to move you to the Manor tomorrow." He raised one large, square hand in a salute to Ninna and closed the door behind him.

"Well!" Lizzie burst out. "There are no flies on that one, that much is certain!"

"Are we all to move to the big house, Ninna?" Matilda reached for the dirty tonic spoon. Lizzie knew she was dying to wash it.

"I think we really are," Ninna murmured.

CHAPTER 2
The Arrival at the Manor

The Manor where Squire Bisselthwaite lived was in the center of Grimstead Compound. The thirteen farms that made up the rest of the Compound fanned out from the large, old house. Most of the fields touched the edge of the Manor grounds at their narrowest points, although all the farms were separated from the Bisselthwaite property by a dark, crumbling wall.

As Lizzie and her family rode through the huge, rusted iron gates set into the stones, she glanced up at the rooftops of the Manor. Her hat slipped down her neck, and she clapped one hand to hold it on as she squinted up at the dark front of the house.

There was a rather grand entrance, but of course the carriage took the family to the back of the house to the kitchen gardens. As the cart jostled over the pebbly drive, Ninna murmured in Lizzie's ear, "Did you see that?" She pointed up to one of the windows on the third or fourth floor.

"What?" Lizzie squinted again. It was all a gray blur to her.

"Oh, nothing. Just thought I saw a face in one of the windows upstairs." Ninna sat back and put her arm around Matilda. On the seat opposite the girls, Mam and Da swayed with the movement over the cobbles. They shared an old rug to keep them warm, and it slipped from their shoulders with the movement of the cart.

The kitchen garden was a small square, also walled in. Washing hung from a line, some shirts and combinations. Matilda giggled and pointed at the pants, and Ninna grinned at Lizzie. "Better than hoeing old clods of earth, I'm thinking; isn't it, girls?" she said.

Mam and Da found it difficult to get down from the cart when it stopped. Ninna had to let go of Matilda and hold onto Da, who swayed when he stood up. Lizzie got a grip of Mam's shoulder and walked her into the garden to tap on a blue painted door. There were gashes and chips in the paint from where the wood had split from age and moisture. The steps were ancient as well. Mam staggered as she stumbled up the uneven flagstones.

Ninna hesitated. She glanced at Lizzie, and rapped on the scarred door with her fingertips.

A tall, angular female opened it. Her dark hair was scraped back into a knob on top of her head. She wielded a wooden spoon in one hand. As the family trooped inside, she waved it at the dark red tiles, also pitted with age, and shouted, "Don't spread grit and rubbish all over my clean floor with your dirty clodhoppers!"

Lizzie made a great show of wiping her boots on a thin mat before she entered. The kitchen was a long, low room with a huge, antiquated stove on one side and a wooden dresser lined with blue and white plates on the other. Low shelves flanked the dresser, loaded with jars and tins. There was also an ancient wooden table at the far end of the room, on which the tall woman must have just rolled out pastry.

Da looked about the kitchen and saw the chairs by the table. He made for one. "No, Da," Ninna said, pulling his sleeve. "Those aren't for us, d'you see?"

"Well!" The thin female closed the door, propped her fists on her hips, and raked them with her eyes. She shook her head in a decided manner. "No, you won't do," she said. "You're too scrawny for Manor work, the lot of you."

Ninna stepped forward and offered her most winning smile. "Oh, please, won't you give us a chance, Miss – ah, Mrs. ..."

"Ellis," the woman snapped. "Just Ellis for me, and no Miss or Mistress about it. And you needn't grin at me like that. No," she continued, with a sharp intake of breath, "my mind's made up. You can't stay here."

"I can almost make bread so that it rises." Matilda raised her huge eyes in a mute plea. The woman called Ellis humphed and folded her arms.

"It was the Squire himself who wanted us to come to the Manor to work." Lizzie felt a bit desperate.

"*And* his son," Ninna added.

"The Squire! Much he knows what's going on about him. This house has fallen about his ears since his wife decided to die in her bed. No, you'll have to go." In a dismissive manner, she turned to the shelves by the dresser and pulled out a bowl of eggs and a small, dark bottle.

"Tonic!" Mam caught sight of the bottle. "Is it time for tonic? Tonic!" Da, beside her, stumbled and resumed his search for a chair.

Lizzie tried to silence Mam, but Ellis stopped and turned. She jabbed her wooden spoon in Mam's direction. "She's one of those tonic fiends," she said. Her knob of hair appeared to tighten on her head, and the skin by her narrow nostrils whitened.

"Sorry," Lizzie said, feeling more desperate than ever. "She'll sit quiet in a chair during the day, if you have a wee room for her."

Ellis jabbed her spoon in Matilda's direction. "And just what are you about, miss?"

Matilda dropped the rag she had picked up. Obviously she just hadn't been able to resist wiping the table. "I am very sorry, Ellis," Lizzie said. "Matilda, my sister, can't help herself. She likes to keep everything clean."

The tall woman sniffed. For a moment they could hear nothing but the loud tick of the clock on the dresser. She jerked her head towards the door to the house, and said, "Third floor upstairs. Two empty rooms. Aprons are in the room for you lot-" pointing at the three girls, "- and you are to keep them *clean*, mind. The mother and father can go in the other room. We'll get them settled later."

"Oh, thank you!" Ninna said. Lizzie nodded, feeling an enormous gust of relief.

Mam and Da were to stay in a tiny, cold little room next to the girls' sleeping quarters on the third floor while Lizzie and Ninna worked. That section of the house was obviously reserved for the servants at the manor, although now the wing had an empty, desolate feeling.

The girls helped their parents down a long, low corridor. The carpet on the floor was so old that Lizzie couldn't tell what its original color had been. Doors lined the passage, most of them closed. The stairs continued up to a floor above them, but what lay up there, or whether that portion of the house was even inhabited, Lizzie had no idea.

When they arrived in the narrow, cold hall, Ninna peeked into one of the rooms with an open door. "This must be ours," she said, and she pointed to the three aprons laid out on the bed. "Ellis probably planned to hire us all along, the old fraud."

Da opened the door next to the Apron Room, as Lizzie now thought of it, and shambled in. He sank into a low seat by a tiny, dirty window. After a minute, Mam followed and joined him in a chair on the other side of the filthy windowpane.

Ninna stood and watched them for a moment. Da stared straight in front of him. His mouth moved, but he didn't make a sound. Mam held one hand up to her lips; even Lizzie could see that her mother's fingers trembled, since the room was so small. "We can clean their window later," Ninna whispered.

"What good will that do?" Lizzie asked.

Ninna turned on her. "Well, I'm sure I don't know!" she said. "At least it's something I can do for them. It's much better than giving them the contents of that nasty bottle!"

"Bottle?" Mam asked. "Tonic?"

"What happened?" Matilda pushed between her sisters.

Ninna scrubbed one hand across her eyes, bent down, and smiled at her sister. "Nothing, love," she said. "Oh, look, now, you've put on your apron! Lovely, isn't it, Lizzie? Ellis will be pleased to have some help in the kitchen, sure as eggs!"

"I wonder what we're supposed to do first," Lizzie muttered. She turned her back on her parents, marched to Apron Room, and grabbed one of the starched, white garments laid out on the bed. She jerked it over her head and knotted the sash in quick, angry motions.

"Best find a good spot for that bottle." Ninna followed her into what was now their bedchamber. She picked up her own apron and put it on. Lizzie stole a look at her and wondered how her sister managed to make everything she did so effortless. She knew her own bow was sideways in the back, her hair was windblown, and her dress was a fright, but Ninna made the uniform look becoming.

"I had better continue to carry it in my pocket," Lizzie said. "You know how devious Mam can get, when she wants a nip of syrup."

"Oh, Lizzie -!" For a moment the two looked at each other. Lizzie closed her eyes and felt something hot and large overwhelm her. She forced her mouth into a straight line.

"Well!" she said in a bright tone. "Matilda, why don't you come with us, and we'll see if Ellis hasn't got a job for you in the kitchen!"

The girl tucked her reddened, fat little paw into Ninna's slim hand, and they made for the stairs. Lizzie listened at her parents' door, but the occupants were silent. She followed her sisters downstairs.

TO BE CONTINUED IN

CROWN PHOENIX:
Lamplighter's Special

ABOUT THE AUTHOR

Alison DeLuca is the author of the Crown Phoenix Series which includes *Night Watchman Express*, *The Devil's Kitchen*, and *Lamplighter's Special*, steampunk fantasies for young adults. She was born in Arizona and has also lived in Pennsylvania, Illinois, Mexico, Ireland, and Spain.

She currently wrestles words and laundry in New Jersey.

Made in the USA
Charleston, SC
06 December 2012